**Praise for *On a Ring and a Prayer***

"In *On a Ring and a Prayer*, Sandra D. Bricker weaves a charming and plucky story of one woman's reinvention after betrayal. When fashionista Jessie Stanton's husband, Jack, goes missing, she is left with nothing but the ring on her finger—and too many unanswered questions. With the help of lovable friends, including a handsome surfing detective and his gigantic dog, Frank, Jessie finds new purpose as she begins to reexamine the life she's been living. Bricker's deftly added narration by Jessie's aged grandfather provides history, perspective, and a warm touch in the midst of trying circumstances. Highly recommended."
—Julie Carobini, author of *Fade to Blue*

"You won't just read Sandra D. Bricker's new novel, *On a Ring and a Prayer*—you'll breathe it in and become part of it. It's a story of overcoming, a story of finding hope, and one you'll remember long after you turn the last page. Novel Rocket and I give it our highest recommendation. It's a 5-star must read!"
—Ane Mulligan, President, Novel Rocket

"I fell in love with these characters and this story and—better still—stayed in love. I have no doubt you will, too. Good news! There's more Jessie and Danny right around the corner!"
—Eva Marie Everson, best-selling, multiple award–winning writer, including *The Road to Testament* from Abingdon Press

**Other Books by Sandra D. Bricker**

*The Big Five-OH!*

The Love Finds You Series
*Love Finds You in Snowball, Arkansas*
*Love Finds You in Holiday, Florida*
*Love Finds You in Carmel-by-the-Sea, California*

Another Emma Rae Creation Series
*Always the Baker, Never the Bride*
*Always the Wedding Planner, Never the Bride*
*Always the Designer, Never the Bride*
*Always the Baker, Finally the Bride*

The Quilts of Love Series
*Raw Edges*

The Contemporary Fairy Tales Series
*If the Shoe Fits*
*Rise & Shine*

A JESSIE STANTON NOVEL

Sandra D. Bricker

*Nashville*

*On a Ring and a Prayer*



ISBN-13: 978-1-63088-926-5

Published by Abingdon Press, P.O. Box 801, Nashville, TN 37202

www.abingdonpress.com



Macro Editor: Teri Wilhelms

Published in association with Books & Such Literary Agency

Library of Congress Cataloging-in-Publication Data

Bricker, Sandra D., 1958-
On a ring and a prayer / Sandra D. Bricker.
pages ; cm.—(A Jessie Stanton novel ; book 1)
ISBN 978-1-4267-1160-2 (softcover : acid-free paper) 1. Divorced women—Fiction. 2. Life change events—Fiction. 3. Chick lit. I. Title.
PS3602.R53O5 2015
813'.6—dc23

2014029817

Printed in the United States of America

1 2 3 4 5 6 7 8 9 10 / 20 19 18 17 16 15

*To Marian—for putting up with it*
*To Rachelle—for knowing what to do with it*


## Acknowledgments

Special thanks to Ramona and Teri.

And to Luke, the rad surfer dude who taught me how to speak Wave.

# Prologue

*Sweet little Jessie was the center of my life. From the day she was born and I held her in my arms—all pink and new, wrapped in a cotton blanket and singin' a song that only she and God knew the words to—it was plain she was gonna grow up into somethin' special.*

*Her dark hair and beamin' blue eyes put off enough light to kindle up a whole room. And not just an ordinary light neither. The kind of light that don't appear without a purpose. No, that kind of light was put there. The Scripture says we know His voice when we hear it. What it don't say, but maybe it should, is we also know His light when it meets our eyes. And Jessie was filled up with His light, no doubt about it. I saw it right away, and then I just kept on seein' it the more time I spent with her.*

*We got to spend some good time together, too. Her mama—my daughter—married a hometown boy, thank the Lord, and they settled just three blocks away from me over on Eaton Street in Slidell, Louisiana. Once she got old enough, little Jessie walked as far as my house every mornin', and I'd be waitin' for her out on the front porch with my coffee, black and strong, and I'd walk her the rest of the way to school. When the three o'clock bell rang at the end of the school day, we'd do the same thing in reverse. She'd walk as far as my house, and I'd walk her home the rest of the way. After we shared a cookie or an apple, she told me what she learned in school. Jessie always liked learnin'.*

*"Grampy, you know what?"*

*"Tell me." This was the way nearly every one of our after-school chats began.*

*"You know that planet with the rings around it?"*

*"Saturn."*

*"Yeah, that's it. Saturn. Well, if you had a big enough bowl o' water, and you plunked Saturn down into it, you know what would happen?"*

*"It might drown, I reckon," I answered her, hidin' my smile behind my coffee cup.*

*"No! That's the funny thing," she said, that light lightin' up her pretty face like a solar flare. "It would float."*

*"Nah, it wouldn't float," I teased. "It would sink like a stone."*

*"No, Grampy, it would float. I promise!"*

*"Well, I'll be."*

*Got me to wonderin' that day—the way grandpops do sometimes—if my Jessie might become the first female astronaut or one of those astronomers who discover new planets. Whatever she did, I knew she'd be somethin' special, and I prayed to the Good Lord every mornin' and every night before my head hit that pillow that—whatever it was that she did—she would do it with faith in the Lord above.*

*That's a child's only hope in a world that changes as fast as this one.*

# 1

Watch this. If I hold my coffee at just the right tilt, the reflection off my ring will blind her."

"Jessie, stop that."

Jessie angled her hand so that the sunlight streaming through the café window bounced off nearly four carats of perfect clarity, ricocheting back toward the window. Just one slight adjustment and—

"There!"

"What are you? Ten?"

"Ten-year-old Jessie would never have this ring."

She grinned as the woman two tables over flinched, squinting as the beam of sunlight hit her right in the eye.

"And why are you acting like this anyway?" Jessie asked in a graveled whisper. "Support me in my cattiness like a good friend should. You know perfectly well that Shea McDermott has been talking smack about my marriage for three years now, since the night of Elton's Oscar party."

They both glanced over toward Shea's table, and Jessie offered the bleached blonde a forced, cursory smile.

Through her tightened, pearly white expression, Jessie muttered, "She makes me crazy."

"I can see that. But you have an unfair advantage, Jess," Piper replied with a serious tone as she tucked her short, streaked strawberry-blonde hair behind one ear. Then a sunbeam grin ignited her face, and her glossy green eyes shimmered with mischief. "You've got nearly two carats on her."

They both snickered just as the waiter approached the table.

"Can I get you ladies anything else?"

His nametag read DIRK. Jessie thought it was the perfect name for an obvious actor-turned-waiter like so many hundreds of them flanking trendy restaurant tables from Malibu to Glendale. Dirk-the-waiter looked like he belonged in a leading-edge fashion layout in *Esquire* rather than schlepping lunch for LA's *hot-du-jour.*

"It happens to be my friend's birthday," Piper told Dirk, and Jessie held her breath and used her birthday wish against Piper revealing which one. "We'd like a generous slice of amaretto cheesecake and two cappuccinos."

"Right away."

"Oh, and—" Piper wrinkled her nose at him and whispered, "put a candle in it?"

"Piper, no."

With one hand, she waved Jessie into submission, and with the other she sent Dirk-the-waiter quickly on his way.

"So what are we doing?" Piper asked. "Twenty-five again?"

"Sounds good."

"Twenty-five it is. And you don't look a day over twenty-four."

Jessie smiled. She didn't *feel* her thirty-seven years either. At twenty-four, she'd been working the fragrance counter at Bloomingdale's in the Beverly Center. Jack had parked outside of the store on his way to pick up a couple of new suits from Hugo Boss. On his way back through the store, he circled Jessie's counter three times before he stopped and asked her to recommend a perfume for his mother's birthday. They made a date for dinner at Moonshadows Malibu that very evening; a patio table at sunset. And Jack had swept her off the size-seven Manolos she'd borrowed from one of her roommates before the panna cotta had been served for dessert. Six dinner dates later, she learned that Jack's mom had passed away in the previous decade, and he'd only summoned up her memory as an on-the-fly excuse to talk to "the pretty brunette with the light blue eyes." But by the time the truth rolled out, he'd already reeled her in and Jessie dismissed his little white lie in the name of true love's course. She'd fallen hard, and they were married that very summer on the white-sand Pacific shore, not far from that patio table at Moonshadows.

"Funny how everything seems to come full circle, isn't it?" Jessie mused as the recollection of her first days with Jack wafted through her mind. "I was just thinking about—"

Dirk-the-waiter's arrival at her table sliced her thought clean through. "Happy birthday," he sort of sang as he set the cheesecake and coffees on the tabletop between them and lit the lone candle sticking out of the center of the dessert. "Make a wish."

Jessie smiled at Piper, closed her eyes—*I wish this perfect life would last forever!*—and blew out the candle before they both dug into the cheesecake from opposite sides of the gilded plate.

"Uh, Jess?"

Piper narrowed her eyes and scrunched up one side of her collagen-enhanced pout as she glared through the window toward the street.

Jessie set down the large white cup after taking a sip. "What's wrong?"

"Isn't that . . . *your car*?"

Jessie's eyes darted after Piper's, and she caught sight of the rear bumper of her Deep Sea Blue convertible 640i BMW . . . just as the large tow truck dragged it around the corner of Cross Creek toward Pacific Coast Highway.

Jessie instinctively smacked her heart to get it beating again, and she willed her wide-open mouth to shut tight when she caught Shea McDermott's Botox-lifted eyes focused directly on her.

"I . . . It couldn't . . . But . . . *Nooo.* It had to be someone else's . . ."

"Ms. Stanton, I am so sorry," Joseph-the-valet whimpered as he approached her table. "He took the keys and he said your lease had been revoked by—"

"All righty, Joseph!" Piper intercepted. "That's fine. We understand." She leaned closer and lowered her voice considerably. "Call us a taxi, will you, please?"

"Of course."

Dirk-the-waiter looked like some sort of canary-eating feline as he set the leather folder on the edge of the table. "Your check."

"Thank you, Dirk," Piper replied.

Jessie tasted a sour version of her coffee at the back of her throat as she plucked a credit card out of her wallet and slipped it into the folder, handing it to him.

"Uh," Dirk muttered. "Isn't it your birthday?"

She shook her head until it rattled. "Yes. Why?"

"Well, normally the *other person* pays for the birthday lunch."

"Oh. Right." Jessie inhaled sharply before continuing. "It's our thing. She'll get the check on her birthday. This one's mine."

"Thank you, Dirk," Piper interjected.

The moment he left them, Piper leaned halfway across the table until her face was about eight inches from Jessie's. "He said your lease was revoked, Jess. What's going on?"

"I have no idea. I need to call Jack."

Her hands trembled as she dipped into her Prada okra-orange Saffiano leather bag and pulled out her iPhone. She didn't take the time to swipe through the address book, and just dialed Jack's cell number herself. When the call failed to connect, Jessie inhaled sharply and tried again, but the shrill three-tone siren sounded again.

"We're sorry," the robotic recording stated. "The number you have dialed is no longer in service at this time. If you feel you have reached this recording in error—"

Jessie disconnected, but she continued to stare at the screen as if she hadn't.

"What happened?"

"I got an out-of-service recording."

"That's weird. Why don't you try his office?"

"Good idea. Okay."

Just in case it had been a simple user error, she used the address book to reach Jack's office. Tears stung her eyes as she took a deep breath and held it tightly in her lungs for a moment. Jack would certainly know what to do. She just had to—

"We're sorry. The number you have dialed . . ."

Jessie's chest tightened, and the rogue tears streamed from her eyes and down both cheeks.

"Jess?"

"Piper, something awful is happening. I can feel it. His office number is disconnected too, and—"

"I'm very sorry, Ms. Stanton," Dirk-the-waiter interrupted, and when she looked up into his eyes, she spotted a flash of . . . almost . . . *glee.* "It seems your card has been denied."

Jessie's eyes widened to the point that the strain of it ached.

"Would you like to try another?"

She couldn't think. She simply turned her gaze toward Piper as the cascade of salty emotion reached her chin and dangled there for a moment before plummeting to the edge of the saucer beneath her cappuccino cup.

"Here. Use mine," Piper said, handing him her credit card.

The next several minutes blurred like a watercolor painting left out in the pouring rain. When Jessie finally blinked, she found herself sitting next to Piper in the back of a hybrid taxicab as they turned onto Malibu Road.

"Right up here," Piper told the driver, and he rolled to a stop in front of the expansive hacienda-style home where Jessie and Jack had lived for the last several years. "Thank you," Piper added, slipping the driver some folded bills before squeezing Jessie's arm and shaking it. "Come on, sweetie. We're here."

She somehow managed to drag herself out of the cab and mindlessly put one foot in front of the other until they reached the arched gate to the front courtyard. It took three tries to punch in the code, but just about the time that Jessie started to imagine that she'd been locked out of this one final part of her life, the gate buzzed and she pushed it open. She jumped as it clanked shut behind Piper.

Thankfully, the front door code worked on the first try, and she stepped inside with a sigh.

"What in the world . . . ?"

She turned toward Piper to find her friend gape-mouthed and wide-eyed as she scanned the conspicuously empty walls of the lavish living room. Every piece of Jack's extensive art collection had vanished, much of the landscape vacant and glaring at her. The remaining furnishings looked strangely out of place without it, like a half-decorated hotel lobby.

"Piper," she said, wincing. "What's going on here? Do you think we've been . . . robbed?"

"And the robbers paused to revoke the lease on your car and cancel your credit cards? I don't think so, Jess."

"What then?"

And with that, the hot tears erupted again, and Jessie's chest began to pound with questions.

"I have no idea."

The two of them stood in silence for several slow-ticking seconds. Jessie labored against the array of panicked and disjointed notions skipping across her brain like plump children playing hopscotch. Beyond the wall of glass at the far end of the living room, the blue Pacific Ocean carelessly cavorted beneath foamy, white-capped waves that tumbled over each other to land on the shore. Nearly two hundred feet of private beach—the attraction that drew her to this house out of all the others they'd toured—seemed to laugh at her now, taunting that it knew something she didn't.

As she surveyed the artless walls one more time, a sudden notion hit her with a thud. She gasped, and then she spun around and clomp-clomp-clomped across the Mexican ceramic tile in the hallway. Crossing the large master suite, she reached Jack's walk-in closet at the far end and thrust open the door.

"Empty," she muttered.

"Jessie?" Piper called from the hall as she followed. "What is it?"

She turned back toward the door and waited for Piper to cross the threshold before she replied. "All of Jack's clothes are gone."

"What? Are you sure?"

Jessie didn't bother to answer. She just shuffled toward the king-sized, four-poster bed and dropped to the edge of the pillow-top mattress.

"Wow, you weren't kidding," Piper said as she peered into the closet. "Not even a dust bunny left behind."

Jessie couldn't react. She just curled both of her hands into fists around the Egyptian cotton comforter beneath her as Piper rushed past her and tugged open the door of the second closet. Jessie held her breath.

"Well, it looks like all of your clothes are still here."

She sniffed. "He left me."

"Nooo. Jack wouldn't . . ."

"He left me, Piper. That's the only answer. He canceled my credit cards, surrendered my car, packed up his belongings, and he left me."

Just then, the front bell rang. Jessie and Piper both gasped.

"See! That's probably him now," Piper exclaimed as she jogged down the hall toward the front door.

"He's not going to ring the bell to his own house," Jessie stated softly.

She grabbed a tissue from the ceramic box on the nightstand and dried her eyes on the way to the door, sniffling as she did.

"You must be Mrs. Stanton," the balding man standing in the foyer said as she emerged.

"Yes. And you are . . . ?"

"Anthony Grana. Your Realtor."

"My . . . what?"

He quickly produced a business card from his jacket pocket and handed it to her. "Malibu Realty. I handled the sale."

Piper said it for her. "The sale?"

"Your husband left his cell phone behind this afternoon, and I thought I'd return it on my way home."

Jessie accepted the phone and just stared at it.

"You were with Jack this morning?" Piper asked him.

"Yes, at the closing."

"The closing," Piper repeated. "I don't understand."

Jessie inhaled sharply before clarifying. "I think what he's saying is . . . my husband sold our home."

"We got a very fair price, too, if I do say so."

Looking over Piper's shoulder at the beckoning blue sea, Jessie shook her head.

*Déjà vu all over again*, she thought, then moved on to consider whether to act on the instinct overtaking her at the moment, and just go ahead and rush over the wooden deck, across the sand, and throw herself into the laughing ocean.

---

The sun had only begun to peek its big head out over the top of the pastel horizon, but the surf had called Danny's name early that day. He'd managed to step into the bottom of the wetsuit, letting the top of it hang down around his waist as he tucked Carmen—the name he'd given his surfboard—under one arm and trekked across the sand, bare-chested. The waves looked inviting, full of the come-hither allure only the morning swells of the blue Pacific could muster in him.

He pounded three times on the side panel of the battered Volkswagen bus parked at the edge of the sand before proceeding toward the beckoning surf. Danny spread out his Zuma Jay beach towel and dropped Carmen on it, face upward. Squatting down to inspect her, he tugged at the leash to make sure the connection to the plug felt secure. He ran his hand down the length of the leash to check for frays, knots, or tears. Reasonably confident, he flipped her over to scrutinize the fin box. The screws looked tight; nothing loose or broken.

He stood upright and slid his arms into the sleeves of the wet-suit and zipped it as he stepped out of blue flip-flops. He dropped to the sand and folded his legs into a sort of lotus position. Inhaling deeply, he closed his eyes and tilted his head back slightly.

*Man, I love mornings out here.*

Before he even had a chance to exhale, however, the clamor of Riggs's approach sent all thoughts of quiet meditation upward into a puff of steam.

"You're early, man," Riggs grumbled as he stalked across the sand. He dropped his bright orange board next to Danny and flopped down on it. "I haven't even had my coffee. What's with the crack of dawn?"

"Sorry. I just wanted to get an early jump."

"Well, what are you sitting here for, then?"

The corner of Danny's mouth quirked as he leaned back and looked at his disheveled friend. Short, curly dark hair, dusky light-brown skin, cropped black beard. Riggs wore his multiethnicity like a permanent tattoo.

"I was waiting on you," he said, pointing out the obvious.

"Well, here I am. We gonna get wet, or what?"

He chuckled. "Yeah. Yeah, let's get wet."

Riggs trailed Danny into the water, letting out a shriek as his stomach hit the cold board. They paddled over fairly meager waves, typical to the Santa Monica area north of the pier at this time of year. Heavy winds the night before had at least pumped the swell a couple of feet, so the morning wasn't a complete bust. With an exchange of nods, they let the first wave pass them by.

"I heard Mavericks is prime right now," Riggs called out as they waited to catch the next one. "You wanna make a run up there this weekend?"

"Don't you have Allie this weekend?"

"She'll go with us."

He and Riggs hadn't made it to Mavericks all year. Truth told, the idea really appealed to Danny. It wasn't like he had any hot cases to keep him rooted in town. But the odds were mounted high against Riggs's twelve-year-old daughter's mother signing off on a six-hour drive to scout out better waves for the weekend.

"This one looks pretty good," Riggs called out, and Danny checked it out before giving him the nod.

"Let's try her out."

Everything else tumbled out of his thoughts as Danny paddled forward, positioning himself positively for the half-built swell. He made a clean entry into the wave, creating enough momentum and speed to set up the ride, then popped up to his feet. He glanced over at Riggs just in time to see his board pearl, its nose digging down into the water. Riggs groaned as he wiped out into it, leaving Danny to finish out the ride alone. Wiping out into a two-foot wave? He made a mental note against ever dragging a precoffee Riggs into the water again.

He'd just started to consider turning back into the surf for a second go of his own when distant, familiar barking called his attention to the shore.

Sure enough, one hundred twenty pounds of harlequin Great Dane stood in the sand, his pointed cropped ears erect, and his deep-throated barks cutting straight across the water. Danny dragged his board by the leash, trudging to the shore.

"What's up, Frank? What's all the racket?"

Frank pounded the sand with his front paw as Danny approached, his typical move when he had something urgent to share. Shielding his eyes from the sun with one hand, Danny spotted the car parked next to Riggs's bus.

"What's a Jag doing parked at our place, boy?" he asked the dog.

"What's up with Frankenstein?" Riggs asked as he plodded out of the water.

"Looks like I've got company." Danny picked up his beach towel and followed Frank, calling out to Riggs over his shoulder. "Be back in a few."

"Nah, I'm headed in, too," he replied. "I need a shower and some joe."

Danny knew he didn't have much of a choice in the matter. Ever since he'd agreed to let his friend park in his driveway, Riggs had slowly infiltrated until he'd become as much a part of Danny's home base as the leaky faucet in the kitchen.

Frank rushed to the passenger window of the white Jaguar and peeled out a tirade of objections to its presence. From beneath the bass drum of his barking, soprano screams hit pitches he hadn't thought possible.

"Frank! Back!"

He dropped his towel and leaned Carmen against the patio post before making his way toward the car.

"Frank!" he repeated. "Get back. Now!" The dog reluctantly retreated, circling around Danny and standing behind him like a ready-and-waiting soldier. A white one. With giant black spots.

He leaned down and peered into the car. His heart bumped a little as a gorgeous brunette with wide, glistening eyes looked back at him. Through the closed window, he thought he heard a muffled version of his name.

"What? I can't hear you."

She lowered the window by no more than an inch. "Mr. Callahan?"

*Is she looking for my father?*

"I'm Danny Callahan. Who are you?"

The driver leaned across the blue-eyed beauty and spoke to the opening in the window. Her very short, streaked hair framed sharper features than her friend's. "I'm Piper Brunetti, Mr. Callahan. I got your name from Vicki Washington."

The name skimmed his brain before coming back around for a landing. Cheating husband. He'd provided her with visual art to support a hefty divorce settlement the previous spring.

"What can I do for you, Miss Brunetti?"

"This is my friend, Jessie Stanton."

Weepy blue eyes glittered at him, and when she forced an unconvincing smile to her apple cheeks, dimples caved in at the base of them.

"She has a situation. With her husband."

He looked back as huge tear droplets escaped her wide eyes, momentarily waylaid by the dimples before cascading from her chin.

"I need to get out of this wetsuit," he told them. "Why don't you come inside."

Both women's attention darted toward Frank, and the crier with the apple cheeks and heart-shaped face shook her head defiantly. "Uh-uh. No."

"Oh, he's harmless," he reassured them both. "Just noisy."

Neither one of them seemed to believe him.

"All right," he said with a shrug. "But I'm going inside. If you want to talk to me, you'll need to get out of the car." When he reached the doorway to his small bungalow, he turned back and called out to them. "His name is Frank. And he's already eaten."

Danny slapped his thigh, and Frank obediently followed him through the door. A stream of fresh coffee dribbled into the pot on the counter, and Frank sniffed the air beneath it before curling up on the large padded rectangle bearing his name angled into the corner of the kitchen. Danny followed the sound of the running shower to find, as he suspected, Riggs had discarded his wetsuit and clothes in a heap in the hallway outside the open bathroom door.

"Don't come out of there in the buff," he shouted through the door. "Females in the house."

"Yeah, okay."

"At least, I think they're coming in," he muttered as he peeled off his wetsuit en route to the bedroom.

---

Jessie poked her head through the open door and timidly tested the waters. "Hello?"

"Go on in," Piper whispered. "He said we should come inside."

"But the cow . . ."

"It's not a cow, Jess. It's a dog." With a sniff, she added, "A really, really big dog."

"With cow spots."

"Cow spots."

"Black blotches on white. Like a cow coat. Oooh, maybe he *ate a cow* and—"

Piper giggled. "You are so—"

The soft, menacing growl of the approaching cow-dog stopped them both in their tracks. At the top of the first full bark, Jessie squealed and pulled the door shut with a slam. Clutching the doorknob to hold it closed, she turned toward Piper.

"Let's run for the car."

"You need to talk to this guy, Jessie."

Leaning away from the barking, she shook her head. "Not enough to be mauled to death. Let's go."

Piper's lips parted in preparation for her objection, but the turn of the knob in Jessie's hand jerked her focus to the only thing standing between her and a horrible, bloody demise. When the turn of the knob unlatched the door and it pulled back from her, Jessie screeched and clutched it with both hands, yanking it shut again.

"Help me!" she shouted at Piper. "It's opening the door!"

With one hard wrench, the door flew open and the knob slipped straight out of her grasp. Instead of the perilous brown gaze of a giant dog on the other side of the jamb, she met the narrowed steel-blue eyes of a surfing private investigator.

Jessie released a bumpy little nervous chuckle. "Sorry. I thought it was . . ." Her words trailed off, and she nodded toward the dog standing silently behind him.

"Frank's a pretty inventive guy," he replied, "but I'm pretty sure it takes the advanced skills afforded by opposable thumbs to turn the knob and open the door."

"Uh . . ."

When nothing of substance followed, Piper elbowed her in the back.

"Why don't you come in and tell me why you're here," he suggested, and he swung the door fully open. But when the dog straightened his big pointy ears, Jessie found her feet cemented to the spot. "Frank!" he said firmly. "Go lay down."

When the dog turned away and trotted across driftwood oak flooring, disappearing into the kitchen, Jessie exhaled and walked cautiously through the door.

The décor astonished her a little, but she tried not to show it as she followed him past a casual assemblage of rustic farm tables and a blue leather sectional facing two light tan club chairs. A compilation of scenic framed photographs depicting blue waters and waves of all sizes and strengths adorned the otherwise bare board-and-batten walls. The mantle of the small corner fireplace had been constructed out of an old vintage beach sign.

"My office is in the sunroom," he said. "Through there. Can I get you coffee?"

"No, thank you," Jessie replied, and she grabbed Piper's wrist as she carefully sidestepped the cow-dog.

"I'll have some water," Piper blurted over her shoulder. "If you have bottled."

The sunroom provided another unexpected surprise. It was surrounded on three sides with light oak louvered shutters. A desk—the top of it made from a short, colorful surfboard—was angled into the corner across from two rattan loveseats cushioned in deep hunter green.

"It looks like nothing but a rundown little beach shack from the outside," Piper whispered. "It's pretty nice in here, huh?"

Jessie softly shushed her friend before nodding. "I know, right?"

Danny Callahan stalked into the room, handing off bottles of cold water to them before scraping the light green distressed wood chair away from the desk and mounting it backwards.

"So what can I do for you?" He slurped hot coffee from a mug. "Husband troubles?"

Jessie lowered her eyes and examined her open-toed Ralph Laurens.

"Cheater?" he asked Piper.

"I wish I knew," Jessie spoke up. "In fact, I wish I knew anything about Jack Stanton at all. We've been married thirteen years, and as it turns out . . . I don't know anything for sure anymore." She fought back the sting of the tears that rose in her eyes and groaned softly under her breath. "My husband has disappeared, Mr. Callahan. And he took my life with him."

"We were hoping," Piper chimed in, "maybe you could help sort it out?"

"He . . . he closed our accounts . . ."

"And sold her house right out from under her," Piper declared, her indignant anger showing. "We were sitting there having a nice lunch when we watched her car being towed down the street, Mr. Callahan. Please. You have to help her."

"Bearing in mind," Jessie added, "that the life he took includes every cent I had."

The surfing detective lifted one eyebrow and stared at her; not for long, but long enough to burn a small hole.

"I don't work for free," he finally stated, and Jessie deflated. "But that's an interesting ring you have on."

*"Grampy! Help me!"*

*My heart just about busted straight through my chest to hear the terror in my Jessie's voice that day. I'd just been sittin' out on the stoop waitin' for her to make her way down the lane to my house when she come tearin' around the corner at a full run. And the biggest dog I ever seen in all my days come barrelin' behind her.*

*"Grampy, heyyy-yelp!"*

*Set down my cuppa joe and stalked straight down to the end of the driveway. Opened up my arms, and Jessie jumped clean into 'em. She crawled up over my shoulder like a monkey in the jungle, holdin' on to my head and screamin' bloody murder.*

*That old hound dog clomped to a stop in front of me like a clumsy horse, his ears pasted back and his tail a-waggin'.*

*"Ain't nothin' to be scared of here, child," I told her, but her vise grip on her Grampy's head didn't budge. "Just a hound dog. Look at 'im."*

*She must have taken a peek because she squirmed a little. "But he was chasin' me."*

*"He's just chasin' yer light," I told her. "He sees it, too, and wants to be buddies."*

*"I don't want to, Grampy. Make him go away."*

*"All righty, child," I said with a laugh as I carried her up the driveway to the porch. "G'on, dog. Git!"*

*"You're always savin' my life," she told me, once inside the safety of the screen door.*

*"Yeah?" I said. "Well, yer savin' mine right back."*

*Jessie found this incredibly funny, and she laughed until her belly hurt. "I can't save you. I'm just nine. How old are you anyway, Grampy?"*

*"A hundred and nine," I fibbed.*

*"You're a hundred and nine?" she cried, her big blue eyes round and shiny as half dollars. "That's really old, Grampy. That's prolly why your whiskers are all silver, huh?"*

*"Could be."*

*My sixty-nine years seemed ancient as all git-out most days.*

# 2

Jessie instinctively tucked her left hand under her right arm and narrowed her eyes, scrutinizing Danny Callahan in an effort to interpret his meaning. Was he going to yank three-and-a-half karats of Neil Lane brilliance right off her finger?

"Relax," he said, pausing to suck back more coffee. "I'm not gonna steal it. I'm just pointing out that you're obviously not completely without resources."

Outrage sloshed from one side of her insides to the other—kind of like the coffee he nursed in that chipped blue mug. Jessie grabbed her purse and stood up. "Thank you for your time, Mr. Callahan."

"Jess," Piper hissed softly. "You need his help."

"I'm not handing over my ring to him, Piper."

Danny chuckled, the mere sound of it stoking the flame of Jessie's irritation. She shifted her entire body and stood over him, glaring at him as he continued sipping his coffee casually, looking so unbelievably smug!

"You find my situation amusing?" she asked.

When he glanced up at her and their eyes met, she thought he may have withdrawn slightly. She took a little pleasure in his apparent astonishment at the sparks of anger in her eyes, but it didn't last long. His pompous smirk returned in a fraction of a second, and Jessie resisted the uncharacteristic urge to slap him.

"Look," he said. "I know a guy who can get you a good price for that ring. It won't solve all your problems, but it will get you more than enough to hire me."

"You'll help her then?" Piper interjected.

"Piper . . . *My ring?*"

"Your ring from the husband who disappeared and left you holding the bag!" she pointed out, and Jessie's heart dropped a little deeper.

"From the look of it, you're wearing a lot of green on your finger there," he told her. "Enough to pay me and give you some walking-around money until I can figure out what happened."

"It was appraised at sixty-two," she said softly.

"He's not going to give you that much on a used ring," he replied.

"What's this about a ring?"

Jessie turned to find a caramel-skinned man—wearing nothing but a bath towel wrapped low around his waist—standing in the doorway to the sunroom, grinning at her.

"I told you about wearing something," Danny snapped.

"I am wearing something. I'm wearing a towel."

"Riggs!"

Extending his hand toward Jessie, he ignored Danny's objections. "Aaron Riggs."

"J-Jessie Stanton," she replied, reluctantly shaking his hand. "And this is my f-friend, Piper Brunetti."

Danny jumped up from the chair and scraped it away as he swooped in and clamped Aaron Riggs's shoulders with both hands, leading him out of the sunroom.

"Go put some clothes on," she heard Danny demand, "and take off."

Jessie and Piper locked eyes. Piper blinked first and cackled softly.

"Let's get out of here," Jessie whispered. Piper nodded and stood up but, before they could head for the door, Danny returned to block their way.

"I'm sorry about that."

"Does he . . . live here?" Jessie asked. "Is he your . . . your . . ."

"What?" he exclaimed. "No, he's not my . . . anything!"

"I just thought, with the towel and everything . . ."

Danny chuckled and shook his head. "He's a buddy I went surfing with this morning."

"Oh."

"Sit down and let's talk about your case."

"You're taking her case then?" Piper asked him.

"I'll do some digging . . . see what I can find out for you."

The three of them awkwardly backtracked, returning to their places in the sunroom. Danny opened a large laptop and punched a few keys.

"I'll need a contact number and address," he said, and once again, Jessie felt her shoulders slump.

"I only have somewhere to live for the next week or two before the new owners move into my home. And I don't really know where I'm going to be yet . . ."

"You can stay with us," Piper told her.

"Oh, Piper, you have a houseful already with Antonio's family in from Italy . . ."

"We'll figure it out. I'm not going to see my best friend homeless!"

"Who's homeless?" Aaron Riggs asked from the doorway, fully clothed. "You're looking for a place to crash?"

Jessie's heart fluttered. She could only imagine what he might have in mind.

"Easy there. I'm not inviting you to join my harem," he said with a chuckle when he saw her expression. "I own a couple of properties. One of them is a duplex here in Santa Monica, and there's a vacant unit that came available yesterday."

"Riggs," Danny intervened. "You promised Charlotte you'd move into that place so Allie would have somewhere to go when you have her."

"She has somewhere to go. We've got my van. We've got the bed in your guest room . . ."

"Riggs."

"Look," he said, staring at Jessie. "If you want to see it, I can take you over there right now. It's nothing fancy, but from what I overheard a minute ago, you can't really afford fancy anyway."

*Well, that's the sad truth.*

Jessie closed her eyes and massaged her throbbing temples as she wondered how this had become her life.

"Chaz, it's Danny Callahan."

"Callahan. Where you been, buddy? Haven't seen or heard from you in three months."

"Oh, you know. Listen, I'm sending a jpeg over right now," Danny said as he hit Send on the email. "It's Neil Lane, three and a half carats, appraised at sixty-two. What can you do for me?"

"Lemme have a look . . ."

While he waited, Danny opened another browser window and clicked on one of the bookmarked pages. He typed in Jack Stanton's name and last known address, and his screen went flush with a wealth of information on Jessie Stanton's missing person.

"Ha!" Chaz clucked. "It's still on her hand?"

"She's not so willing to part with it until I talk to you and get the straight dope."

"Got yourself a new girl, Callahan?"

"New client. The husband vanished and took their assets with him. Pretty much all she's got left is this ring and some expensive shoes."

"Clarity looks pretty good," he said slowly, obviously lingering over the image. "The band going with it? I can give her more for the set."

"Let's talk about the set then."

"I'll have to see it in person, you understand."

"Sure."

"I might be able to do ten."

"Ten," Danny spat. "C'mon. You can do better than ten grand, Chaz. It's nearly four carats. And I'm no expert on upscale jewels, but even I know Neil Lane is a pretty big ticket."

"She got paperwork to prove it's Neil Lane?"

"You can't verify that online or the logo in the ring or something?"

Chaz paused for a long moment, sputtering and mumbling; typical song and dance. Finally, "Where's the hand now?"

"She went with Riggs to check out one of his crash pads."

"Gimme the address, and I'll meet you there."

"Not for an offer of ten grand, buddy," Danny objected. "It's a sixty-thousand-dollar ring."

"Maybe I can do twenty-five."

"Or thirty-five."

"Nah, not thirty-five."

Danny shook his head. "Chaz. This woman's in a choke hold here. She needs to catch a break."

"Not to mention that there's a big price tag on her PI," he pointed out.

"Thirty-five?"

"Lemme have a look. I'll do the best I can."

"Personal favor, buddy," Danny told him. "Let me check in with Riggs and find out where they are. I'll text you the address."

Danny disconnected the call and composed a quick text to Riggs to verify the duplex address.

*Duplex scared her*, Riggs texted back. *On the way to the Pinafore property.*

If the duplex freaked her out, he could hardly wait to see her reaction to Riggs's Pinafore apartment building. Danny laughed at the mental picture of prim and proper Jessie Stanton coming to terms with the idea of living in an eight-hundred-square-foot apartment with a closet the size of that big bag she carried around.

*Hang there. Bringing Chaz to look at the ring.*

*10-4.*

Thirty minutes later, Danny parked his Jeep behind Riggs's VW bus on Pinafore Street. The shiny white Jaguar on the opposite side near the Coco Avenue intersection looked glaringly out of place amidst the row of Toyotas, Fords, and Buicks with dented fenders and dull paint jobs. He hadn't been to the property since he pitched in to help Riggs finish off the corner unit a couple of years back when he'd first bought the apartment building.

"My second rental property, dude!" Riggs had declared. "I'm officially a real estate magnate."

Danny had questioned his friend's decision to invest in rental properties around the time the economy took a dive, but it had worked out pretty well for him. He'd always been a handy guy, so it seemed like a good fit for Riggs; not to mention the landlord role left free time for a lot of surfing, and generated enough income to keep Charlotte in their former La Crescenta hillside house and Allie in private school. So what if Riggs had to do it from the inside of a Volkswagen minibus?

Jessie Stanton appeared somewhat shell-shocked to Danny when he made his way to the vacant apartment and walked inside. He could hear her friend chattering about morning light and parking spaces with Riggs in the adjacent bedroom while Jessie stood in the middle of the living room—pale and fragile—looking like Dorothy in her first few seconds outside the front door of her fallen house.

"You all right, Mrs. Stanton?"

Delayed reaction. When she finally looked up at him and blinked, she brought a sluggish internet connection to Danny's mind.

"Yeah," he said, taking a stab at a reassuring smile. "It's not Malibu, is it?"

She didn't reply. She just blinked at him again and faintly shook her head.

Danny scanned the small living room, trying to look at it through the eyes of the likes of Jessie Stanton, lingering over chips in the windowsill paint, two-toned brown shag bearing a striking resemblance to a roadside bear he'd once seen in Angeles Crest. The single light bulb dangling from the loose overhead socket created an interrogation-room ambience.

"You know, I can maybe help you fix the place up a little," he said. "I mean, some paint and a good shampoo for the—"

He sliced his own words in two. No use continuing when she'd already turned and left the room. With a shrug, Danny followed her to the doorway of the narrow galley kitchen where she mindlessly opened the refrigerator and stood there glaring at the inside of it.

"Yo, Callahan," Chaz called out from the front door. "You here?"

Danny took one last look at the bewildered woman still staring into the fridge before he returned to the front room to greet Chaz.

"Dude. Riggs is trying to rent this place to a skirt with a Neil Lane ring?"

"She's a little out of other options," he growled in a low voice. "Hang on, I'll get her."

She hadn't moved a centimeter, still staring blindly into the old, empty refrigerator.

"Mrs. Stanton?"

Jessie's attempt to shut the crooked door to the Frigidaire was met with resistance, and Danny stepped forward to help her.

"Maybe we can get Riggs to spring for new appliances before you move in," he commented. "Listen, my buddy is here to have a look at your ring." She looked a little zombie-esque as she obediently turned and put one foot in front of the other.

"Chaz, meet Jessie Stanton."

Chaz brushed coarse, dark hair away from his face and nodded. "Charles Decker, at your service." Jessie hardly flinched. She just stood there gawking at him. "You got a ring set you want to sell, yes?"

"Chaz thinks you can get much more if you sell the set," Danny pointed out. After another moment of queer silence, he picked up her hand and displayed it for Chaz. "Let's give her a break, huh? What's your top dollar?"

Chaz produced a gem loupe from his shirt pocket and inspected the ring on Jessie's motionless finger.

"This is really good quality," he commented, sounding a little surprised. "How old is it?"

When Jessie didn't respond, Danny nudged her wrist.

"Oh. It's . . . uh . . . my hus—J-Jack . . ." She paused and swallowed noisily before continuing. "He gave it to me for our tenth wedding anniversary. A few years ago."

Chaz turned the loupe and leaned in until Danny guessed she could feel his breath on her fingers.

"Three and a half carats, platinum setting," she managed. "Our insurance broker had them appraised for sixty-two thousand last year."

Chaz chuckled as he slipped the loupe into his pocket again. "I might have a buyer in mind. I'll have to check with him and get back to you."

Danny shot him a glare.

"Wait right here. I'll step outside and give him a jingle."

As Chaz took off in one direction, Piper and Riggs appeared from the opposite one.

"Is that Decker?" Riggs asked.

"Yeah, he'll be right back. He may have a buyer for the rings. He's checking in with him."

Piper hurried to Jessie's side just as an ounce or two of tears spilled down her face.

"I know, sweetie," her friend reassured her softly. "I know. But it's going to be okay."

"So what do you think about the apartment?" Riggs asked, clueless. Danny wanted to slug him.

Jessie shook her head, her eyes locked with her friend's and brimming with desperation. "I can't . . . live here, Piper. It's just awful."

She probably hadn't meant for Riggs to hear her, but he absolutely had. "Hey!" he exclaimed. "If you're not into it, lady, fine. But there's no need to throw around words like *awful*!"

Jessie wiped her eyes before looking up at Riggs. "I'm sorry, Mr. Riggs. It's just not . . . what I'm used to. And this is all just a little bit overwhelming for me."

"You'll come home with me," Piper repeated. "Antonio's mother is making manicotti, and his aunt brought over a case of Italian wine from their vineyard. We'll have a nice dinner, and you'll—"

"I just want to go home while I still have one to go to," she said, sniffling. "Will you take me home?"

Piper nodded and led Jessie toward the front door, but Chaz reappeared and blocked the way.

"Okay," he stated. "I have good news. I've texted over that photo Callahan sent me, and my buyer is interested. I'll tell you what. I'll give you eighteen grand for the set."

Jessie stared at him blankly, and Chaz finally lifted his hand and snapped his fingers in front of her face.

"Yes? No?"

"I . . ." Her mouth stayed propped open like that, not a peep escaping from it.

"Fine. I'll give you twenty."

Jessie glanced at Piper before fixing her light, glistening eyes on Danny. He felt the weight of them somewhere deep in his gut.

"Do you have a card?" Piper asked Chaz, and he blurted out a cackle.

"No. I don't have a card."

"I have his number," Danny interjected. "You go ahead and get her home. I'll check in with her tomorrow."

"Thank you, Mr. Callahan."

"Danny."

Piper led Jessie out the front door like a medical aide leading a blind patient. "Come on, sweetie. Let's go home."

"What about the apartment?" Riggs called after them, but the women didn't hesitate for even a moment. "Are you even interested . . ." He didn't bother to finish once they disappeared around the corner; he just tossed his head and chuckled.

"Let's give her a little time to think it all through," Danny suggested. "I'll call you tomorrow."

Riggs nodded. "Yeah, she's a little PTSD, isn't she?"

"She is."

"Well, there's a time clock on the offer for the ring," Chaz cut in. "If she wants to sell it, I will need to hear from her within twenty-four hours."

"Why? You got more pressing offers to sift through?" Danny snapped. "Just give the woman a break. I'll call you tomorrow."

Chaz smacked the doorjamb and shrugged. "All righty then." And with that, he left.

"Same old Chaz," Riggs commented. "Ever the empath."

"Said no one about Chaz Decker, ever," Danny added.

Riggs stepped into the kitchen and flipped off the overhead light, then he did the same in the bedroom. Danny walked outside with him and waited while he locked the dead bolt.

"What happened to her . . ." Riggs commented. "She never saw it coming?"

"I don't think so."

The two of them ambled down the broken concrete driveway, and Danny stopped at the end next to a tall palm tree.

"If she moves in here, how about we work together to clean up the place a little?" he suggested, and Riggs grinned at him.

"I hope you haven't gone all sweet and sappy on this one, Danny. She's the walking wounded."

"So that makes it all the more important to help her out, does it not?"

Riggs turned and headed toward his bus. Halfway down the sidewalk, he called to Danny over his shoulder. "I've been meaning to give the place a little attention anyway. Now's as good a time as any."

*That's the spirit.*

"I'm headed out to take Allie to dinner and see her school play rehearsal. I'll catch you waveside in the morning."

"See you then."

---

Jessie didn't know how long ago she'd stepped out of her shoes, thrown open the glass doors, and crossed the deck, climbing up on the railing and sitting there like a fat, pathetic lump of anxiety and remorse; but she'd been staring at the ocean so long it felt warmly imprinted on her retinas. She'd apparently hung out a sign on her brain—Temporarily Out of Order—and simply stopped thinking about Jack or their house or the BMW she'd seen bobbing around Cross Creek and up Pacific Coast Highway. And most of all, she'd evicted all thoughts of crummy apartments with mangy carpet in the living room, loose floorboards in the bedroom, and zero water pressure from the single faucet.

Hadn't she already lived through the worst abandonment of all when she was a kid? Did she have to go through it yet again?

She considered the idea of wandering into the house and breaking out a glass of wine, but since she couldn't be certain it wouldn't turn into a bottle or three, she thought better of it. And suddenly a random thought crept up on her.

*Did Jack even leave the wine collection? Or did he take it with him?*

Acid rushed through her stomach in a wave that rivaled the one heading for the shore beyond the golden sand beneath her. Jessie pushed her legs over the railing and hopped down to the deck. Her feet pushed her through the great room, around the dining room, and into the kitchen, where she yanked open the French doors to the wine closet.

*Nothing.*

Empty shelves, floor to ceiling; empty wine cooler; not a bottle left behind. Not even the snooty bottle of chardonnay he'd given Jessie for her birthday. Jack had taken it all.

She'd never really liked wine all that much, let alone appreciated swirling it around in her mouth and discussing its undertones and top notes. In fact, she didn't really know why it bothered her so much that he'd taken it with him, but that big empty closet stung like an unceremonious, no-holds-barred slap across the face.

She opened the pantry door—half expecting to find that he'd taken all the snacks with him as well—but to her relief, the pantry remained fully stocked. She grabbed a bag of Cool Ranch Doritos first, but reconsidered. The Cheetos would leave that annoying orange residue on her fingers afterward; all the better to smear on the cushions of the pale sage Tommy Bahama sofa Jack had apparently sold to the new owners of her beloved home.

Jessie stopped in her tracks and sighed. As satisfying as the rebellious act might leave her, she couldn't do it. She stamped her foot on the ceramic floor tile beneath her and groaned, trading the bag for the chips after all.

"Fine," she muttered as she padded into the living room and flopped onto the sofa. "But I'm not taking out the trash before I leave."

*"Grampy, I can't do it. Don't make me."*

*"I won't make you, child. But if you don't put the worm on the hook, you ain't gonna attract the fish. You wanna fish, don't you?"*

*"I don't think so, Grampy. Can I just sit here next to you and you do the fishin'?"*

*"Sure thing."*

*My Jessie was always the sensitive sort. She never did learn to bait the hook, but she liked to cast the line for me, and she made for some good company on the river bank out toward Picayune. We ate egg salad sandwiches and potato chips and talked about everything under the sun while waitin' for a speckled trout or a big ole catfish to amble by my line.*

*"S'posin' you could only fish for one kinda fish for the whole rest of your life, Grampy. Which'n would you want?"*

*Jessie liked her s'posin' game. We played it often.*

*"Why would I wanna cast for only one kinda fish, huh? S'posin' you could only wear one of your frilly dresses every Sunday for the resta yer life. Could you pick which one?"*

*She curled up her little face in a real puzzle. "If I hadda," she said, bitin' on the corner of her lip, "I think I'd hafta pick my blue checkered dress. The one with the pretty petticoat under it."*

*"Yeah? Why that'n?"*

*"I like the way it looks when I twirl."*

*Yeah, Jessie and me'd made an Olympic sport outta her twirlin'.*

# 3

Realtor Anthony Grana's irritating voice had serenaded Jessie for most of the night, and it was a sad song indeed.

*Until the end of the month to move out.*

*The furniture and appliances stay.*

*So generous of your husband to throw in the office safe.*

Jessie's focus perked. *The office safe.* Setting her coffee on the table next to the sofa, she popped up and hurried down the hall into Jack's home office.

She rolled up the top on the massive desk and sank into the leather chair before it. Not even a Post-it left behind. She yanked open the drawer of the cabinet beside it to find nothing but a lone hanging file wobbling there like a pathetic one-armed man. She swiveled the chair and tugged open the closet door to Jack's barren supply shelves and shook her head with a bitter groan. He'd taken the reams of paper, boxes of file folders, cartons of pens; nothing at all remained.

Jessie knelt down inside the closet and lifted the false bamboo floor, folding it back to reveal the floor safe hidden there.

1-16-47. His dead mother's birthdate. With a crank of the lever, she opened the steel door and peered inside. Unlike the rest of her cavernous life, something had actually been left behind in there. Jessie tugged out the leather portfolio tucked inside and collapsed backward to a sitting position and leaned against the closet jamb before she opened it.

Her birth certificate . . . several copies of her mother's death certificate . . . random letters and papers, none of which gave any real hint of the husband she'd thought she had or the life they'd led together. Aside from the lonely marriage license tucked into the back of the stack, of course. Nice of Jack to leave her proof that she hadn't dreamt him up.

Stuffed down into the bottom, she found a fat envelope with her name scrawled across it in Jack's recognizable handwriting. Jessie's heart thumped hard as she tore it open in the hope that a letter might explain what she couldn't figure out without him. Why had he done this? Why had he left her with nothing?

In place of the letter of explanation he clearly hadn't left, Jessie found a large wad of cash. She counted out ten thousand dollars. A strange valuation of her worth.

When her cell phone buzzed, Jessie reached down into her pocket and pulled it out.

"Hello?"

"Mrs. Stanton, it's Danny Callahan."

It took her a moment to settle back to the present, to find clarity. "Please call me Jessie."

"Well, Jessie, I have some news. Can I stop by?"

"Sure," she sputtered. "I guess so. Do you know where I live?" *For now, anyway.*

"Yep. I'm about three minutes from your driveway."

Jessie folded the envelope of cash and stuffed it into her pocket before pushing the papers back into the leather portfolio and dropping it to the seat of Jack's desk chair on her way through the door. She barreled down the hall, through the bedroom and into the bathroom. She grabbed her brush and ran it through her bedhead hair as she glared at her unfamiliar reflection in the mirror. She hadn't slept more than a few hours the night before, and every bit of the restless worry that kept her awake now showed in shadows on her weary face. The front bell chimed as she glided gloss across her bare lips, and she tossed the tube into the drawer before rushing to the door.

"This is quite a place," Danny said as she tugged open the door.

"Yeah." She couldn't think of anything else to say, so she settled on, "Coffee?"

"Please."

Jessie waved her arm at the couches in the living room as she passed. "Make yourself at home . . . while I still have one."

Danny walked over to the open glass door instead and stepped out onto the deck. Jessie imagined the view as some sort of Nirvana to a beach bum like Danny Callahan. Although his own view from that shack of his up Pacific Coast Highway wasn't much different.

"I have pumpkin spice, hazelnut, or French vanilla," she called out to him, and he sauntered back inside with a confused glaze across his handsome face.

"Just coffee," he told her. "You don't need to feed me."

"Those *are* coffees."

"Oh." He paused momentarily to mull it over before asking, "You don't have just plain black coffee?"

"I don't know," she admitted. "I'll check."

She spun the K-cup storage rack until she found the single offering of the Columbian that Jack used to drink before he gave up caffeine.

"Cream or sugar?" she called out.

"Black."

When she left the kitchen with the steaming cup, Danny had returned to his previous spot on the deck and he stared out at the surf as if gazing at a long-lost love.

"Black," she told him, and he turned around and smiled at her.

"Excellent."

"Do you want to sit out there?"

The small web of wrinkles on the outside of both his eyes ignited as he squinted at her. "No, inside is fine. Just admiring the view for a minute."

Jessie tapped her foot while he made his way to the couch. Sat down. Sipped his coffee. Adjusted the cushions . . .

"You said you had news?"

One corner of his mouth tilted upward and quirked slightly. "Yeah," he said, setting down the coffee. "First things first, Chaz has agreed to go thirty-five on your rings."

"Both of them?"

"The set."

She instinctively twirled the precious Neil Lane mementos around her finger while she considered the offer. "Do you think that's good?"

"I think it's the best you're going to get in a hurry. From the looks of things, and given your situation, I'd say fast money is the way to go."

She snorted out a bitter chuckle and nodded. "I guess you're right."

"We can get a check for you by the end of the day."

"About that." She twirled her rings for a moment longer before admitting, "It looks like I don't even have a bank account. I checked this morning and my life is locked up tight." She tugged the envelope from her pocket and opened it. Her eyes betrayed her, and tears popped out and ambled down her cheeks as she counted out a thousand dollars and handed it to Danny.

"What's this?" he asked.

"It seems Jack put a price tag on my worth," she snapped. "He left me some cash. Wasn't that nice of him? At least he didn't leave it on the nightstand, right?"

"I'm . . . sorry."

"Anyway, here's a down payment on whatever you're doing to help me find him. Is this enough? It's a thousand dollars."

"It's fine."

She wished he wouldn't look at her with such sympathy emanating from his steely blue eyes. Her heart fluttered gently as she wondered why this total stranger looked at her that way.

"And on that subject, I ran over to Jack's office this morning," he said, and she froze, wide-eyed, waiting for the second large boot to drop. "He left his assistant high and dry as well. After insisting she take a few days off, she returned to the office today to find the locks changed and the phones shut off."

She tried to imagine Jack doing much of anything—much less an undertaking of this size—without Claudia's help or knowledge.

"No cash left for her?" she cracked. "I guess that makes me *special*."

"I've spent some time trying to follow the money trail, but I haven't really gotten anywhere yet. I'll keep at it though."

She tried to choke back the mist of emotion taking over, but as she gave him a blurry stab at a smile through the tears, Danny Callahan leaned forward and locked her gaze with his own.

"Look, I'll get to the bottom of this. Meanwhile, what's your thinking this morning about moving into one of the places Riggs showed you yesterday?"

"What's my thinking?" she repeated softly.

"I know it's not what you're accustomed to," he said as he looked around. "But it's a roof over your head."

She sighed. "Not the duplex."

"You prefer the apartment building—"

"I wouldn't exactly call it a preference . . ."

"I'll call Riggs. You get started on your packing, and we'll get the apartment ready for you before you have to vacate this place."

Jessie massaged her temples for several moments before a sharp intake of oxygen pierced her chest. "Thank you, Mr. Callahan."

"Danny."

"I'm not sure why you're so decent to me, but I don't think I could face any of this without you. Without what you're doing for me."

"Look," he said with a lopsided grin, "I'm an epic failure at a lot of things. But I do try to be decent. You've been dumped on and you need a break."

"Well . . . Thank you."

She continued massaging the lump of tension at the side of her forehead as she dropped back into the cushions behind her. "I keep hoping it's a bad dream," she said softly, her eyes still closed. "You know that stretch of time between when your mind wakes up and you open your eyes for the first time in the morning?"

"Yeah."

"I found myself thinking how relieved I was that the nightmare I'd had wasn't my reality." A sour burst of a chuckle escaped her throat as she opened her eyes and looked at him. "And then I realized . . ."

As Jessie's words trailed away, Danny just stared at her blankly. He didn't appear to know quite what to say. For that matter, neither did she. She simply gave her rings one last yearning look and a quick twirl before slipping them from her finger. When she extended them toward him, he raised both hands and shook his head.

"Nah. I don't want to take custody of them," he said. "You keep them on your hand until we meet Chaz for the check."

*Must I?* She peered down at the traitorous rings resting in the palm of her hand.

"That way, there's no room for error."

"Lose your keys a lot, do you, Danny?" she asked as she pushed them back down her finger. "Leave your cell phone behind at restaurants? Afraid you'll set them on some random windowsill somewhere and forget all about them?"

"Been known to do a little of all that," he replied, and he stood up. "I'll call you with a time to meet."

"About that. I don't . . . have transportation either."

"Oh, right. No worries. I'll pick you up."

---

The fact that Dogtown Coffee used to be a surf shop came as no surprise to Jessie. The moment they walked in, she pegged it as a natural hangout for the likes of Danny Callahan with its colorful murals and cool hipster vibe.

"What kind of coffee?" he asked her.

"Something caramel," she replied.

He didn't disappoint when he returned to the table and set down two mugs. He kept the thick black brew for himself and slid the foamy one toward her.

"Salted caramel coffee with sea-salt foam," he sort of grunted.

Obviously not his taste, but he'd chosen well. One sip elicited an appreciative moan from somewhere deep within her.

He grabbed a napkin and wiped away the foam mustache she hadn't realized she'd acquired. "Thanks," she said with a giggle. "You should really try some of this. You don't know what you're missing."

His only reply came with a lift of his own coffee as he took a few gulps.

"Chaz should be here any time," he told her. "Then I'll run you home before I head over to Pinafore."

"You're going to the apartment building?"

"Yeah, we're planning on tearing out the living room rug today."

"You are?" She almost didn't recognize the surge of joy when it shot through her. Joy had been a little distant and unfamiliar to her these days.

"Unless you're set on keeping it."

"Oh no!" she blurted, and he grinned at her. "No. You just feel free to tear that sucker out and send it far, far away."

Danny chuckled, and a sudden thought tased her heart with an electrical pulse. "Uh, what are you planning to replace it with?"

"Oh, you'll love it," he told her. "We scored a nice remnant of lime green shag. It'll really brighten the place up."

"Lime . . ." A foamy wave of sea salt rose in the back of her throat as the *thump-thump-thump* of her heart accelerated. "Shag?"

Danny's serious expression cracked slightly, slowly giving way to a broad grin.

"Would I do that to you?" he asked her.

"Not lime green shag?"

"No."

"Oh, thank God!"

Danny took another gulp from his coffee before telling her, "Riggs got a line on some Pergo."

Jessie swallowed around the lump in her throat. "Pergo," she repeated. "Isn't that . . . *laminate*?"

Danny narrowed his steely blue eyes and stared at her for a moment before he asked, "I think it is. But you know what it's *not*?"

"Two-toned brown carpet that smells like bad breath?" she said with a squirm.

"That. Yes. It's also not costing you anything, so I wouldn't complain in front of Riggs."

"Got it. No complaints from the ungrateful homeless person. Do you think I could go over there with you? I'd like to have another look at the place in the light of day."

"Wasn't it daytime when we were there?"

"Not up here," she answered, tapping the side of her head. "It was all kinds of dark up here."

"And this is you in the light of day?"

"What do you mean?" she asked him.

Danny curled up his face before releasing a rumbling little groan. "Isn't that . . . *lam-in-ate*?"

It took a moment to process. "Oh," she finally said. "Is that your impression of me?"

"Pretty good, huh?" he replied with a mischievous smile before he took another drink from his coffee.

"*No*," she retorted. "It's not accurate *at all*."

He set down the cup and nodded toward the door. "There's Chaz."

Jessie leaned into Danny's direction and looked up at him, her light blue eyes brimming with an innocence he wasn't completely convinced she had.

"And you're sure this is all I'm going to get for my rings?"

"This ain't no charity I'm runnin' here, lady," Chaz piped up. "I gotta be able to make something too."

Danny gave her a nod. "It's fair for such a fast turnaround."

"Okay."

She slipped the rings from her finger and set them in Chaz's outstretched hand. After inspecting them carefully, he pushed them down his pinkie atop the brass ring already there and handed Jessie the check.

"Cashier's check," he said. "All official and everything."

She took it from him and smiled timidly. "Thank you." After a moment, she tilted her head toward Danny and, wide-eyed, mouthed the same to him. "Thank you so much."

Jessie wasn't sure why, but she felt a sense of relief as she watched Chaz saunter out of the coffee-house with her rings sparkling on his fat pinkie. Maybe because she didn't want to spend any more time with him than necessary? Despite the fact that he was a friend of Danny's—a fact in itself that didn't seem to fit—she just didn't like the guy. Something about him. The way his eyes narrowed and turned to small slits whenever they made eye contact, and the greasy stuff in his thick black hair. And then there was the shiny pleather jacket. She felt certain he thought everyone else believed it to be leather, but she knew better. In her eyes, it made him look like a refugee from one of those present-day mobster movies Jack used to like.

The fleeting thought that perhaps her relief at Chaz's departure came from the subsequent departure of her wedding rings tickled the back of her neck and she brushed it away.

"First stop, a bank account," Danny announced, standing. "Any preferences?"

"Just not Wells Fargo," she replied. "Apparently, I'm dead to them."

Danny chuckled, took a last swig from his cup, and gave her a nod. "I know just the place."

She gathered her things and followed him out. An hour later, Chaz's cashier's check and most of the cash Jack had left behind was safely deposited in her new account, checks with a monogrammed J and a Pinafore address had been ordered, and she tucked $200 into her wallet. Jessie couldn't remember the last time she'd walked around with cash in her purse, but it seemed like a good idea to have some now. She wasn't exactly sure why.

By the time they arrived at the apartment building, they had to step over the stacked piles of laminate flooring outside the open front door to get inside. Riggs had already pulled up the living room rug and rolled it into a monstrosity in the corner, and they found him in the smaller of the two bedrooms. Jessie hadn't even remembered there was a second bedroom; not that it would fit anything more than a desk and a chair, of course.

*Oooh. Or perhaps it would make a nice walk-in closet!*

Riggs pushed a large, thundering machine that looked like a cross between a vacuum and a carpet cleaner along the corner of the small room, and when he didn't respond to Danny's efforts to call out to him over the clamor, Danny did the next best thing and pulled the plug.

"Oh, hey," Riggs greeted him. "When did you get here?"

Danny nodded toward his friend's project. "What are you doing?"

"I thought I'd see if I can make any improvements to the existing floor back here, but the boards are pretty loose. We may need to bring in the nail gun."

Danny smiled at Jessie. "Any excuse to use the nail gun, and this guy is all over it." He moved to the corner of the large, empty bedroom and wiggled a floorboard or two with the toe of his shoe. "Yeah, I see what you mean."

Jessie stepped up behind him as Danny crouched and tugged at one particularly warped strip that came up easily. "Oh dear," she remarked. He pulled up another two and tossed them into the corner. "Maybe you should quit while I'm ahead?"

"There seems to be a lower subfloor or something," he commented, and he sprawled on his stomach and reached down into the floor all the way to his elbow. A moment later, he pulled out a small stack of books and a dusty velvet drawstring bag.

"What is that?" she asked, and Riggs joined them as the three formed a circle around the substantial hole in the floor.

"It looks like some kind of chamber built underneath," Danny told them.

"Like a Priest's Hole," she said, a rush of adrenaline coursing through her.

"I don't think you'll find a priest down there," Riggs said with a chuckle.

"In the 1500s," she told them, "priests in England had hiding places built into their castles and country houses. Some were big enough to conceal the priests themselves; others held secret treasures or papers or their sacred vessels."

Danny gazed at her over his shoulder with one arched eyebrow.

"What?" she commented. "I like to read."

"I can see that."

"It might be a handy place to have, don't you think? How big is it? Maybe I could put a safe down there."

"I'm guessing three feet squared," he surmised. "Maybe a foot deep."

"What're you gonna hide down there?" Riggs inquired.

"You don't need to know that."

She picked up the books and examined them, blowing away the dust from the cover of the first one with a hearty puff. "*Madeline's Rescue*," she read. "By Ludwig Bemelmans." Flipping through it, she noticed the publication date. "It's a children's book," she stated. "Published in 1953."

"This must have been the kid's room," Riggs remarked before turning his attention back to the opening in the floor.

"Are they all children's books?" Danny asked her.

Jessie separated the dusty books, stopping to sneeze as she did. "It looks like it."

*Time of Wonder* by Robert McCloskey.

*Little Bear* by Else Holmelund Minarik.

And the last one: *Charlotte's Web* by E. B. White.

"Oh my!" she exclaimed. "This must be a first edition." When Danny moved closer to inspect it, she glanced up at him and grinned. "This was my favorite book as a child. The publication date says 1952."

"What's in the little bag?" he asked, and Jessie balanced the books in the crook of her arm long enough to pull open the velvet bag and shake the contents out into her hand. A domed round locket rested there, only about an inch and a half in diameter. It looked to be genuine gold with small red-and-white stones set into the dome and tiny aged pearls forming a circle around the edge. Jessie flicked it open with her fingernail and a yellowed photograph of a woman tumbled out from inside. Danny quickly retrieved it from the floor and placed it in the palm of his hand so they could look more closely.

"She's lovely," Jessie remarked. "Very exotic."

"Sad eyes."

With no regard for their discovery, Riggs cranked up the floor sander again and went about his work. Covering her ears and grimacing, Jessie gladly followed Danny's lead as they made their way out of the small room.

"I didn't even notice there was a second room," she told him as they headed for the living room. "What do you think about turning it into a walk-in closet? Do you have any shelf-building skills?"

Danny grinned at her. "You want your private investigator slash pawn broker slash Realtor to become your carpenter as well?"

"I could hide my jewelry down in the floorboards where that little girl hid her treasures. I think it's a good sign, don't you? They stayed safe all these years. I wonder when she lived here. Do you know when these apartments were built? You can find that out, can't you? Being a big investigator and all?"

His grin broadened, and he laughed right out loud.

"Well, can't you?"

"I can look into it, yes. In between finding your husband and building out your closet."

"Oh, goodie."

"Goodie," he repeated. "I don't think I've met anyone in the last twenty years who says *goodie*."

"Well, now you have. And what about building those shelves? Do you think you could do that? Do you have any paper? I can draw you a picture of what I have in mind."

"Oh . . . *goodie*," he stated dryly.

*"I gotta write two paragraphs about what I wanna be when I grow up," Jessie told me, her mouth full of half-chewed cinnamon toast.*

*"And?"*

*"And I don't know what to say. I mean, I'm only eleven. How do I decide now?"*

*"Well, what're your favorite things to do?"*

*She thought it over for a minute. "I like twirlin'."*

*"Maybe you wanna be a dancer then. You used to like those ballet classes of yours."*

*"Mrs. Krieger didn't like it when I twirled though. She said I ain't got discipline."*

*"You're a free spirit, that's why," I pointed out, and she seemed to like it 'cause she nodded her head and smiled at me. "What else you like doin'?"*

*"I'm a good speller."*

*"Yeah? Maybe you'll write the Great American Novel, huh?"*

*"I don't think I like words that much."*

*"Why dontcha think about what you* do *like that much."*

*She chewed her lower lip and considered it with great consternation on her pretty little face.*

*"I like dress-up, Grampy. You know, like pretty dresses and high-heeled shoes like Mama wears sometimes. Maybe I could be one of those models on the front of the magazines down at the drugstore?"*

Lord above, *I started thinkin'.* Gimme strength.

*"Jessie-girl," I said, "I want you to remember this your whole life what I'm about to say to you."*

*"Okay, Grampy. What is it?"*

*"There's a lotta folk in this world who are gonna try to show you that what you have in the cupboard and the closet and what you drive down the street is the measure of your importance. But don't be fooled."*

*"Okay, I won't," she said, studyin' her toast more than her talk with her grandpa. Then she looked up at me with the light in her blue eyes a-twinklin'. "How do I measure then?"*

*On the walk home that day, I told Jessie the Bible story of Samuel when he anointed young David to be king.*

*"God didn't care nothin' about how he was just a little kid out in the field with the sheep 'cause the Lord don't look at the clothes a man wears or the way a lady fixes her hair. He looks straight into the heart, Jessie-girl. So you guard your heart and keep your eyes fixed on the Lord, and you'll be a-okay."*

*"Okay," she said, and she kissed my cheek. Before she ran inside, she turned back and added, "Do you think I could still wear my pretty gingham dress if I grow up to work in the field with the sheep, Grampy?"*

# 4

Jessie closed the flap on the last cardboard box, and Piper taped it down into place.

"There you have it," Jessie said, standing back to survey the skeleton of a room. "Everything I have left, packed into nineteen boxes."

"Plus the six in the kitchen," Piper added hopefully.

Jessie found it so hard to digest. Her entire life had changed in an instant. Well. One instant plus the weeks on end Jack must have been planning it without her knowledge.

Danny had called to give her an update just that morning, and he didn't know much more than he'd known when she hired him, aside from the fact that Jack had tied up all of his loose ends more neatly than those cardboard boxes stacked in the corner of the bedroom. On the upside, he and his friend Riggs would be around in an hour or so with a truck and some muscle to move her twenty-five boxes including the ones in the kitchen. Never mind the dramatic shift in ZIP codes at the bottom line of her move.

She sat down on the edge of the massive bed and sighed. Running her hand over the satiny surface of eighteen inches of luxurious thickness, Jessie said a silent good-bye to the finest bed that had ever graced a Malibu bedroom. Out of everything she'd lost in one fell swoop, she felt certain she would miss the comfort of her four-poster bed most of all. She'd spent eight hundred dollars of her ring money to purchase a replacement bed from a place called *Rest Well Mattress* located in West Hollywood, but she had limited hopes about resting well on it—despite the promising name of the establishment that had sold it to her.

Three hours later, Jessie Stanton closed the doors of her Malibu home for the very last time, hoping her black cloud of misery cleared by the time the new owners arrived. No sense in everyone suffering, after all. Contrasting how ecstatic she and Jack had been when they moved into this house with the way she felt as she left it—and him—behind, she climbed into the passenger seat of Piper's Jaguar and closed her eyes. After buckling the seatbelt, she dropped her head back before the tears could escape her eyes. Piper reached across the seat and squeezed her hand, however, and that was all the catalyst the tears needed to force past the barrier of her eyelids and stream down her cheeks.

"It's going to be okay," Piper promised.

"Have you lost your mind?" she asked her friend softly. "I don't even know how you can say that with a relatively straight face."

"You are going to be fine, Jess. You're going to work through this, and I'll be there to help you. It will be okay. You'll see."

She darted a quick, disbelieving glance toward the driver's seat and sighed again. "If you say so."

If one didn't compare the two residences, past to present, the condition of the small apartment on Pinafore seemed almost . . . inhabitable.

Riggs and Danny stood there like two goofy—albeit eager—sentries as Jessie and Piper passed through the front door. The hideous shag carpet in the living room had been replaced by a smooth-toned attempt that resembled actual hardwood floors, and the blotchy, yellowed walls had been painted with an appealing shade of light gray that stretched out its fingers toward ice-blue. Against the stark-white trim around the baseboards and windows and the almost-new charcoal chenille sofa against the largest wall, it gave the room a pleasant, clean quality. An understated navy-blue ivy pattern scrolled its way around the borders of a pretty gray area rug, and a small flat-screen television sat atop a plain black table.

"Where did this come from?" she asked no one in particular.

Jessie wrestled a gasp from escaping her throat as she glanced into the kitchen. The dilapidated refrigerator was gone, and in its place stood a noble stainless side-by-side.

"We installed the filter," Danny offered. "For the icemaker and the water."

She imagined she looked to Danny Callahan like a woman who didn't drink ordinary tap water. Accurate as the impression was, Jessie wished he hadn't so easily discerned it.

The kitchen cabinets looked to have been sanded and repainted a fresh, clean white, with brand new knobs and drawer pulls of brushed nickel. The chipped brown linoleum floor did nothing to meet the buttery walls halfway, but Jessie figured a nice rug might help it disappear a little. Too bad there was nothing that could do the same for the ancient, scraped butcher block counters; but the charming little bistro table and two chairs tucked into the other end of the room almost made up for them.

"You've really worked hard on this place," Piper commented to Riggs, and he half grunted humbly in reply. "No, really. It was so kind of you to try and make the apartment comfortable for Jessie. Thank you so much."

Riggs whispered something that Jessie couldn't decipher and, as she turned toward them, Piper elbowed him nonchalantly and smiled.

*Are they . . . flirting?* Jessie wondered, watching them for a moment with newly discriminating eyes. No, she knew that couldn't be. Piper and Antonio were the most solid couple she knew.

"You haven't seen the best part," Danny said with a nod and a strange glint in his eye.

She allowed him to lead her past the bedroom—now painted a muted slate blue and completely bare aside from an overturned cardboard box and the stark new mattresses and frame she'd bought. Danny yanked open the door to the tiny second bedroom, flipped the light switch just inside, and waved his arm. Jessie's mouth flew open and just hung there. Soft grunts of surprise somehow made their way from the base of her throat, but she couldn't speak a single coherent word beyond them.

"Oh my!" Piper expressed for her. "That is just . . . amazing."

Danny Callahan had taken the crude drawing of a walk-in closet she'd made for him on her last visit to the apartment she would now—like it or not—call home, and he'd built an exact replica and painted it all glossy eggshell white.

"You . . . You did this?" she managed, and Danny grinned.

"It's what you wanted, yes?"

"Y-yeees!"

"Go on in. Have a closer look."

Like Alice, Jessie stepped gingerly through the looking glass and into the depth of the thick remnant of dark blue carpet inside the closet. She didn't know where to look first; at the small crystal chandelier hanging where the dingy, cracked overhead lamp had once been . . . at the rows and rows of cubbyholes for her handbags . . . or perhaps the double rods awaiting her hangers of clothes. But no.

It was the half wall of shoe cabinetry that completely did her in.

"Ohhhh," she moaned as she stepped up before it and caressed several of the openings. "This is so . . . *beautiful*."

An ornate carved wooden dresser with five long, deep drawers had been topped with a small slab of blue and gray granite and placed beneath the shoe cabinets. A bench, cushioned with a blue and white paisley design, sat angled into the corner next to it.

Danny stepped past her and pulled up a corner of the rug to show the secret beneath it. "Your Priest's Hole," he told her as he tapped on the floorboard beneath. "I cleaned it out and lined it with some tile inserts. It's all ready for whatever treasures you want to hide."

A shadow of confusion crossed over Jessie's consciousness, and she tilted her head slightly and stared at him. Why was this stranger going to all this trouble for her? It wasn't like she had anything reciprocal to offer him. Nope, nothing to offer him . . . or anyone else, for that matter.

"Wait until you see the bathroom," Piper said softly. "It's so much improved."

Jessie arched an eyebrow and stared into Piper's eyes as she sauntered past her; stared so hard, in fact, that their gazes seemed locked up tight. Had she even seen the bathroom before?

The pale yellow bathroom walls responded reasonably well to the branches of sunlight pouring through the window, and the sheer floral shower curtain seemed to attract the light to it. The floor and countertops, both pretty much abysmal, could be ignored if she tried very hard—and squinted. But that blue bathtub!

*Oh. That's just . . . horrible!*

"Maybe we could replace the seat?" Piper asked, nodding toward the toilet in the corner.

"Yeah, whatever you say," Riggs replied.

And there it was. The confirmation she'd been awaiting.

"Hold on just one second. Whatever *she* says? What's going on here?"

The three of them exchanged fleeting glances, each of them looking more pathetic and guilty than the others.

"Piper?"

"Better come clean," Danny muttered before he stalked down the narrow hallway.

"They didn't make these improvements out of the kindness of their hearts, did they?"

"Yes!" Piper objected. "They absolutely did!" One look from Riggs, and she added, "I may have financed a thing or two, but—"

"Are you kidding me?"

"Come on, sweetie. I knew you'd react like that. But it's just something Antonio and I wanted to do for you. It wasn't much, really. Just a little something to make things a little easier."

"How much did you spend?"

"Jess."

"How much, Piper?"

"A few dollars, really. We have the money to spend. It's not worth the big deal you're making of it."

"That closet alone . . . That cost more than a few dollars."

"Oh, no! That wasn't me. That was all Danny. He wanted to do it for you."

Jessie's stomach lurched slightly. "Are you serious?"

Piper nodded. "Yeah."

Jessie squeezed between Piper and Riggs and made her way down the hall to the living room where Danny stood in front of the window, his arms folded across his chest and his full weight shifted to one of his jeans-clad legs. His muscular arms pressed against the sleeves of the dark gray T-shirt he wore, and she noticed for the first time the tattooed ring of barbed wire around the bicep of his left arm. She stepped a little closer for a better look at it.

"That's an interesting tattoo," she said, and he seemed startled to find her standing beside him. "Barbed wire is an odd choice for a laid-back surfer like yourself."

"Nah. It's thorns," he corrected.

"Thorns."

"A reminder of my faith," he clarified. Well. Clear as sludge.

"Oh," she mumbled. "Listen, about the closet. Piper said you did that on your own, and I'm just wondering . . . You know . . . Why did you do that?"

A long few moments ticked past before he angled his head downward and replied, "Because I could."

She didn't know how to respond to that. "But why?"

Danny raked his hand through his long, straight blond hair and asked, "Do you like it?"

"Yes, of course," she admitted. "It's beautiful."

"It's just what you wanted."

"Well . . . yes."

"Do you want to thank me?"

She stumbled over the question. "Of course. Thank you."

"Then we're square."

"But I—"

"That's the thing about being square with someone, Jessie. You move on, discussion over."

"I feel like I should pay you for—"

"Now see there? The discussion's not over. Why is that?"

Jessie giggled. "Sorry. Thank you. And that's all."

"Good. I'll get Riggs and we'll start unloading the truck."

---

It took all of two hours to unload most of her personal belongings into the closet Danny had built for her. When Jessie emerged, Piper had unpacked the kitchen boxes for her. She opened the refrigerator to find it stocked with a few minimal necessities as well.

"Piper. Thank you."

"For what?" she asked without looking up from arranging some fresh flowers into a plain glass vase on the counter.

"For all of it."

"We're best girlfriends," she said with a broad grin and a nod. "You'd do the same for me if Antonio turned out to be a louse."

"Which he's not," Jessie chimed in.

"No. He's not. And speaking of Antonio, I have to get home. His mother is cooking. Will you be all right here on your own?"

"Well, if I have any problem at all, it certainly won't be for your lack of planning." After a sudden thought, she grinned. "Come look at my closet before you leave."

She led her friend by the hand down the hall and into . . . Nirvana.

"Good grief," Piper said with a sigh. Then, in a whisper, she added, "It's like Fashion Week at Bryant Park was shipped to the ghetto."

Jessie giggled. "It's a great closet, isn't it?"

"It really is."

Piper smiled. She stepped toward Jessie and paused to brush her hair away from her face before clutching Jessie's shoulders and pulling her into an embrace. "I love you. You're going to be fine. I set up the Keurig," she said. "I made up your bed with a pair of those Egyptian cotton sheets you love, and there are some snacks here if you get hungry. Just call if you need anything at all."

"I will."

"And don't forget dinner at the restaurant tomorrow night. You, Danny, Aaron, and me."

"You don't have to do that . . ."

"What's the use of being married to a man with a restaurant if you can't use it to say thank you to a couple of guys who have been kind to my BFF?"

"Well, I can't think of one thing to say to that."

Piper smiled and kissed the side of Jessie's head before turning to leave.

"Danny will pick you up at seven o'clock. Wear something pretty."

She followed Piper to the door. "Don't I always?"

Jessie flipped the lock on the doorknob, turned the two deadbolts, and slid the safety chain into place after Piper left. Before walking away from the door, she turned the knob and yanked. Sure enough, that door wasn't going anywhere.

Jessie turned around and leaned against it with a sigh, surveying her minimalist surroundings. Nope, that door wasn't going anywhere. And sadly, neither was she.

She flopped down on the sofa and leaned against the arm as she retrieved the remote and flicked on the small television. After flipping through the channels for a few minutes, she turned it off again and fell back into the sofa cushions. Before she could sink too deep beneath those *What am I going to do now?* thoughts plaguing her, she hopped up and stalked down the hall. After entering her new closet, she closed the door behind her, sat down on the plush bench and sighed.

Vacant as it was, inside that closet she did at least sense the very remote feeling of having come home. And now that she'd lost her husband, her home, her car and her gold-standard four-poster bed, Jessie Stanton would take whatever she could get.

---

"Piper met Antonio on a wine tour in Italy," Jessie explained as Danny merged onto Santa Monica Boulevard toward Beverly Hills. "He was a really successful vintner then with a winery in Tuscany. They fell in love almost immediately, and she said by the time she headed back to the States, she actually considered picking up everything and moving to Italy to be with him."

The world of vintners and restaurateurs—and Jessie's Malibu mansion and designer labels as well, for that matter—were utterly foreign to Danny. He wished he hadn't agreed to this dinner, but Piper had been so charming when she invited him that he couldn't quite manage to decline. Besides, Riggs had been all over the invitation before it had even been completed.

*"Dude. She wants to thank us. It would be rude to turn up our noses."*

Yeah, that was Riggs. Never one to be rude. *Not.*

"Fortunately for me, she didn't do that," Jessie went on, "and he followed her here instead. He commuted back and forth for a few years after they married, but now they just go back to Italy a couple of times a year. He spends almost all of his time running the winery long-distance and tending to his restaurant."

"Tuscan Son," he remarked. "Catchy name."

"It's only been in business a few years," she told him, "but it's one of the best reviewed and most highly regarded dinner spots in Beverly Hills."

Danny took a deep breath and glanced over at Jessie's impeccable appearance before asking, "Am I underdressed?" Even though he'd chosen to wear jeans, he'd topped them with a new-ish black sport coat and charcoal shirt, but still.

"You look great. Wait until you try the calamari. Do you like calamari?"

"Squid?" he cracked. "Uh, no."

"Oh, but it's so good," she insisted. "It's baked in these spicy breadcrumbs and tomato sauce. It's really amazing."

If this was the kind of thing on the menu, he could hardly wait to see what Riggs—his pizza and beer counterpart—might order.

"Oh, and they have this *life-changing* bread broiled with gorgonzola and garlic."

*Life-changing bread*, he thought, and he cast a quick grin in the direction of the passenger seat. *A wave at Mavericks . . . a sunrise run on the sand with Frank . . . a break in a case that hasn't had one in a month . . . the touch of God's hand. These are the things that change lives. Not bread. Not even bread with garlic.*

He wondered what this Antonio might be like; this Son of Tuscany who named his restaurant after himself and his heritage, who thought he changed lives with gorgonzola bread. Piper married him, Danny considered, so he couldn't really be all that bad. Despite the snooty looks of her, she'd turned out to be pretty chill. Maybe this Italian husband of hers would, too.

"There," Jessie interrupted his thoughts. "Pull up over there."

A uniformed kid with perfect hair approached Jessie's door before the Jeep even came to a full stop, and he yanked it open, flashing those bright white teeth as he did.

"Mrs. Stanton, it's good to see you again."

"Heath," she said, stepping out of the car. "How's school going?"

"One semester to go," he called over his shoulder as he rounded the Jeep. He nodded at Danny and handed him a numbered stub. "Enjoy your evening, sir."

Jessie waited on him at the arched wood and beveled glass entrance to Tuscan Son. A sharply dressed host greeted them in the spacious entry where colorful hand-painted tiles formed a vibrant sunflower at the center of the floor.

"Mrs. Stanton," he said. "We have your party seated right this way."

"Thank you."

Bright stucco walls clothed in climbing ivy led the way to the wide-open restaurant. A wooden pergola strung with strands of small white lights and flowering vines disguised the very tall lighted ceilings and gave the place the appearance of an outdoor patio. Large thick-padded leather chairs in green and beige flanked distressed wood tables, and pristine chandeliers resembling groups of flickering candles hung low over each of them.

Danny nodded at Riggs as he followed Jessie to the large round table where he was seated across from Piper. The man next to her stood and greeted Jessie with a kiss to the cheek before extending his hand toward Danny.

"You must be Mr. Callahan," he said through an unmistakable Italian accent.

"Danny," he replied as they shook hands.

"I am Antonio Brunetti. Welcome to Tuscan Son. I believe we owe you a great debt of gratitude for your kindness to our Jessie."

Danny didn't quite know what to say to that, so he just smiled.

"Please, sit down, both of you," Antonio urged them. "We're serving *aperitivos*, and appetizers are on the way."

Danny sat down next to Piper and grinned when she rested her hand on his forearm for a moment. "I'm so glad you came."

A waiter appeared at Danny's elbow and leaned forward, placing a glass on the table.

"What is this?" he asked.

"Negroni," the waiter replied. "Red vermouth, gin, and bitter Campari. It's a traditional Italian predinner cocktail."

Danny leaned in and softly told him, "I don't drink alcohol. Could I get a club soda with lime?"

"Certainly, sir."

As the waiter removed the glass and hurried from the table, Jessie angled closer and asked, "Is something wrong with your drink?"

"No. Not at all. I just ordered something else."

She regarded him carefully for a moment before nodding. "Okay."

"Jessie," Antonio remarked as the waiter delivered Danny's club soda. "Tell us. How are you adjusting to your new surroundings?"

The slight hesitation before answering amused Danny. She wasn't about to admit that she'd probably checked the locks on the front door half a dozen times that first night alone, or that she'd likely stubbed her perfectly manicured toes on the uneven kitchen tile a time or two.

"I'm settling in," she said in an unexpectedly bright tone of voice. "Piper and Danny and Aaron have really worked hard to make it pretty for me." She lifted her glass and shared a shiny smile with each of them. "Thank you so much to everyone at this table. I couldn't have survived any of what's happened without you."

"Pretty good for a woman who thought moving into my apartment building was something akin to living under a bridge," Riggs cracked.

"*Per giorni migliori a venire*," Antonio said, tilting his glass in her direction.

"Yes," Piper agreed with a nod. "To better days ahead."

Danny raised his glass and clinked several others. He really did hope that for Jessie Stanton. "To better days," he chimed in.

---

*"What do you think of it, Grampy?"*

*Little Jessie had just been invited to her first boy-girl dance to put an exclamation point on the end of her eighth grade year. Her mama took her shoppin' three different times before the arguments stopped and they agreed on a dress. She looked pretty as a picture in it, too. Reminded me of her gram back in the day.*

*She stood there in the middle of the living room waitin' on a nod from her old gramps, and when she finally got what she come for, she sent out a beam of light that could guide ships. That's when she started up her twirlin'.*

*"I know, Grampy, isn't it di-viiine?" she sang as she made her circles.*

*Her mama stood watchin' in the doorway to the kitchen, and she gave me a secret little smile before she told her, "Go take that off, Jessie. Before you get it dirty."*

*"Okay, Mama," she beamed, and went runnin' off.*

*"She's headed for high school in the fall, Daddy," my April—Jessie's mama—said. "I hope she's ready. Her head's still so far up in the clouds."*

*My April had a scowl on her face on the day she was born, and she'd been starin' down the troubles of life ever' day since. Not like Jessie whose best days were spent twirlin' and dreamin' of party dresses 'n' fancy shoes. I reckoned that day that a combination of my two girls might be safest out there in the world, but on their own . . .*

*Well, I sent a prayer upstairs for 'em both.*

# 5

Jessie gazed at her reflection in the ladies' room mirror and couldn't help noticing that the woman looking back at her appeared almost . . . happy. Come to think of it, her heart felt immensely lighter as well. A strange new feeling, she acknowledged. In fact, she hadn't thought of Jack or her new situation even once through the exquisite dinner.

A young Dior-clad woman stepped up next to her, primly washing her hands. They exchanged polite smiles through the mirror.

"Is that Armani?"

Jessie gazed at the woman. "I beg your pardon?"

"Your dress. I thought I saw it at Armani on Rodeo."

"Oh." She glanced down at the beaded crepe dress. "Yes. It's Armani."

"It's fantastic."

"Thank you." She loved the dress, but couldn't help wishing she had that eighteen hundred dollars back. The days of extravagant shopping sprees, designer labels, and shoe therapy had disintegrated along with Jack.

The pretty blonde reached out and ran a finger along the seam of Jessie's handbag. "Gucci?"

She nodded.

"Broadway leather evening clutch. It's exquisite."

"You know your designers," Jessie said, touching up her lipstick.

"I'm all about fashion. I just wish I had the income to fund my obsession."

Jessie snickered. "I understand."

"I'm Amber Davidson," she said, offering a demure hand toward Jessie.

"Jessie Stanton."

When Amber dropped her hand, she bent slightly and leaned against the counter with one hip. "I just have to tell you . . . I really love your style."

"Thanks. But you look really beautiful. That's Ralph Lauren, isn't it?"

Amber brightened and ran her hand over the satin French cuff. "His Blue Label tuxedo wrap dress. It is pretty, isn't it?" Her smile dropped slightly as she looked into Jessie's eyes. "I borrowed it from a friend for this date tonight. The girl who set us up said he's got boatloads of money, and he's very particular about elegance in women."

"I see."

"Elegance is the prerogative of those who have taken possession of their future," Amber said. "Coco Chanel said that. Or something like it. I thought this dress said *elegance*. What do you think?"

"Very," she said in an encouraging tone. "But can I give you a word of advice?"

"Of course!" she exclaimed. Deflating slightly, she added, "It's the shoes, isn't it? The shoes are all wrong?"

Jessie glanced at them. "No. They're fine. I just wanted to say that your love of fashion is one thing. But making yourself over in the interest of winning a man's heart . . . it's not the way to go. It can only end in heartache. You're a lovely girl, Amber. Be yourself."

Tucking her honey-blonde hair behind her ear, Amber lifted her eyes and looked at Jessie emotionally. "No offense, but I think that's pretty easy for someone like you to say. You've probably got the rich guy and the mansion and the car."

Jessie snorted. "You'd be surprised."

"If you *don't* have all of that, then you're right. I'd be very, very surprised."

The inner debate on whether to share her unfortunate life with a total stranger in a ladies' restroom raged, but still . . . Amber's sweet smile made the decision for her. Maybe a good dose of her own reality would jolt the girl into wearing Ralph Lauren for her own edification; not to meet someone else's lofty expectations. If only someone had administered similar warnings to her, perhaps she'd have listened to those alarm bells that went off the first time Jack had stopped at the entrance of a party long enough to fix Jessie's hair. When he'd stepped back to admire his work, something inside Jessie dropped, and that inner voice whispered to her about a man who looked at her like a prize pig he planned to show at the fair.

"I was a fragrance clerk when I met my Prince Charming, Amber. But recently, I watched my car being towed down the street and went home to discover that my perfect, rich husband had sold the house, closed his business, and disappeared without a trace."

Amber gasped. "That's . . . horrible."

"All I have left in the world are the labels that once seemed so important to me."

"Well, at least you have them."

Jessie sighed. "For all the good they do me."

"Too bad you can't rent out all of your adornments to wannabes like me," Amber commented with a chuckle. "There's enough of us out there that we might be able to keep you in the lifestyle to which you've become accustomed. Or close to it anyways."

A freight train of thoughts barreled through her brain, and Jessie grinned. "You know, Amber, you might be on to something there."

"Sure!" she exclaimed excitedly. "And hey, I've been a sales clerk in every chic boutique in Los Angeles and Orange Counties. You could hire me to help you! We could set up a killer little shop, Jessie. Girls would come all the way from out in the valley to rent a Chanel bag or a pair of Jimmy Choos."

"When can you start?" Jessie asked, completely in jest.

"Hey, I make eleven bucks an hour at my current job. If you can top that, I'm there."

The random conversation in front of the bathroom mirror stuck with Jessie after she returned to the table for coffee and tiramisu. By the time the waiter refilled their cups, Jessie excused herself, grabbed a restaurant business card from the host at the front and scribbled her cell number on the back. When she went in search of Amber Davidson, she spotted her seated at a table with none other than Remy Kade, the smooth serpent-like acquaintance of Jack's who had pinched her thigh under the table at a fundraiser last Christmas.

"Pardon my intrusion," she said timidly as she approached the table.

"Jessie Stanton," Remy exclaimed, and he tucked his linen napkin under the plate in front of him and rose to his feet. "How are you, dear? It's been a long time."

"It has. How are you, Remington?"

"Very well. This is my new friend, Amber. Would you like to—"

"Yes, Amber is my new friend as well. I actually came over to give her something." Handing her a card, Jessie smiled. "Call me tomorrow, will you?"

She seemed happily stunned. "Of course!"

"Good. We'll talk."

"O-okay."

"Remy, nice to see you. Take care."

Jessie left their table, then paused behind Remy. Waving a finger at Amber, she shook her head vehemently and mimed, "No, no, no," and pointed to her date. "Absolutely NO."

Amber lowered her face to hide her wide grin.

"Everything all right?" Piper asked when she returned.

"More than all right," she told them. "I think I might have made a very important decision about my future."

"While you were in the ladies' room?"

Jessie giggled. "Actually, yes."

"Where all the best ideas originate," Riggs piped up, and Danny shook his head and laughed.

"I sure hope you're right."

---

The Santa Monica sky was unusually clear, and the Santa Ana winds had summoned up a breeze strong enough to push the stars around along with Danny's straight blond hair. At a stoplight, he grabbed the elastic band wrapped around the gearshift and raked his hair back into a ponytail. Jessie smiled. He'd probably waited all night to do that.

Jessie closed her eyes and dropped her head back for a moment, inhaling slowly, deeply. Was it her imagination, or had she actually begun to breathe again without thinking about it?

When she opened her eyes again, she focused on Danny's profile, tracing it with her gaze. A strong stubbled jaw . . . not dimpled exactly—more like indentations really; little parentheses that formed around his mouth when he smiled . . . a distinct, thin nose that pointed down ever-so-slightly . . . and those eyes. Blue steel, narrow and intense, made more so by the thin lines extending from their outside border.

Danny must have felt her gaze on him because he turned toward her and smiled, setting those parentheses into motion around it. "What's up?" he asked her.

"I was just thinking how strange it is that I feel so relaxed."

"I guess it's been awhile."

"Longer than I'd even realized, I think."

Danny nodded and returned his focus to the road ahead. "So you want to talk about it yet? Your big idea?"

"Kinda."

"Think of me as a sounding board. I won't speak until you tell me to."

Jessie chuckled. "I'll bet you get a lot of women with that line."

He flashed those steely blues in her direction, and something grabbed her stomach at the same time.

"I met this young woman in the ladies' room. Amber," she told him as she crossed her leg and shifted toward him. "We were talking about my dress and her shoes; you know, ladies' room chat."

"I'll take your word for it."

"She said something that really got me to thinking. She said I should put all of my designer labels into a shop where women with Armani tastes and Target budgets could come and rent them. For special occasions, for a hot date, that sort of thing."

Danny eased to a stop at the corner and turned toward her. "Is there a market for something like that?"

"Well, I know there are a few shops like it in New York. Then a website—Bag, Borrow or Steal—became a really big thing a few years back for women all over the country. All those girls migrating to the big city and paying outlandish rent for shoebox apartments couldn't afford the fashion dictated by a city like New York or Chicago. So they rented label handbags and accessories by the week or month for prices they *could* afford, and they were shipped directly to them."

Danny shook his head as he made the turn on her street. "If you say so."

"Anyway, I don't know if there's a market for apparel, too, but I imagine if there's a niche anywhere, LA would be the place. Don't you think so?"

"I'm out of my element here," he admitted. "But I'd say it's worth looking into. Judging by the size of your new closet, I'd venture a guess that you have plenty of inventory."

Jessie giggled. "Yes, I do. But it's all in my size. I'll have to think about that."

Danny shifted into neutral and yanked on the parking brake before Jessie realized they'd arrived in front of her apartment building.

"Do you feel like a cup of coffee?" she asked him. "I even have some plain black K-Cups, just for you."

"Sounds good."

They headed up the driveway, and Jessie noticed a shiny sand-colored car parked ahead of them with a large red bow wrapped entirely around it.

"Look at that," she exclaimed. "Someone has a birthday surprise in store for them."

"How do you know it's for a birthday?" he asked as they approached it.

"Look, there's a card."

They peered at the card taped to the driver's window of the shiny Ford Taurus.

JESSIE STANTON.

"What does that say?" she asked him for the sake of clarity.

"It's for you."

"Me. Who would get me a car?"

"Piper?"

"Maybe. But why wouldn't she have said something at dinner?"

Danny flicked the card away from the tape and handed it to her. "Why don't you find out."

She tore open the envelope and yanked out the card as adrenaline surged through her.

*You can't make a new start without transportation. It's no BMW, but it will get you from here to there. The key is in your mailbox. Enjoy!*

"Who's it from?" Danny asked her.

"I have no idea. They didn't sign it."

Danny took the card from her and read it for himself. "Well, they know you well enough to know what kind of car you used to drive."

"It has to be Piper," she mused. "Who else would do such a thing?"

"No clue, sister. But you'd better move it out of the driveway before Riggs sees it. There's no parking in the drive."

"Do I even have a parking spot?"

"Around back. Go unlock your mailbox and grab the key. I'll show you where to park."

She started away before turning back for another sweeping look at the car in front of her. Excitement pulsed through her as she asked him, "Who would buy me a car?" With a sigh, she leaned down to see what kind of car it actually was. "A . . . Taurus. Who would buy me a Taurus?"

Danny lifted one shoulder in a shrug.

"A Taurus. Is that a . . . *Ford*?"

"I think it is."

"My dad used to drive a Ford, I think."

"And now you'll drive one. It came full circle."

Jessie nibbled on her lower lip and nodded tentatively. "Yeah. It looks like I, uh, come from a long line of . . . *American* cars then."

Jessie scurried over to the rows of metal mailboxes and turned her key in the third lock. Two Ford keys dangled from a flimsy ring, and as she examined them she figured the row of vent openings on the box must have been barely wide enough to slide them through.

"Find it?" Danny asked as he yanked the last of the huge red ribbon from the top of the car and wrapped it into a manageable coil around his arm.

"Yes, right where my benefactor said it would be. There's a slot on the box where she must have poked them through."

"Well, go ahead. Unlock the doors then and let's see what you've got here."

Jessie poked one of the keys into the door and turned it. She slipped behind the wheel and pressed the button on the door to unlock the passenger door for Danny. He slid in and slammed the door. "What do you think?"

Jessie ran her hand over the beige leather seat and peered up at the night sky through the closed glass of a sunroof.

"It's kind of great for a Ford, don't you think?" she asked him, and Danny chuckled.

She turned the key and started the car, then scanned the dash for a way to turn on the headlights while Danny produced a remote control and an owner's manual from the glove compartment.

"You'll want to put this on your key ring," he said. "It's a remote for locking the doors and popping the trunk, probably arming the alarm if it has one." He flipped open the manual before adding, "Looks like a 2010 with a V-6 engine, cruise control, and an alarm. Still under warranty. How many miles on it?"

She peered at the dash. "Thirty-six thousand twenty-seven."

"Nice. Pull down the driveway and make the turn behind the building. I'll show you where to park."

Jessie shifted and touched the gas pedal. She thought it had some power for a Ford.

*But who would give me . . . a Ford?!*

---

"You promise on our friendship?" Jessie squealed into her cell phone.

"I promise on our friendship," Piper humored her. "I did not buy you a car."

"Then who?"

"Maybe Jack?"

"Jack!" she choked out. "He left me homeless, carless, husbandless, and then—what?—he was so filled with remorse that he sent me a used Ford?"

"Mm," Piper surrendered. "Who then?"

"I wish I knew!"

They both remained silent for several beats before Piper chimed, "It has to be Jack, Jess. Who else could it be? No one else really knows, do they?"

"No one who might find it in their hearts to worry about my lack of transportation."

"Exactly. It's Jack. Have you told Danny? Maybe there will be a clue there that he can follow."

"He was with me when I found it parked in the driveway. But we both assumed it was you."

"Well, call him. Tell him it wasn't me and see if he can follow the paper trail to Jack."

"Follow the paper trail," Jessie repeated. "That sounded so PI of you. Look, I've gotta go. I have an appointment."

"Where are you headed?"

"I'll tell you all about it later. Want to come over and help me christen my new kitchen?"

"Seven-thirty?"

"Perfect. See you then."

Jessie grabbed a quick shower and, while still wrapped in a towel, rooted through one of the wardrobe boxes she'd yet to unpack until she located her favorite Wolford dress, the V-neck fourteen-gauge knit. She loved the light sheen of the fabric, and she hung it on one of the display hooks in her new closet before stepping back to admire it. Twenty minutes later, with her hair and makeup fixed for the day, she slipped into it and added a wide leather belt that fastened in the back. She adjusted the holed and studded pattern in the front and chuckled out loud as she recalled Piper's words the day she'd tried it on at the Wolford store.

"No wonder they call it the Magic Belt. It does magic for your waistline!"

She slipped into black-and-leopard Barbara Bui low-boots with four-inch spiked heels, stopping to admire them for a moment before hurrying out of the closet and down the hall. She'd already transferred the essentials into the Bui Nappa bag she'd bought the same day as the shoes and left it on the arm of the sofa. She grabbed it and headed out the door.

Once she settled in the front seat of her Taurus, Jessie pushed back the panel from the sunroof and looked up at the gray-blue sky overhead. She hoped she remembered how to navigate from Pinafore Street over to the Third Street Promenade where she'd agreed to meet Amber; she so seldom made it to this side of town. Twenty minutes later, though, she reluctantly turned off Santa Monica Boulevard. If she kept driving, she'd reach Ocean, then Pacific Coast Highway, which led to Malibu. Her heart sank. She wouldn't be heading home to Malibu ever again; the thought hovered like a bitter, dark cloud all the way into Starbucks.

"Jessie!" Amber called out to her from a small table, and she waved her arm. "Come on over."

Jessie raised a finger and nodded toward the counter, stopping to order a skinny caramel macchiato from the adolescent clerk.

"Thanks for meeting me," she greeted Amber as she dropped her bag and sat down.

"You look killer," Amber replied. "Love the shoes. Who are they?"

"Barbara Bui."

"They're awesome. I wrote a piece for a fashion blog last month about Barbara Bui."

"Oh, you're a writer?"

"Aspiring. I've published a dozen or so articles, even had a feature in *Today's Style Magazine*."

"That's a great publication."

"Yeah, they pay pretty well, and they seemed to like what I turned in, so I'm hoping for another chance to write for them soon."

"So that's the career you're hoping to build? As a writer?"

"I don't want to write the Great American Novel or anything. Fashion is always where I've aspired to be, but that doesn't pay very well at the entry level either, so I just make a dollar here and a dollar there in hopes I can keep my teeny little roof over my head."

Her smile beamed with sweetness and sincerity. There was something about Amber Davidson that Jessie really liked.

Amber had pulled her honey blonde locks back into a sleek ponytail, held in place with a section of braided hair. She looked pretty in the dark emerald mock turtleneck sweater with elbow-length sleeves and brown pleated trousers; the color of the sweater had turned her bluish eyes a shade of deep, foamy green.

"So what are your thoughts?" Amber asked excitedly. "Am I giving notice on my job to come to work for you? Are we going to storm into the lives of girls like me and give them a fashion boost?"

Jessie smiled. "Let's talk about that."

"Ooh, let's do."

"I've done a little research, and I've found that there are several shops like what I have in mind in major cities across the country, but I haven't found one in the Los Angeles area. I'm not sure if that would be a good sign for us, or a bad one." Jessie opened the leather-bound notebook she'd tucked into her bag and slid the pen from its loop on the spine. "I called three different places and asked some general questions about how they work, and I was most impressed by this shop I found in Dallas called Queen for a Day. They started out just renting accessories—shoes, bags, jewelry—and they did that for about three years. Then they expanded to a consignment shop as well with apparel. They're more strictly vintage clothes, but I don't see us limiting ourselves like that. Especially because we'll be starting out—literally—with just the clothes in my closet."

"This is so exciting. What are you going to call it?"

"Well," Jessie said, and she paused to take a sip of her coffee. "I was thinking about what you said to me in the ladies' room when we met."

Amber's eyes grew round and wide. "Why? What did I say?"

"Something like, 'It's too bad you can't just rent out your own adornments to wannabes like me.'"

Amber giggled. "Did I say that?"

"You did," she replied with a nod. "I was thinking of calling it Adornments. What do you think?"

"I think I'm a genius."

They shared a chuckle, and Jessie sipped her coffee in silence for several beats. Her head had been buzzing with details, questions, plans, and wonderings about this venture ever since Amber had suggested it.

"Is there enough in my closet to warrant a rental shop?" she said, more thinking out loud than asking Amber's opinion. "And with everything in my size, maybe we won't have enough diversity for customers. I don't know. Is this an insane idea?"

"I'd say the first thing is to do an inventory of what you have and are willing to part with for the cause," Amber stated. "I mean, you're going to want to have clothes to wear yourself, right? You can't rent out *everything*."

"Mmm," Jessie mumbled.

"But maybe you have some friends who might want to donate to the cause, or do it like a consignment situation where they get a portion of the rental each time one of their garments is borrowed."

"Oh, that's an idea."

"We can set up a software program to inventory and categorize everything."

Jessie's heart fluttered slightly. "Do you know how to do that?"

"I'm your girl," Amber returned with a grin. "I'm available today. Do you want to take me home with you and show me your closet?"

"Only if you don't judge where I live now."

"Please. I live in a one-room apartment off Melrose that looks more like a closet, with a futon in the corner where I sleep."

"Tell you what," Jessie said. "I'll pay you for your time today, and then we'll decide if there's actually a workable idea here for us to build upon."

"Okay."

She recalled Amber saying she only made eleven dollars an hour at her current position, and she wondered about that. The girl obviously had considerable skills. Jessie realized she'd forgotten what it was like out there in the real world with real paychecks while she spent all those years in the beach castle with the prince and all those charge accounts he afforded her.

"Fifteen dollars an hour?"

"Are you joking? Sold!"

Jessie glanced at the clock behind the front counter. "It's five to eleven now," she said. "Starting at eleven."

"Oh, good. Five minutes left on my break."

---

"I haven't completely unpacked yet, so maybe we could start by hanging everything up and hauling these wardrobe boxes out of here. That way, you can get a good idea of what I have."

When Amber didn't reply, Jessie turned back to find her standing just inside the door, her mouth gaping open.

"*This* is . . . your closet? It's . . . magnificent! Where did you find this place?"

"Well, it's actually the tiniest second bedroom in the known world," she said with a laugh. "But I have a handy private investigator. He transformed it into a closet."

"You have your own private investigator?"

"That's a story for another day. Ready to get started?"

Amber nodded. "How many pairs of shoes do you think you have?"

"I wondered that myself last night when this whole idea was churning me awake, so I hopped out of bed and came in here to count. I'm a little embarrassed to admit to you that this massive closet doesn't even have enough cubbies to contain all of my shoes. In all, I own eighty-six pairs of shoes, Amber."

"Eighty-six!"

"Please don't be impressed. I suddenly find myself feeling embarrassed about it."

"Are you joking?"

"I wish I was. So how should we start? My laptop or a pad of paper?"

"Let's see your laptop. If you have a database program, we can use that to get started on inventory, and then I can migrate the information to whatever program you decide to use for your business."

"Here's what I heard," Jessie teased as she headed for the doorway. "Blah blah blah, inventory, blah blah blah, your business."

Amber snickered. "Grab your laptop, and I'll start moving the hangers out of the boxes."

*I'm pretty sure I love this girl.*

---

*There's an old bridge on the Slidell side of the Irish Bayou just right for crabbin', and I like makin' a day of it out there. Jessie was about six the first time she rode along, and she's been comin' with me now and again ever since. Long about eight years old, she started puttin' together that little crabs got faces just like her, so boilin' 'em up for supper seemed akin to makin' a meal outta her. Far as I know, she never connected them dots to cows, or we'da been eatin' a lot less hamburgers.*

*"Joellen don't look like the others, Grampy," she said to me, peerin' down into the trap. "She's a good bit smaller."*

*"Joellen . . ."*

*Took me a minute or two 'fore I realized the child was givin' those crabs names. By the time we took 'em home and started the water boilin', Jessie had planted her two feet firm on the floor, crossed her arms, and declared she'd be havin' cereal for supper.*

*"In protest, Grampy. I'm eatin' cereal in protest."*

*The next time, my little union representative had macaroni 'n' cheese, and it become a family tradition. On crabbin' days, we gathered everybody up and had steamed crabs in butter, a little Cajun rice, and a big ol' bowl o' macaroni and cheese.*

# 6

I thought we were christening your kitchen," Piper said as she stood in the doorway to Jessie's new closet. "That usually implies that you invited me over with the thought of making me dinner."

"Oh, I know, and I'm so sorry," Jessie told her from the floor in the far corner. "We just got so involved here that I completely forgot I'd asked you. Will you forgive me if we order Chinese takeout or pizza or something?"

"Possibly. Who was the young woman who let me in?"

"That's Amber. My new best friend."

"I've been replaced?"

"Only for a while. Is it all right?"

"That depends."

Their banter fell short as Amber stepped past Piper. "Excuse me," she said, moving into the closet and plopping down on the floor across from Jessie. She picked up the open laptop and typed something into it. "I heard you say you wanted to order takeout," she said when she finished. "There's an amazing Thai place not too far from here. I know someone who used to work there. They don't deliver, but I could go pick it up."

Jessie looked up at Piper with a grin. "Thai?"

"Can she be my new best friend, too?"

"Sure. I'll share."

"Great then. Thai food it is." Piper entered the closet and sat down with them before extending her hand. "Hi, Amber. I'm Piper."

"Hi," she said as she shook Piper's hand. "I'm Jessie's new employee."

"Employee?" Piper's expression elongated as she looked at Jessie. "While Amber retrieves our Thai food, you, my friend, have some talking to do."

Jessie nodded and laughed. "I really do. Wait until you hear this ridiculous idea I have."

"It's not ridiculous," Amber corrected her. "It's genius. Risky, but genius."

Piper's gaze swept the closet. "I'm guessing it has something to do with clothing?"

Amber turned the laptop screen toward them. "Here's their menu. Tell me what you want first so I can call in the order."

Piper raised her hand. "I don't really have to look if they have Mee Krob."

"It's her fave," Jessie informed Amber.

"Okay." Amber scanned the menu. "Sweet, crispy noodles with shrimp, chicken, and bean sprouts," she read. "That sounds delicious. I'll have that too. Do we want some crab rangoon?"

"Oh. No," Jessie piped up immediately.

"Jessie doesn't eat crab," Piper pointed out, and Amber giggled as Jessie wrinkled up her nose, closed her eyes, and shook her head emphatically.

"Then what do you want, Jessie?"

She took a moment to glance at the menu before deciding. "That pineapple fried rice looks fun," she told them. "It's rice, shrimp, chicken, cashews, raisins, and pineapple, all of it served in a real pineapple shell! I want that."

Amber wrote it down. "You eat shrimp, but not crab?"

"It's a personal choice," she said.

"Any drinks?"

"I have Diet Coke and bottled water," Jessie told them. "Oh, let's get some veggie eggrolls too."

"Done."

"There's about forty dollars in cash on the kitchen counter. That should be enough, right?"

Amber scribbled on a scrap of paper before leaving the closet. Jessie heard her greet someone on the phone in another language, presumably Thai.

"She's adorable," Piper whispered.

"Isn't she?"

"Do a background check."

"Really?"

"Absolutely. This is LA."

"Do you think Danny could do that?"

"Absolutely. Now tell me, please, about your terrible idea."

"Not terrible. Just ridiculous."

Piper snickered. "Okay. Tell me."

"Well, I met Amber the other night at Antonio's restaurant. And by the way, she was on a first date with Remy Kade."

"That letch?" Piper exclaimed in a hushed voice.

"I know. Anyway, we got to talking while we were in the ladies' room . . ."

---

The three women made fast work of their dinner, despite the fact that they hadn't stopped chattering even once throughout the meal. Jessie had been so eager to get Piper's take on every thought she had about this possible venture, and Piper easily contributed a few dozen ideas to expound upon her plans.

Adornments had unanimously been approved as the business name, and Piper committed an appointment with Antonio's attorney to help with the legalities. Amber would set out on her primary assignment the very next morning by narrowing down three or four storefronts available for a reasonable monthly rental amount. When asked what "reasonable" might look like exactly, Jessie and Piper sounded off in stereo: "Cheap!"

Meanwhile, Jessie had learned the basics of the database program she never knew she had on her laptop, and her part of the plan began with completing an inventory of garments, handbags, shoes, and jewelry. After that, Piper would be Jessie's first test case of consignment rentals when she agreed to choose some items from her own closet and deliver them to Adornments in return for a 55 percent return on every rental. At least her size four dresses and size five shoes would lend a little variety to Jessie's size sixes and eights.

Amber agreed to weed through her own size ten closet as well, but she warned that she had far less from which to choose than either of her dinner companions.

At midnight, the containers still strewn around the living room floor between Jessie and Amber, Piper had sprawled out on the sofa with two cushions propped under her head.

"I've got to get home," she muttered. But she made no move to leave.

"Me too," Amber said, popping to her feet and gathering the containers. Jessie collected their glasses, used plastic utensils, and wadded paper towels, and she followed Amber into the kitchen.

"Yeah," Piper said to the ceiling through closed eyes. "I really gotta get home." And with that, she turned over to her side and curled into a petite little ball. Jessie watched her from the kitchen doorway and chuckled.

"Want to spend the night?"

"Could I? I'm too sleepy to drive home."

"I'll call Antonio and tell him."

"Mm-hmm. That's a good idea."

Jessie walked Amber to the door and whispered, "We'll need to start keeping a time sheet on your hours. How long were you here today?"

"I've already set it up in your laptop," she said, tossing the strap of her purse over one shoulder. "I went off the clock around eight. Thank you for dinner."

Jessie tugged Amber into an embrace. "I'm so grateful you crossed my path."

"We're going to have a ton of fun."

"I hope so."

"It'll be great," Amber encouraged her. "You'll see. It's meant to be."

It had been such a long time since Jessie had given credence to those sorts of thoughts about higher purposes and all that, but she had to admit meeting Amber did feel like something more to her than just a random coincidence.

After covering Piper with a blanket, Jessie double-checked all three locks on the front door before turning out the lights and shuffling to her bedroom. The mountains of plans for Adornments slipped from her mind somehow, and her last thought of the night centered around how comforting it felt to know someone—especially with that someone being Piper—slept in the next room. Jessie hadn't had a lot of experience with being alone.

It seemed like a few minutes later that the familiar fragrance of coffee wafted beneath her nose and whispered seductively until she opened her eyes.

"Morning," Piper sang from the edge of the bed. "Rise and shine?"

"Coffee?"

"Caramel vanilla cream."

"I'll rise, but I won't shine for at least an hour."

"Fair enough, but I have to go. We've got a planning meeting for the spring fundraiser."

"Don't forget to make time to go through your closet," Jessie reminded her. "And be generous."

"Am I ever anything less than generous?"

Jessie sat upright and tugged her friend toward her. As she embraced Piper, she softly said, "You're the most generous person I know."

"Ah," she replied with a chuckle. "Thank you, sweetie." She tried to pull away, but Jessie held on for a few extra seconds.

"I mean it, Piper. I really love you."

"Jessie. I love you, too," she said with a tinge of surprise.

Piper had only just closed the front door behind her when Jessie's cell phone rang. When she picked it up, she noticed Danny Callahan's name on the screen.

"Hi, Danny. I'm glad you called."

"I didn't hear from you yesterday," he said.

"I know, I'm sorry. I got so involved that I lost track of nearly everything. Piper even showed up for dinner last night, and I'd completely forgotten that I invited her. We ended up ordering takeout."

Danny chuckled. "Nothing wrong with takeout."

"I wanted to tell you though . . . Piper didn't give me the car."

"Are you sure? Maybe she just didn't want to—"

"No, I'm sure! She didn't do it. So we were thinking maybe it was Jack."

"Your husband," he returned in monotone.

"Well, who else could it be? I mean, no one really knows much about what happened, certainly not that he had my car surrendered . . . other than the valet at the restaurant where I was when it happened. So Piper thinks maybe Jack felt guilty or something."

"And what do you think?"

"I don't really know, but if it is him . . . wouldn't that provide you with some sort of lead toward finding him?"

He remained silent for several beats; considering the possibility, she figured. Finally, "I can look into it."

"Also . . . do you do background checks? Being an investigator and all that?"

"I can. What did you have in mind?"

"Is it expensive?"

"We can work it out. Hey, can I stop over in a bit and have a look at the paperwork in the glove box? And you can tell me who you're looking into."

"Sure. I'll just be in my closet."

"Your closet."

"I'll tell you all about it when you get here."

"I'll bring lunch. Are you opposed to In & Out burgers?"

"Not in the least," she admitted. "And guess what I have! I have cookies."

"What kind?" he asked with an air of mischief.

"Oatmeal raisin and chocolate chunk. I saw them in the bakery case at Albertsons."

"Thirty minutes."

Jessie ran out to her car and retrieved the paperwork in the glove compartment. She used the rest of the time to finish entering the last of her handbags into the database Amber set up. She had just a few minutes to tidy up the area—and then herself—before Danny arrived at the front door and she led him into the kitchen.

"Do we need dishes and utensils or—"

"I'm good eating right out of the wrappers," he interrupted.

The two of them sat down at the bistro table, and Jessie handed him the paperwork on the car. Danny pushed a thick cheeseburger and a small bag of fries toward her before he thumbed through it.

"Do you think there's anything there that will lead you to Jack?" she asked. "Or to at least narrow down who gave me the car?"

"Not sure on either count. But it's worth a shot."

After another few minutes, he tucked the paperwork into his shirt pocket and grabbed a couple of fries.

"You're eating those without ketchup?" she cried.

"I'm not much for condiments. So tell me about the time you're spending in your closet."

"Oh! Okay. Get this . . ."

"Tell me again how I let you talk me into this."

Jessie giggled and opened the bakery bag of cookies and extended it toward Danny where he sat behind the wheel of his Jeep.

"Well, one minute I was telling you about my business idea, and the next you were telling me you had to leave to go on a stakeout. I've only seen them on television, and so I bribed you with these delicious cookies into letting me come along."

Danny grabbed another one and nodded. "Yeah. It's all coming back to me."

"So, what happens now?" she asked, picking up the small binoculars from the bucket between their seats. "We just sit here until . . . what?"

Danny snatched the binoculars from her hand the moment she raised them to her face. "What did I say to you when we parked?"

She tapped her temple playfully with one finger. "Let's see if I can remember. Don't touch anything. Don't do anything. Don't say anything. No ifs, ands, or buts."

"Very good. So why are you touching something already?"

Jessie groaned. "I just wanted to look around."

"That's why God gave you eyeballs."

"Yeah, but—"

"That sounds like a *but* to me."

Jessie clicked her tongue in disappointment. "Fine. Can I at least ask you a question?"

"Shoot," he said as he peered through the binoculars himself.

"What are we watching for?"

"See the computer repair storefront?"

Jessie scanned the overhead signs at the strip mall across the street from where they had parked. A convenience store. A nail salon. A used bookstore. "Oh! Stiller Computers?"

"Yep."

"So we're watching for stolen equipment to be delivered?"

Danny gave a hearty chuckle. "No. David Stiller is the owner. We're watching for any activity there at all."

"Why? What did he do? Jump bail or something?"

He lowered the glasses and looked at her with an amused grin. "What do you know about jumping bail?"

"Nothing. Or stolen computers either, for that matter."

"David Stiller and his wife are divorced. She lives in Henderson, Nevada, and has full custody of Ian, their ten-year-old son. Two weeks ago, Ian disappeared off the playground at his school, and his mother thinks he may have been snatched by the father. The cops searched the guy's house in Glendale as well as his place of business, and they found no evidence that Ian had been there."

"So she hired you to see what you can find out."

"Exactly."

The germ of an idea dawned, and she turned to him, excited. "I know! You want me to go in there?"

Danny blurted out an immediate, "No!"

"Hear me out. I could just go in with a few questions about my laptop, have a casual look-see around, and—"

"Absolutely no look-sees, Jessie."

"What are you going to do then?" she objected. "Just sit here indefinitely?"

"That's kind of the way a stakeout works. You watch someone do the same thing each day and hope they break their pattern at some point."

She sighed and stared out her window for several beats before muttering, "Not very proactive, if you ask me."

"Yeah. There's not much proactive about a stakeout besides the snacks you bring along."

Jessie peered into the back seat to look for snacks other than those she'd brought along, and she frowned. "Good thing you have me then. Without my cookies, you'd be up a creek, wouldn't you?"

Danny dropped his head back and laughed unabashedly. It sounded sort of musical to Jessie, and she couldn't help but join in. When Danny jerked the binoculars back into place, she caught up with what had drawn his attention back to the strip mall as a lanky, thirty-something man emerged from the computer repair store and locked the door behind him.

"Is that him?" she exclaimed.

"Yep. Every day at four, he closes up shop, gets some snacks from the store next door, chats up the woman who runs the used bookstore for a while, and then heads home. You could set your watch by him."

"It doesn't sound like the actions of a guy with something . . . *or someone* . . . to hide, does it?"

"Nope." Danny trained the glasses on the convenience store and watched through the window as Stiller moved about. "But I get paid to watch him, anyway."

"While eating cookies. Nice work if you can get it," she muttered seriously, then she shot him a quick grin.

Stiller emerged from the store with a bag tucked under one arm as he waved at the clerk through the glass and sauntered down the sidewalk, past his own shop, and into the bookstore.

Danny checked his watch. "Ten minutes after four. Right on schedule," he remarked. "I've probably got a good ninety minutes before he breaks free of his girlfriend in the bookstore. Do you want me to run you home?"

"No," she blurted without thinking. "I mean, do you mind if I stay?"

"Why would you want to? You can see this is pretty boring work."

"Oh yeah," she said with a nod. "It's a snooze-fest. But don't you need me to keep you from nodding off and missing his next move?"

The truth was Jessie enjoyed the distraction of sitting in a car with Danny Callahan, talking about his case and bantering back and forth. Much to her surprise, she actually liked him. She and Jack had never had the kind of relationship that nurtured playful conversation or interesting observations. She couldn't remember a single time when he'd said anything that made her think beyond making a note to her calendar or making a special order at the butcher's counter.

"Have you ever"—she said as her thoughts turned back toward David Stiller—"seen what he buys at the convenience store?"

"What do you mean? Snacks, a magazine, that kind of thing."

"What kind of snacks? What magazine?"

Danny scratched his jaw and shrugged one shoulder. "He seems to have a penchant for their bean burritos. And he buys a lot of chips and sodas. The occasional Yoo-hoo. I don't know what the magazines have been."

"Does that sound like dinner for a guy Stiller's age? I mean, every night?"

Danny looked into her eyes so deeply that she could almost hear the grind of his wheels as they started turning in his brain. "Well, he's a single guy. A lot of single guys rely on junk food."

"From the same place, every single night? I mean, why wouldn't he just drive through Del Taco on his way home once in a while?"

"He wants to eat with the woman in the bookstore." His tone of voice said he wanted to convince himself more than Jessie.

"Have you seen her?" she asked casually. "What's she look like?"

"Fifty, maybe. Pretty for an older woman."

"Funny that he'd want to eat convenience store burritos with a fifty-year-old woman each day."

He thought it over. "He hasn't got anybody else?"

"Maybe."

Danny sat there stewing for a few minutes, and it thrilled Jessie to no end as he seemed to catch up to her line of thought. She gasped when he suddenly sprang into action by yanking open his door.

"You stay here," he said as he climbed out. "I'll be right back." Once he closed the door, he leaned in through the driver's window and glared at her. "I'm not fooling around here. Do not leave this car."

"I promise."

Her pulse palpitated wildly as she watched Danny jog across the street toward the bookstore. Her heart clanked along with the distant bell attached to the front door as he opened it . . .

*If I ever actually get a store up and running, I want bells on the door like that.*

. . . and then it stopped again while she waited for any further sign of him.

---

*"Grampy, did you know if you take an empty glass and put it up against a wall or a door, you can hear what they're sayin' in there?"*

*"And just how did you discover such a thing?" I asked little Jessie as she chugged down the last of her milk.*

*"I saw it on TV. You wanna try it?" she asked with hope brimmin' from her eyes as she held up her empty glass. "Let's go next door and see what Miss Beauchamp is sayin'."*

*Maizie Beauchamp lived alone, so if she was sayin' much of anythin', she sure didn't want a little girl and her grampy hearin' it.*

*"There's laws against that," I told her. "You can't go around listening at people's doors with your milk glass."*

*"The boy on TV did it, and he uncovered an evil plot. Maybe Miss Beauchamp is plannin' somethin'."*

*Took an hour o' talkin' to persuade Jessie to help me paint the garage door instead.*

*"Not much adventure in paintin', Grampy."*

*"But the police ain't gonna haul us in fer it."*

*"Well, that's true, I guess. Can we at least paint it a pretty color?"*

*"How's red strike ya?"*

*"Like the fire engine we saw last week?"*

*"Just like that."*

*She brightened up and raced to the back door. "Well, c'mon, Grampy. What're ya waitin' for?"*

# 7

The proprietor of the bookstore smiled at Danny as he approached the counter where she sat perched on a padded metal stool. The scent of old books and worn leather permeated the charming little store.

"Good afternoon. How can I help you?"

Danny returned her polite smile. "I'm looking for something by Frank Peretti, or maybe you have something by other authors like him."

"We have a large selection of inspirational fiction along that wall," she pointed out. "The second section is mystery-suspense."

"Thanks."

Danny scanned the aisles as he made his way through the store, but he didn't spot Stiller; or any other shoppers for that matter. He stood under the SUSPENSE sign for a minute or so and randomly grabbed a couple of books, both of which he'd read before.

As the woman rang up his purchase, a scuffling noise drew his attention to the drawn curtain behind the counter. His ears perked and he clearly heard it as someone hissed out a soft hush warning.

"That's sixteen dollars and thirty-seven cents," she told him, and fresh inspiration pinched Danny at the center of his throat.

He pulled out his credit card and extended it toward her and—just as her fingertips touched it—Danny let go, flicking it slightly until the card fell, bouncing off the corner of the counter and to the hardwood floor.

"Sorry," he muttered.

"I'll get it."

When the woman bent over to pick up the card, Danny leaned around the edge of the counter and peered through the small opening in the curtain, catching sight of about six inches of the face of a young boy with dark, curly hair and crooked front teeth.

*Ian Stiller.*

There was no mistaking it. That was the boy in the photograph Teresa Stiller had emailed him.

Danny recovered just an instant before the older woman straightened with a soft groan. The hum of adrenaline coursed through him, but he tucked it behind a nonchalant smile as he signed the credit card slip and accepted his purchase.

"Thanks."

"Have a good day, young man."

"You, too."

On his way across the street, Danny pulled out his cell phone and scrolled for Rafe Padillo's number.

"So? What happened?" Jessie badgered him the minute he climbed behind the wheel. "Were they sharing a burrito?"

Danny held up a finger as Rafe answered. "Detective Padillo."

"Rafe, it's Danny Callahan."

"*Ah, hola, amigo. ¿Cómo estás?*"

"I'm good, thanks. Listen, remember that abduction case we talked about last week? Ian Stiller."

"*Por supuesto.* From out Nevada way," he confirmed in Spanglish.

"Right. Well, I've got a location on the boy. Can you send someone out to pick him up?"

Jessie grabbed Danny's arm and squeezed. "I knew it!"

"I'm texting you the address of a strip mall," he said. "The boy and his father are in the back room of a used bookstore. There's no one else on the premises except the shop owner, a middle-aged woman."

Within the hour, the cavalry arrived and Rafe went in through the front while two of his men circled around to the back. It took no more than ten minutes for him to emerge with Stiller in handcuffs, Ian at the side of a female officer, and a third officer leading the older woman out of the shop. After glancing at Danny and nodding, Rafe spoke to the officers for a moment and headed across the street. As he approached, Danny's thoughts tripped over each other, trying to land on an explanation of Jessie's presence.

"That's good work, Callahan," he said, leaning down to smile past him. "Take on a partner, didja?"

"Rafe Padillo, meet Jessie Stanton," he stated.

"Pleasure." Rafe straightened. "Looks like Stiller played on the sympathies of the bookstore owner by telling her stories about an abusive mother and the good of the child. We'll find out the rest of the details at the station. You can call your client and tell her to expect a call from me within an hour or two."

"She'll want to get started to come and pick up her son. Thanks, Rafe."

Rafe nodded before leaning down to the window again. "Take care, Ms. Stanton."

"Thank you!" she sang after him as he crossed the four-lane street. Turning to Danny, she squeezed his arm again and bounced several times in her seat. "We did it. That little boy is going home!"

"That little boy is going home because of you," he reluctantly admitted. "That was good insight. Maybe your new business should be investigating instead of dressing . . . what did you call them?"

"Fashionistas."

"Right."

"Are you looking for a partner?" she teased.

"Sorry."

"I can be the Executive Investigator in Charge of Stakeout Snacks."

Danny chuckled. "I may have to reconsider."

"Oh, that's rich, bud."

"Don't I know it."

Danny and Riggs straddled their boards, side by side, waiting for a wave that might or might not show. Frank stood guard at water's edge, pacing back and forth and casting furrowed glances across the surf toward them, periodically shouting out one lone bark.

"I've been surveilling the guy every day for more than a week," Danny managed over the boulder-sized pit in his stomach. "Watching him walk in and out of that bookstore carrying snacks and magazines for his son, and it didn't even occur to me . . ."

When he didn't complete the thought, Riggs spoke up. "But Malibu Barbie takes one look at him from across the street and puts it all together."

"Hey. Don't call her that."

Riggs shook his head and clucked. "That's tragic, man. Makes you question everything, right? Like maybe all those cases you've solved, maybe they were all just flukes, and it all comes down to this one case, proving your deepest fears: You are a fraud."

Danny glared at Riggs. "Shut it."

"Have a little perspective," his friend pointed out. "It's one case, bro. And it wouldn't bug you nearly as much if a rookie hadn't caught what you missed, right?"

He glanced over his shoulder at the lackluster wave heading their way. "It's not much," he said, thankful for the diversion, "but let's ride it home."

"Nah. You go on. I'm gonna wait on a real ride."

Frank welcomed Danny to shore by pacing as he paddled in. Danny tugged on Frank's ears and ruffled the top of his head before dragging his board a few yards and tossing it down. When he dropped to a seated position, Frank towered over him, nudging Danny with his nose and rubbing the side of his massive head against Danny's cheek.

"All right, all right," he said with a laugh. "Lay down, boy."

Frank complied, and Danny noticed Riggs still bobbing out there in the foamy blue-black surf. Straightening his back, he filled his lungs with warm morning air before releasing it slowly and closing his eyes. Gratitude and worship came easily to him on mornings like this one, and he spent several minutes sweeping the events of recent days around in his mind, searching the remnants for guidance . . . insight . . . wisdom; the kind of thing that only emanated directly from the Creator of such things.

When Jessie crossed his mind's eye, Danny smiled. Her glossy brunette hair with streaks of gold that framed her pretty heart-shaped face glimmered, and something in those glistening light blue eyes of hers pierced his chest.

*What about this business idea of hers?* he silently prayed. *Is it divine inspiration from You, or is it desperation that will sink her even further?*

Danny knew starting a business of any kind in the midst of devastation seldom turned out to be a stellar idea, but what else was she going to do? Jack Stanton took everything—the house, the car, the income, the status—and she could hardly afford to simply stand idle, waiting to see what happened. Liquidating the diamond symbols of her connection to the man who had burned her and turning the rings into something solid on which to rebuild purported an undeniable pliancy, not to mention being symbolically satisfying. But this business model—Adornments—for someone who seemingly knew nothing about building something from the bottom up this way, well, it seemed like a pretty risky proposition.

*But if anyone can take what little she has and make it into something more, I have a feeling it's Jessie.*

He didn't know quite why he felt that way, but something about Jessie Stanton spoke to his heart about restoration and resilience. She'd endured such a shocking and disappointing series of events, and yet she'd managed to retain a degree of innocent joy and an air of cautious hopefulness that he admired.

*Give her strength and wisdom, Father. Carry her through this time, and help me get the answers she needs so much. Where did this guy disappear to?*

Riggs's familiar, high-pitched caterwaul pushed Danny's eyes open, and he laughed as he watched his friend ride a pretty fair-sized wave with unusual balance and poise. When he hit the shore, he called out to Danny. "Let's take another lap."

"Nah," Danny returned as he stood up and grabbed his board. "I've got work to do." He smacked the side of his thigh, and Frank galloped after him. "See you later."

Danny stowed Carmen and stood under the makeshift outdoor shower he'd erected to the far side of his driveway. Icy water flowed over him, and he shook his head like Frank often did, sending a spray of water in every direction from his shaggy hair. Using the handheld shower tool, he washed away the excess sand from his bare chest and legs before shutting it down and drying off with a towel stowed in the storage cabinet under the stairs. He thought for a minute about taking off up those stairs to the roof for a little more quiet time, but the mission before him held the greater draw.

He changed into khaki shorts, and he pulled a black T-shirt over his head as he stalked into the kitchen—Frank close on his heels—to brew some coffee. He seized the full cup, along with a cinnamon bagel out of the bag on the counter, and headed into his office to fire up the computer. For the next ninety minutes, he aimed laser focus at Jack Stanton.

*Search known aliases.*

*Identify property holdings.*

*Research related property transactions.*

*Retrieve possible trackable records, such as bankruptcies, federal and civil lawsuits, familial history, current or past registrations of automobiles, aircrafts, or boats.*

The only item that came up with any sort of red flag at all was the purchase of property in Indonesia back in March of last year under the name of John Fitzgerald Stanton. Danny clicked on the link for further information and dialed Jessie's number.

"Hey, it's Danny."

"Oh, hi." She sounded a bit breathless.

"Is this a bad time?"

"No, not at all. I'm clearing some things out of my closet and into wardrobe boxes. What's up?"

"Two things. I finished Amber's background check, and she's clean as Nebraska snow."

"No surprise there. Thanks, Danny."

"Second. What's Jack's full legal name?" he asked.

"John Fitzgerald Stanton," she replied. "Why?" He heard the off-key chime of her doorbell in the background, and Jessie reacted. "Sorry, Danny. That's my door. Can you hold on a sec?"

"Nah, go ahead. That's all I needed for now. I'll talk to you later."

"So how did your appointment with the attorney go?" Amber asked as she slipped out of her jacket and draped her purse and backpack over the arm of the sofa.

"Really good. He's the one who helped Antonio get his restaurant up and running," Jessie replied as she headed for the refrigerator. "Water, tea, or soda?"

"Nothing, thanks."

She grabbed an iced tea and twisted off the top on her way back into the living room. "He knew all the right questions to ask and helped me make a list of about six dozen things I need to do before I can open the doors."

They sat down on the sofa, and Amber grinned at her. "Well, I think I can help with one of them."

"You found something?"

"I actually found a couple of places."

Amber opened her backpack and produced a slick, neon pink file folder held shut with an elastic clasp. She pulled out several pieces of printed paper and leaned toward Jessie so they could both review them at the same time.

"This one is off Melrose a block over from those vintage shops, like Slow and Wasteland."

Jessie slipped the page from Amber's hand to examine it more closely. "I didn't really want to go that far out, but it's cute, isn't it?"

"They're offering a two-year lease, and it's already got a whole wall of built-in cubbies and racks. The other thing they have that only one of the six places I toured has is a really unique sales counter at the back of the store."

One of the photos showed an interesting, high-gloss counter with carved detail at each corner. "That's really pretty."

"Look at the second one. It's here in Santa Monica."

"Better," Jessie remarked, taking the next page.

"This one's on one of those side streets, not too far from the Promenade. It has a longer lease. You have to sign on for three years, but the rent is far more reasonable than the Melrose location because utilities are included." Amber leaned closer and looked over her shoulder. "It needs some attention, like paint . . . but check out those windows."

Jessie's train of thought derailed for a moment when the bass notes from a neighbor's stereo blasted through the walls.

"Wow," Amber commented with a chuckle. "You didn't tell me your place came with entertainment. Do you pay extra for that?"

"Only in patience."

They shared a laugh as they looked at the third and final page.

"Okay, this one is up the boulevard toward Wilshire . . . but not close enough to endure the Wilshire price tag."

"A plus."

"Yeah. It's about the same price as the second place, but the utilities aren't included."

"It looks like it needs a lot of work."

"Yeah, the floors are a bit of a mess and there's no sales counter there. Also there's a portable wall on the far end that needs to be repaired if we want to use it to separate the dressing rooms."

Jessie spread the pages out in front of them across the coffee table.

"Hey. You have a coffee table."

"Yeah," Jessie replied with a shrug. "It's not too horrible, right?"

"Not at all." When Jessie lifted an eyebrow and grinned, Amber giggled. "Well, it's not . . . *completely* horrible."

"It turns out I have a small storage locker that comes with my apartment. I went out back this morning and opened it up to see how scary it was . . . you know, in the daylight hours . . . and I found this inside it. So I scrubbed and disinfected it for about an hour straight, and dragged it in. Once I make sure there's no one coming back to claim this treasure, I was thinking I'd give it a coat of paint or something."

Amber regarded the coffee table closely. "Is it . . . lopsided?"

"Oh!" she exclaimed, kneeling down on the floor to tuck the folded piece of cardboard back under the front leg. She tried rocking it as a test. "There. That's better."

Jessie's heart dropped a little. *Oh, how the mighty have fallen*, she thought. *But let's hope the table doesn't.*

"Do you feel like taking a ride?" Jessie asked.

"Sure. Where?"

"Show me where this second one is. I want to see it in person."

"You won't be able to get inside," Amber warned. "We'd have to make an appointment with the owner."

Jessie grinned and crinkled her nose. "Yeah, but we can peek in the windows, right?"

The two of them grabbed their bags and filed out the door. When Jessie struggled with closing it behind them, Amber joined in and it took the both of them to yank it shut so that she could lock one bolt after the other.

"I'm parked in back."

The two of them chatted amiably on the drive over, which only took about fifteen minutes—a bonus for Jessie. Even if the commute might be the only easy thing in her new life, she'd take it.

"It's the third one over," Amber said. "There's street parking, and then there's the small lot in front."

Jessie turned off the engine and leaned down to survey the stretch of small stores.

*Decent curb appeal, nothing competitive on either side, great windows.*

"Let's go snoop," she said, and the two of them climbed out of her Taurus and headed directly for the third storefront from the end.

Jessie cupped both hands around her eyes and pressed against the glass to peer inside. She recalled that the information sheet said it was only around nine hundred square feet, but the place looked larger than she'd imagined.

"Do you think we can fill all that space?" she asked Amber. "I mean, I don't really have that much inventory coming out of my closet, do I?"

"It just looks so big because it's empty. I can pretty much guarantee, once we get set up, you'll wonder how to fit everything in."

"You're sure?"

"I'm sure," Amber replied, and she rubbed Jessie's arm briskly. "Remember, we have to utilize space for at least a few dressing rooms."

"Oh. Right."

"See that door at the very back?"

"Is that an exit?"

"No," Amber explained. "There's a tiny hall that leads to a storage room and a very small office. It's hardly big enough to turn around in, but I think it's a good starting place."

Jessie placed her hand on her heart, closed her eyes, and tried to control her racing pulse. "Are we really doing this?" she whispered.

"I hope so," Amber told her. "Because I think this is the most exciting venture I've ever been involved in."

Jessie gulped around the lump in her throat and nodded. "Me, too."

---

Danny knew where Indonesia sat geographically, but aside from the fact that he'd heard myths about the quality of the waves near Bali, he didn't really know a lot more. He fired up the computer and googled the country.

*Consists of over sixteen thousand islands, but only about thirty percent of them are even inhabited . . . The dominant ethnic group: the Javanese . . . Diverse, with a commercial center in the capital of Jakarta, yet widespread poverty elsewhere throughout the country . . . Recent political reform . . . No extradition policy with the United States . . .*

The hair on the back of Danny's neck stood on end, and he read through the paragraph again.

*Despite the fact that Indonesia does not have an extradition policy with the United States, exceptions are made in cases of drug crimes, such as smuggling and significant dealing.*

He'd never met Jack Stanton, but Danny felt pretty confident in wagering that he hadn't been involved in drug trafficking. If he'd gotten himself embroiled in some other type of crime, he might have made certain preparations for disappearing if the need arose. Purchasing property in a nonextradition country like Indonesia could easily have been a cog in that wheel of escape.

Danny tried to imagine the type of man who could do such a thing, leaving someone like Jessie behind. From his purview, she would have blindly hightailed it right along with him if the situation became so critical that they had no other choice. Before his actions came to light, she'd told Danny herself that she had no idea their marriage was on the rocks or that he even had it within him to do such things to her as surrender the lease on her car and sell the house right out from under her. She'd thought her marriage was rock solid. And Jessie Stanton certainly wasn't the kind of woman from whom a guy sailed away unless under threat of bodily harm. What could Stanton have been thinking? He wasn't going to be able to just replace her.

Unless he already had.

A wave of nausea crested at the thought. Perhaps John Fitzgerald Stanton had already begun assembling his new life, complete with the replacement wife, before he'd given even a hint that he might soon vanish without a trace. Danny suddenly imagined the guy kicked back on a Bali beach, a cold beer in one hand and a hot exotic beauty in the other. All while Jessie flailed around in his aftermath, trying to put her life back together.

The urge to hunt the guy down and drag him out into the open to face the music became almost overpowering, and Danny grabbed his phone and dialed.

"Steph. It's Danny. Are you available for a little lunch?"

*About two weeks into the summer before Jessie's high school year, we rode into town to pick up a few things. She wanted to pay a visit to the soda shop for a handful of ten-cent candies while I took care of business at the hardware store.*

*I watched through the window as a messy-haired boy in dirty dungarees and a torn T-shirt walked up to her. They had quick words and then Jessie stuck her nose in the air and walked away from him. When I asked her about it later, she says, "Grampy, some boys just aren't worth the trouble of takin' a breath to talk to 'em."*

*"Some girls neither, I expect. Who was that boy?"*

*"Aaron Mansfield," she said like a lemon seed she spat out.*

*"Ain't he the boy who took you to the eighth grade dance?"*

*"Don't remind me. I don't want to think about him ever again. He doesn't even like New Kids."*

*"Which'uns?"*

*"Huh?"*

*"Which new kids don't he like?"*

*"New Kids on the Block. I got their pictures up on my bedroom wall, remember?"*

*Buncha kids with dungarees wearin' their hats sideways. "Didn't know they was new."*

*"Oh, Grampy."*

*Seems the truth of the matter was that Mansfield boy had added a couple more little girls to his dance card that night, and my Jessie weren't havin' none of it.*

*I only wish she'd stayed so smart when it came to boys.*

# 8

Jessie lowered herself into the tub of scented water, and the warmth embraced her and melted off a bit of the stress almost immediately. She bent her knees and raised them so that she could sink down far enough to allow the steamy cloak to settle in and snuggle her around the shoulders. Wisps of hair had already snuck out of the clip that shackled them, and they floated on the surface of the bath water.

She inhaled the lavender-vanilla fragrance and closed her eyes, resting her head on the back of the small blue tub. She decided to erase the memory of how many times she'd scrubbed it before deciding to take a chance on bathing in it, instead picturing the free-standing hammered copper tub in the master bathroom of her former home. If she filled *that bathtub* all the way up, she might have drowned. Halfway filled with steaming, scented water, she'd soaked for countless hours over the years in the Malibu house, staring out the floor-to-ceiling window and getting lost in the blue of the Pacific Ocean on the other side.

*Well, this tub is blue*, she reasoned.

Since there were no luxurious copper tubs in her immediate future, that would have to suffice. Jessie took another deep breath, holding the soothing scented balm in her lungs for a moment before stretching out her legs and exhaling it. She moaned softly as she propped her feet on the faucet, crossing them at the ankles.

Just as the corners of her mouth crept upward into a contented smile, a sudden creak preceded a rocking motion beneath her feet, and the faucet snapped right off the wall and fell into Jessie's bath.

---

Danny and Stephanie Regnier grew up next door to one another in Newport Beach. They played basketball together, learned to appreciate the ocean together, and wiped out more times than either of them could count while learning to master the surfboard. Not long after high school graduation, Steph enlisted in the Marine Corps while Danny staggered along a short stint in the Navy. She stayed with the Marines for about ten years, stationed or on tours of duty in unexotic locations like Lebanon, Germany, and Guantánamo. Then one year she came home for Christmas and announced she'd left the Corps and been recruited by a security company. That New Year's Eve, at the annual neighborhood shindig their families never missed, she confided in Danny that she'd actually gone to work for the FBI as an intelligence analyst. She'd been based at the Los Angeles field office ever since. She swore him to secrecy, and he'd kept her confidence the way they'd done for one another ever since the night they'd sneaked off to his family's boathouse to smoke their first cigarette together at the age of twelve.

There'd never been anything romantic between them, but there was a special something there; something indefinable and yet tangible. He'd been an only child, but Danny imagined if he had a sister, he'd have felt about her the way he felt for Steph. And whatever that emotion was, it rose up inside of him the second he saw her push open the door at Shoop's European Deli down on Main Street. It had become their go-to spot over the years, and Danny knew what Steph would order before she even met up with him at the counter.

"Salmon BLT and raspberry tea," she told the clerk before wrapping her arms around Danny's neck and planting a noisy kiss on his cheek.

"For you, sir?"

"He'll want the Jason," she answered for him.

*Hot roast beef, provolone, roasted red peppers, grilled mushroom and onion, horseradish and mayo, served on a crusty baguette.* She really knew him well.

"And an Arnold Palmer."

*Half lemonade, half iced tea.*

The clerk glanced at Danny, and he grinned. "Oh yeah," he confirmed. "She nailed it."

Once they had their food and settled at a table, Danny took a long look at Steph.

"You haven't called me in six months," she declared. "What's up with that?"

"Sorry, I've—"

"Been busy," she completed for him. "You're always busy."

Danny bit into his sandwich and nodded at her over it. "So how's life at the Bureau?" he asked her.

Steph waved her hand and shook her head. "You don't care about my job, Danny. Don't pretend."

They shared a laugh, and he pointed out, "You couldn't tell me anything anyway."

"True," she quipped.

Danny tried to remember the last time he'd seen Steph with her dark blonde hair down. It looked pretty. Normally, she kept it swept back in a tight ponytail. Like usual, though, she wore little to no makeup and a dark tailored suit jacket and trousers; this time, paired with a pale blue blouse underneath. He hadn't noticed her shoes, but he knew he could win a bet on a sensible pair. Not like Jessie with her tall, thin heels, open toes, buckles, and designer labels. He couldn't imagine how women learned to walk atop shoes like those.

"You need my help on a case," Steph stated, and Danny smiled.

"I do."

With no further comment, Steph produced a small spiral notebook from the inside pocket of her jacket. "Got a pen?"

He handed one over and sighed.

"Name?"

"John Fitzgerald Stanton," he told her. "Goes by Jack."

"Who'd he kill?" she asked as she scribbled on the blank page.

Danny loved the way Steph always popped out questions or comments like that with nothing but a deadpan look on her face.

"Nobody that I know of. He dissolved his business, sold his house, surrendered the cars, and disappeared in about eleven seconds, leaving a wife of ten or twelve years behind holding the empty bag. While trying to locate him, I came across a property purchase in Indonesia, finalized a few months back."

"No extradition."

"Right."

"And you want to know what we might know about crimes that might have sent him quietly running into the night."

"Very much," Danny replied.

"Got a social?"

He nodded, pulled up the notes file on his phone and handed it over.

She lifted her grayish eyes momentarily and flashed him a smile as she transferred the information to her notepad. "So . . . you said you wanted me to look at a locket?"

"Right!" He produced the locket they'd found in the floor of Jessie's apartment and placed it in the center of his palm to show her. "What do you think of this?"

Steph's eyes brightened, and she carefully removed it from his hand and held it up toward the light. "This is stunning. A real find. Where did you get it?"

"Hidden in the floorboards of one of Riggs's apartments. Anything you can tell me about it?"

"I think so, but first . . . the thing is . . . I'm getting married."

Surprise lurched within him and Danny laughed. "Just like that? 'I'm getting married.' Expound, Steph."

"He's head of Tactical Collection and Reporting at the Wilshire office. We've been involved for about eight months, seriously for six. He proposed on a transport flight to Hezbollah." She displayed a plain round solitaire diamond and shrugged. "He gets me."

"Name?"

"Vince Neff."

He chuckled. "Let me get this straight. You're going to be *Steph Neff*?"

"Shut it," she said with a wince. "I'm keeping my name for just that reason."

Danny leaned back in his chair and crossed his arms over his chest. "Steph Neff. And he gets you."

"Yeah, so I was thinking you could be my Guy of Honor, if you're up for it."

He puffed out a chuckle of surprise. "What if I hadn't called you today? You were going to just hit me up the weekend beforehand and tell me where to be?"

"Maybe. I don't know. This whole wedding thing . . . you know . . ."

"It's the marriage that cuts the mustard, Steph, not the wedding," he remarked. "And yeah, I'll be your Guy of Honor. When is it?"

"Six weeks. On the boat dock at my folks' house. Nothing elaborate, just twenty guests, a cake, probably some sandwiches or something. My mom's handling all that."

"Do I need to wear a tux?" he asked, holding his breath for the answer . . . until she glared at him.

"What you're wearing now is fine."

Danny looked down at the washed-out blue jeans he'd owned since 2009 or so, and the black cotton shirt with the cuffs rolled to the elbow to hide a small tear.

"Well, I think I can do a little better than this," he commented.

"Not much better," she warned. "If you look better than the bride, I'll pull out my gun and shoot you."

Danny leaned forward and looked Steph in the eyes. "You're going to make a beautiful bride."

"Oh, hush up and eat your roast beef," she said, returning her attention to the locket.

"Jessie?"

Piper's voice lifted Jessie's spirits immediately, and she crawled toward the open door of her beautiful closet and called out to her. "Back here!"

While she waited for her friend, she taped shut the last box of handbags and grabbed the Sharpie pen on the floor next to her to label it.

"Finished!" she exclaimed when Piper stood in the doorway. "I have officially packed and inventoried every item out of my closet. Now what did you bring me?"

"It's all in the car," she replied. "Do you want to do it here, or wait and take it over to the store?"

"I've only just signed the lease, and the store needs a ton of work before I take anything over there. I'll have to do all the inventories here."

Piper deflated. "Then we have to carry it in?"

"Hello?" The man's voice struck Jessie only slightly familiar as he announced himself at the front door. "Ms. Stanton? It's Aaron Riggs."

"Oh! He's here to fix the faucet in the bathroom," Jessie said before calling back to him. "Come on in. I'll be right out."

"I'm just going to head into the bathroom to fix the tub."

"Ooh, maybe we can get some help carrying in those boxes and wardrobe bags!" Piper brightened, and she hurried into the living room to greet him. Jessie listened in as her friend turned on her considerable charm. "Mr. Riggs, I have some things in my car that need to come inside. Is there any chance I could get you to help me?"

"Sure thing. Let me just drop this in the bathroom."

Jessie chuckled softly. Piper was a force.

She shoved the last box into the corner with the others and a satisfied smile wound its way upward as she straightened the others. By the time she finished and strolled out to the living room, several large boxes took up the space between the coffee table and the wall, and four or five vinyl wardrobe bags lay draped over the arm of the sofa. And . . .

"What's that?"

A lovely taupe chenille chair flanked the other side of the table.

"Uh, did I somehow gain a chair?" she asked.

"Isn't it pretty? I remembered this morning that we had it just sitting in the storage room at the restaurant, and I thought it would look really nice in here. What do you think?"

Jessie sauntered toward it, sat on it, and crossed her legs with a sigh. "It's wonderful. Thank you, Piper."

"Oh, good. I hoped you'd like it."

"It's almost starting to look like a real living room," Jessie said with a snicker. "With furniture to fill the empty spaces and all. And hey! I thought you said you were just bringing a few things."

Piper shrugged as she sized up the boxes and bags. "Yeah. I only *meant to* bring a few things, but Antonio has been nudging me about my closet lately anyway. And once I got started, knowing it was going to a good cause . . ."

"And I'm the good cause," Jessie surmised. "Nice. I wonder if you can write me off on your taxes as a charitable contribution."

"Stop."

"Well, there's always the added bonus that you might make some money back on rentals to fund more shopping for some new things to fill your closet and irritate Antonio again. Let's have a look," she said, popping to her feet and grabbing one of the wardrobe bags.

With a ginger touch, she unzipped it and removed four garments draped over velvet hangers.

"Oh, Piper . . . Your Stella McCartney?"

Piper ran her hand along the single shoulder of the flower macramé black dress with nude lining. "Yeah," she stated, and Jessie sensed a twinge of regret in her voice.

"You can't."

"No," she replied, almost convincingly. "The thing is, I could never pull off the single shoulder thing. If I had Michelle Obama's arms, maybe. But I think you'll be able to make better use of it at your store than I can with these arms."

"It's stunning," Jessie breathed. "I've always loved this dress."

"Well, admire it from afar as someone else is trying it on," Piper teased.

Jessie poked her tongue out at her friend before picking up the next garment and admiring it. "Oh, I remember this dress. You wore it to the Westfields' anniversary party over the summer."

A painful twinge pinched the base of Jessie's heart as she remembered dancing with Jack under the glistening chandelier at the Four Seasons' ballroom. Michael Bublé had agreed to perform that night, and Jack had held her so tightly. She could almost feel his warm breath on her earlobe again now.

"Jessie?"

"Sorry."

She hadn't even realized Piper had taken the hanger from her. She focused on the dress held up in front of her. A soft white knit sleeveless with a hint of metallic shine in a pattern of flames. The gown featured an elongated V-neckline and a lovely flared hem.

"Missoni," she said with a sigh. "It's so pretty. Are you sure?"

Piper nodded. "Again with the arm situation. I don't feel so confident in sleeveless anymore."

She shook her head and chuckled. "You're crazy. But I'll take it. Thank you."

"Oh, I brought you the shoes I wore with it too."

"Gianvito Rossi open-toes, right?"

"Yeah, with that pretty metallic glitter. And before you ask me, yes, I'm sure. They hurt my feet something awful. I think I'm getting bunions."

Jessie sat down on the sofa and opened her laptop on the coffee table. "Help me start adding these to the inventory. Do you remember what you paid for the Missoni?"

"I do as long as you never breathe a word to Antonio."

Jessie crossed her heart and lifted three fingers in a faux Girl Scout pledge.

"It was marked down," she justified. "From thirty-five hundred to twenty-six."

"What about the shoes?"

"I have no idea. But they're from the 2014 season. Maybe you can check the website."

She started to do just that, but the intention fell flat as Piper lifted the next dress from those in the garment bag. Instead, she fell backward into the sofa cushions and sighed.

"Vintage Chanel," she managed, just above a whisper, and she cleared her throat before clutching it with both hands. "The fringed trouser suit. Piper, are you insane?"

The black fringed trouser suit featured a jacket with notched lapels, long sleeves and the most exquisite pleated silk detail over tailored wool trousers. Jessie recalled seeing Piper wearing it with a simple strand of pearls—she couldn't remember where—and she'd thought her the most stylish and chic woman in the room.

"You cannot give this up!"

"It doesn't fit right anymore. Justin, the stylist I work with sometimes, has had his eye on it for ages, but I just had the inkling to hold on to it, for some reason. I'm thinking that reason was you," she added with a twinkle.

"Can I try it on?"

"No. This is not a shopping expedition for you. We are stocking your new business venture, remember?"

"Please," she pleaded. "I've always loved it so much. I promise this is the only one."

Piper groaned, and Jessie decided to take it as a yes. She leapt to her feet, snatched the hanger from Piper's hand and raced into her closet and slammed the door behind her before she had the chance to object.

---

"Why didn't you just ask Danny to help you out?" Piper asked as Jessie sat on the floor in the far corner of nine hundred square feet that would soon transform into her future. She hoped.

"He's my private investigator, not my carpenter or my friend, Piper."

But as she sat hunched over, examining the "easy to assemble" instructions for shelving that she'd printed off the internet, Piper's suggestion carried a little more weight.

"Where do you buy precut wood, anyway?" she asked, tunneling her fingernail into the messy nest of hair in order to scratch her head.

"Home Depot," Piper told her. "Or Lowe's, I guess. But Jessie—"

"I think I can do this," she said, but not convincingly, so she tried again. "I do. I think I can do this!"

When the front door whooshed open, Piper growled. "Oh, thank the Lord!"

Jessie glanced up to find Danny standing in the doorway.

"Piper, you called him?"

"I had to. Somebody had to keep you from nailing your hand to the wall, or worse."

She frowned. "I have directions right here," she told him before he asked. "I just have to go to *Home Something* and buy the wood and some"—she paused to check the battered page on the floor in front of her—"braces."

"Uh-huh," he replied, and he stalked toward her and held out his hand. His expression told her he wasn't joking around. "Come on. Get up from there."

She blurted out a moan of complaint before taking his hand and allowing him to tug her upright. She stamped her feet once she was right on them.

"Give me those plans of yours," he said, and she scooped them up and pushed them into his chest. "Now, let's head over to Lowe's and get what you need to get started."

"Fine. But I'm putting them together," she informed him.

"Uh-huh."

Piper squeezed Danny's arm as he passed her. "Thank you."

"I heard that," Jessie barked.

"Good!"

On the way out to Danny's Jeep, Jessie noticed Amber climbing out of her car and heading toward them.

"You're going to love this," she blurted as she approached. "I found a dry cleaner not three blocks from here willing to give us a special deal on bulk jobs."

"And you can tell her all about it when we get back," Danny said, and he grabbed Jessie's arm and led her down the curb.

"Piper's inside," Jessie called back to her. "You guys can get started with the cleaning crew. They should be here"—Danny nudged her through the open passenger door, and she quickly called out—"in thirty minutes or so!"

Amber waved her arm, and Danny closed Jessie up tight inside his Jeep.

"You can be so rude," she told him after he'd rounded the Jeep and slipped behind the wheel.

"My apologies." But he didn't seem the least bit sincere.

Once he steered them out to Santa Monica Boulevard, Danny glanced over and grinned. "So I did a little digging about that locket of yours. Do you want that first, or would you rather get talk of your husband out of the way?"

"You found Jack?" Her heart began to pound so hard that it left an ache in her chest.

"Maybe, but—"

"Where is he?" Jessie blurted.

"I don't know for sure. What I do know is that he bought some property a while back in Indonesia."

"Indonesia!" she exclaimed. After thinking it over for a moment, she asked him, "Where is that?"

"Southeast Asia."

She sighed. "Asia. Why would he go there?"

"I'm still trying to figure that out."

"But your gut feeling?" She hadn't learned a whole lot about Danny Callahan since they'd met, but she'd certainly learned that he tended to live by his gut.

"Well," he said, pausing for a moment to scratch the stubble of his beard. "My first thought is that Indonesia is a nonextradition country. If he committed any crimes and suddenly became concerned about being arrested, he might have wanted a safe place to land."

"Crimes," she muttered, her head spinning a little.

"Can you think of any crimes he may have committed?"

"Aside from murdering our life together? No. What kind of property did he buy?"

"A small island, really. About a hundred acres near the coast of Bali."

"Bali." That rang a significant bell. "He wanted us to go to Bali on our anniversary last year. He said it was a good place to disappear from the world for a while!"

"Did he now?"

"He said it's . . . *paradise*."

Even though the car appeared to be safely stopped at a red light, Jessie wondered how she could simultaneously somersault like that—head over heels over head—at such an accelerated speed.

"I don't really know much more," he stated. "But I'll keep digging."

"Oh." The *thud-thud-thud* of her pulse drummed in her ears. "Okay." She felt sick.

"Do you want to hear about the locket?"

"Sure," she lied.

"I showed it to a friend of mine with a penchant for vintage jewelry. She said it's circa 1950s, a fourteen-carat gold domed locket. The red stones encircling it are flat rubies—thirty of them, I think she said. And the stones set inside the five cut stars are genuine diamonds, about a tenth of a carat each. The pearls on the flip side are real, too, as are the larger diamond and the rubies on the dome."

"Danny!" she exclaimed.

"I was so hoping to hear you say 'Goodie!' again," he teased.

Jessie giggled. "You're crazy. Hey, that had to be a family heirloom. How could they have just left it in the floor like that?"

"I'm guessing they forgot about it, or some tragedy drew them away from the place and they couldn't go back for it," he surmised. "But I'll do a records search to find out who lived there in the fifties and sixties and see if we can track it to a little girl who might have also owned those books you found. Maybe we can get that locket back to its rightful owner somehow."

"Wouldn't that be wonderful?"

The shroud of shock and humiliation about Jack had somehow lifted at the mere thought of finding the little girl—a grown woman by now—and placing her beautiful gold locket back into her hands after so many years. Jessie couldn't help wondering how long she'd been without it, envisioning how heartbroken she might have been at its loss. Her imagination cranked at full capacity until Danny's Jeep came to a stop in the Lowe's parking lot.

"Listen to me," he said, turning in his seat toward her. "I want to warn you about this ahead of time. Piper sent me the measurements for the store and asked me to help you out."

"I can't believe—"

"See, this is what I wanted to avoid," he stated. "She knew you were in over your head, and she asked me to help you out. That's all."

"Danny, I can't let her keep footing the bill for everything I need to build my new life."

"She's not. You're paying. I'm building."

"Uh . . ." She hadn't expected that. "Oh."

"Riggs has a discount here, and he's right over there." She followed his nod and spotted Aaron Riggs leaning against his ugly blue VW bus in front of the store. "He's meeting us with his van to load it up. You'll get a good rate, and you've got skilled labor in me."

"Danny, I—"

"You really have to learn to accept a kindness, Jessie. Can't you ever just say thank you?"

A flush of embarrassment heated her face and she lowered her eyes. "I'm sorry. Thank you."

"That's the spirit. Now let's go use that debit card of yours, shall we?"

She giggled as she unbuckled the seatbelt. "Okay."

The two of them got out and headed across the lot toward Riggs, and Jessie yanked on Danny's sleeve. "Hey, do you think I could go in and get some paint and supplies while you load the wood?"

"Knock yourself out."

Jessie excitedly ran ahead of him, waving at Riggs as she scampered into the store.

*My Jessie was always such a happy little girl, least ways 'til the high school years. It used to didn't take much more'n some colored wildflowers to braid together or a frilly dress 'n' some twirlin' to brighten up her whole day, but as she started growin', so did her yearnin' for somethin' more'n the borders of Slidell, Louisiana.*

*"Someday, I'm gonna have a glamorous life, Grampy," she says to me one lazy afternoon out on one of the piers at Lake Pontchartrain. "Someday, I'll have pretty things and a house where every room is a different beautiful color." My girl always did like her colors. "And folks'll*

*think I'm pretty, too," she added, and my heart just 'bout sank like a rock.*

*"What're you yappin' about, child? Ever'body in Saint Tammany Parish says what a beautiful girl you are."*

*"Yeah, but in Slidell they got nothin' much to compare me to, Grampy. They don't know from nothin'."*

*"They see yer light a-shinin', child. That ain't enough fer ya?"*

*"I guess it should be. But somehow it just doesn't feel like it is."*

*"Then you better get to thinkin' about why that is, huh?"*

*Yeah, Jessie got to thinkin', and her old gramps got to prayin'.*

# 9

She chose *Sterling Grape* for the office walls," Piper said as she pressed the roller into the tray, "because she says it makes her feel happy."

Danny smiled as he put the final touch of pale gray on the baseboard trim.

"I'll tell you the truth," she confided as she finished up the last portion of the wall, "I wasn't convinced she'd ever be happy again. So I'm all for purple walls, or anything else that helps her recover from this mess Jack has left behind. Every time I think about him, I just . . . Oooh! I'm so mad at him!"

He dropped his brush into the hood clamped onto the side of the paint can. Adjusting the sheet draped over the desktop, he leaned against it and drained the last of the cold water from a plastic bottle Jessie had delivered earlier.

"Anyway, I think you're a big part of her recovery, Danny."

He lifted one eyebrow and looked at Piper seriously. "I'm just doing what she's paying me to do."

"That's not true, and you know it," she exclaimed with a flash of amusement in her greenish eyes. "You've gone above and beyond. And I just wanted to tell you . . . I'm grateful."

Danny shrugged one shoulder and looked away, uncomfortable. "Look," he finally responded, "she didn't deserve what she was dealt. I just believe, when someone like that comes across your path, you're designed to help them out if you can."

She pushed back her short, streaked hair with the back of her hand while still holding the roller. "Simple as that, huh?" The quirk in her smile put Danny on edge.

"If you're hinting that there's something more behind it," he assured her, "there isn't. As far as I'm concerned—and I know as far as she's concerned as well—Jessie Stanton is a married woman. I don't pursue married women."

Her smile dissolved and she looked him squarely in the eye. "I didn't mean to offend you."

"No offense taken. I just don't want there to be any misunderstanding."

"Okay," she surrendered. "I get it. You're a good guy. I guess we don't encounter too many of those any more. Maybe we just don't know what to make of you when we do."

The cluster of metal bells, ribbons, and small flowers Jessie had attached to the front door jangled to announce her return.

"Dinner is served!" she exclaimed over the rattle of plastic bags as she entered.

"*Carissima*?" a man's voice followed.

"Speaking of those good guys there are so few of," Piper brightened, "there's mine now!"

She placed the roller into the tray and hurried out of the small office into the store. By the time Danny wiped his hands and joined them, he found Piper in the arms of her husband, Antonio.

"Good to see you again," Danny greeted him.

"Jessie and Amber stopped in to pick up some dinner for you all," he said in his distinctive Italian accent, and he planted a kiss on the top of Piper's head. "I thought I'd break away and see what I might do to help. Besides, I couldn't stand the idea of you all dining on such magnificent cuisine while seated on the floor of an empty store."

He waved a hand toward the window, and two uniformed waiters entered, each of them carrying folding chairs and tables which they quickly set up. Amber covered the tables with paper cloths while Jessie unloaded plastic containers of pasta, salad, and bread, and Antonio filled clear plastic cups with sparkling water.

"We're all going to feel like napping after this meal!" Amber exclaimed. "Who's going to want to keep on working?"

"You are," Jessie joked. "And so are the rest of us!"

"Sir, yes, sir!" Amber returned with a salute.

"Following the meal," Antonio told them as he guided his wife to a chair, "you have three more sets of hands to help in whatever ways are needed."

"*Three* more?" Jessie asked, and Antonio pointed out the willing-and-able waiters he'd brought along. "Oh, thank you so much. All of you!" She sat down next to Danny and reached over to squeeze his forearm. "This is . . . lovely!"

A sudden pit formed at the center of his stomach, a rock of anxiety that anchored him to the chair. Maybe Piper's assumption about his intentions had been driven by some very real hope emanating from her best friend. He'd seen it before. A wife whose worst fears about her husband had been confirmed turned to the nearest male in her life—often the very investigator who had brought her the news—suddenly all those broken dreams and disappointments pinned on his chest like a battered badge. An honorable mention. *It didn't work with that guy, but you'll do.*

"Danny?"

Jessie touched his hand to draw his attention back to the table. He flicked off the thoughts and glared at her.

"Sorry. What?"

She lifted the basket in her hand and chuckled. "Bread. Would you like bread?"

"Oh. Yeah. Thanks."

Danny felt thankful that the various conversations humming around the table didn't include him beyond an occasional comment or smile. Antonio had suffered a mediocre review on his wine in some international magazine, Amber had secured a hefty discount on bulk dry cleaning for the store, and Jessie seemed generally overwhelmed at the fearful prospect of all her hard work culminating in failure.

"It's like when you're in high school," she said, turning to Danny to include him. "You're excited about the party you're planning, but the real concern is that no one will come."

"Oh, sweetie," Piper interjected, "people always stand in line to come to your parties. This won't be any different."

She wilted slightly and tried to push a smile upward. "Promise?"

"Promise."

"You know what would probably help?" Danny added.

"What?" she asked, unfiltered hope brimming from her crystal eyes. "What would help?"

"If you had some shelves and racks to display things on. Why don't we get started."

Jessie sighed. "That's a great idea."

"Come see the walls," Piper said as she, Amber, and Jessie retreated to the office to clean up the paint and supplies while Antonio sent one of his waiters to the back to retrieve cleaning supplies. He instructed the other to clean up the remnants of the meal.

"After, you two can cast lots to see who gets the restroom," he told them with a glimmer of amusement. "And the other cleans the storage room at the back."

A sudden reminder of his brief time in the military flicked Danny's memory. A leader's effectiveness could always be measured by his men's attitude and blind willingness to follow his orders. Antonio's employees showed no trace of regret about the mission; only an eager resolve to accomplish it. That said a lot to him about the man.

"Can I help with the building?" he asked Danny. "I don't have your skills, but I have some muscle if you need it."

"Sure. Let's get started then."

Danny moved to the front corner of the store where he'd deposited his tools and supplies next to the stacks of wood he and Riggs had unloaded earlier. Antonio's wide-eyed expression at the sight of the nail gun amused Danny to no end. A restaurateur and vintner wouldn't have much use for such things, he imagined.

"I've taken some measurements and used Jessie's rough idea of what she has in mind," he said, spreading the sketches out over the sawhorses before them. "I thought display racks and cubby-holes on this wall, and a couple rows of rods over there. Also—" He stopped mid-thought and scratched his jaw as it occurred to him that Antonio certainly hadn't come dressed for construction. "I think I have some coveralls in the back of my Jeep. Do you want me to run out and see?"

"Oh," he muttered, looking down at his expensive black trousers and black silk shirt. "Yeah. It's going to get messy, is it?"

Danny chuckled. "I can guarantee it. I'll be right back."

He couldn't really fault the guy. He'd followed Jessie back to the store with the blind idea of lending a hand. Although he did appear to have the "muscle" to back him up, he sure didn't have the first clue what the offer had entailed. Despite the fact that they had nothing whatsoever in common, Danny liked him.

When he returned with the coveralls he'd worn to help Riggs last month, he found Antonio standing there like Stallone—but with a big, stupid grin on his face—holding the 18-gauge nail gun like an AK-47.

"Uh. That's not plugged in, right?" Danny asked him.

"Oh, certainly not!" he replied with a warm laugh.

"Let's start with some wood glue, shall we?"

---

Jessie clamped the Keurig shut and pressed the button, inhaling deeply as her cup filled with fragrant cinnamon coffee. Amber stood next to her at the kitchen counter, doctoring her own cup with vanilla creamer and too much sugar.

"Would you like some coffee with your sugar?" she teased.

"Oh, I know. It's awful, right?"

They took their coffee along into the living room and sank down to the floor on opposite sides of the coffee table.

"Okay, so here's what I'm thinking," Amber said, getting straight down to business. "We start with Facebook. Their ad space is completely customizable, right down to the amount of money you want to spend per day and the type of person who sees it. It's based on clicks, and you can choose the demographic as well as the days and times it will show up."

Jessie raised her hand and shook her head. "Do we have a Facebook page then?"

Amber giggled as she retrieved her iPad from her bag. "We will after today. But while I'm pulling up my own page to show you, let's talk about flyers. In that pink file folder are some sample flyers that I thought we could pass out or put on cars or something over on Melrose where all the wannabes—*like me!*—shop. I mean, let's face it. I'm your sample customer."

Several sharp knocks on the door severed their focus, and Jessie hopped up to answer it.

"What's going on? Are you all right?" Piper exclaimed when she opened the door.

"I'm fine. Why?"

Piper pushed past her into the apartment. "I've been calling you all morning and getting some strange recording. I finally had them check your line, and the operator said it's disconnected."

"What? That's impossible."

Jessie looked around and spotted her phone on the kitchen counter next to the Keurig. "There has to be some mistake."

Before she reached the phone, however, her stomach clenched with an all-too-familiar sensation. When the cold, nonresponsive phone confirmed it, Jessie's heart dropped with a thud.

"What's the date?"

"The sixth," Amber replied. "Why?"

"The wireless contract runs through the fifth of each month."

"Jack," Piper muttered.

"He canceled my cell phone, too."

An appropriate expletive flew out of Piper's mouth, and Amber snickered.

"The hits just keep on coming," Jessie said on a sigh, and she dropped back into the sofa cushions. "That's just great. I have no phone."

Piper sat next to her and massaged her hand for a moment. "Let's go have lunch."

"What a great idea," Amber said. "I'm starved."

Jessie lifted an eyebrow and glared at them.

Piper smiled. "And on the way back, we'll take care of this little bump in the road."

Jessie wondered what she might do without a friend like Piper. How could she have managed to meet someone in a me-first, upwardly mobile community like theirs whose friendship would turn out to be such a cornerstone for her? A fast-forward rush of everything she had taken care of, inspired, and encouraged Jessie through in the last weeks lifted the corner of her mouth into half a smile.

"You're the best."

"Oh, I know! And you're going to love me even more when I tell you my news."

"What news?"

"That's why I've been calling you all morning," she announced. "Do you remember my friend Cynthia?"

"She does those style segments for the news."

"Cynthia Ross?" Amber exclaimed.

"Yes. And she's doing a special on dressing in red carpet fashions on a linoleum budget, or something like that. So I told her about you and Adornments. She's going to include you guys in the piece, and cover the store opening!"

Amber flew to her feet and danced around. "That is amazing!"

"We just have to call her and set up a time for the initial meet."

Jessie sighed. "And if I actually had a working phone, I would call her right now."

Piper laughed as she grabbed Jessie's wrist and tugged her upright. "Let's go. First sustenance, then wireless."

Piper and Amber ambled ahead while Jessie wrestled with her front door.

"Oh good! Gabi," she heard Amber exclaim. "Jessie, this is your neighbor, Gabriela Cruz." She turned to find a beautiful Hispanic woman standing between Piper and Amber. "This is Piper Brunetti and Jessie Stanton. Gabi lives in the apartment at the other corner of the building."

"Nice to meet you, Gabi," Jessie said, amused. "How did you two cross paths?"

"We parked next to each other on the street the other day, and we got to talking on our way up the driveway," Gabi explained in a thick Hispanic accent.

"By the time we reached your doorway, we'd exchanged all of the pertinent information," Amber teased. "Fast friends."

"Fast friends, *chez*."

"You're the first one of my neighbors that I've met," Jessie told her. "Leave it to Amber to do it for me."

"Maybe you'll come over later?" Gabi invited. "I'm making tamales."

"We're headed out to lunch right now," Amber told the woman. "Catch you later, Gabi."

They piled into Jessie's Ford Taurus and headed down the road before Amber leaned forward from the back seat. "Gabi's really sweet, and I was thinking it would be good for you to know someone in your building. She's your age, too, which is a plus."

Jessie and Piper turned toward each other and shared a lingering gaze before they both burst out laughing.

"I didn't mean it that way. It's not like I think you're geriatric or anything."

"Stop right there before I fire you."

"Oh, come on. I didn't mean anything by it."

"No, it's fine. You're a full decade younger than we are. We understand," Piper teased in a shaky, elderly voice. Turning to Jessie, she added, "Where did I leave that hearing aid of mine?"

---

Frank stood up and stretched before making a couple of circles atop his navy-blue bed and curling into it again.

"Another nap, huh, boy? A dog can never catch too many Zs."

Danny refilled his coffee cup and headed back to his office. Before he even had a chance to sit down in front of the desk, Frank flew upright, planted all four paws on the floor, and growled.

"What is it, buddy?"

The first fraction of the initial rap on the door, and the giant dog flew into a rage, for the benefit of the perceived intruder no doubt. Danny padded across the floor in bare feet, tucking his denim shirt into the waistband of his jeans.

"Stand down, Frankenstein," Steph called out as Danny pulled open the door. "It's friend, not foe."

Frank circled her twice, rubbing her hip with the side of his face.

"Come on in," Danny said, brushing the tips of Frank's ears with the palm of his hand. "You heard her, Frank. Go on!"

The Great Dane gave Steph's leg one final nudge before he trotted off to the large rectangle embroidered with his name and collapsed there.

"Coffee or something?"

"No, thanks. I only have a couple of minutes," she replied, and she followed him to his office.

"Come to school me on the something-old-something-blue stuff?" he teased, leaning back in his chair.

"I was hoping you knew how that went."

Danny chortled. "You picked the wrong gal then."

"I came over to tell you what I found on Jack Stanton."

Danny's pulse kicked up a notch. He'd only just learned about his latest shenanigans a few minutes before Steph arrived. After everything else, they really should have expected it, he supposed, but leaving Jessie without even a cell phone?

"John Fitzgerald Stanton was an investment advisor," she began.

"His wife used the title *Financier.*"

"Interrelated. Anyway, the asset management section of his business has been under investigation for the last year when a deal he brokered between two corporate entities red-flagged some fabricated gains."

"A Ponzi scheme."

"Precisely. Further investigation uncovered a massive amount of missing funds for up to three dozen of his top-tier clients."

"Define 'massive amount.'"

"Well, we know it's in the millions. It could be into a few hundred million over twelve years. Just about the time we feds were ready to bring him in and serve warrants for all of the Stanton Financial records, he went off the grid."

"Taking the gazillions with him?"

"Every last gazill."

"Anybody have a solid line on where he made off to?"

They said it in perfect two-part harmony. "Indonesia."

"Now, he did have an executive assistant whose name keeps coming up . . ."

"Claudia Stern," he interjected.

"Yeah. They brought her in this morning for questioning."

"I met her," he recalled. "She seemed genuinely stunned that he'd disappeared and locked her out of the offices. I don't think she's got much intel to give."

"I suspect you're right. I wish I had more to tell you."

"That's plenty, Steph. Thanks."

One steak and bleu cheese salad for lunch. *Check.*

One new cell phone. *Check.*

One afternoon of laser-focused work on advancing toward an actual store opening. *Check and check.*

By the time Amber left at five-thirty, Jessie had already shifted gears and headed into the kitchen to forage for an early dinner. The landscape of the half-empty refrigerator offered nothing enticing at all, and a knock on the front door distracted her from the grocery list she began scribbling while leaning over the kitchen sink.

"Hi, *Jheshee*," Gabi said with a warm smile when Jessie opened the door. "I made tamales for my brother Reynoldo, and he never showed. I wondered maybe you would like some."

Jessie didn't think she'd ever had authentic tamales before. Oh, she'd had the frozen kind back in her twenties, the kind that came on a microwavable plate next to mashed beans and crunchy rice. She bought them three for two dollars at the Albertsons store near her first apartment. After marrying Jack, she thought she'd never see those lean times again in her life, but they'd come back around and backed her straight into the corner of another battered old apartment.

"Thank you so much," she said. "Come on in."

Gabi followed her to the kitchen, set the plate on the counter and removed the aluminum foil covering. "They're still in the husks to keep them warm. You just remove the meat and drizzle some of the chili sauce over it. I find a lot of *gringas* like to add sour cream, so I brought you a little."

*Gringas.* Jessie laughed.

"This was so nice of you."

Gabi stood next to her, looking around the kitchen. "Your *keechin* is much nicer than mine. Did Aaron fix it up, or did you do it yourself?"

"Oh, it was really my girlfriend Piper. You met her today."

"Ah, *si*. She is *muy bonita*."

"Inside and out," Jessie said with a smile. "She covered the expenses, and Danny and Riggs did the work."

"Danny Callahan? You know Danny?"

"Yes, he's a new acquaintance of mine."

"Is he your"—she struggled to find the word—"*amor*? Your . . . *boyfriend*?"

"No, no. Just someone I know."

"Danny Callahan, he is *muy caliente*, no?"

"*Caliente*?" Jessie repeated. "Oh, you mean he's good-looking. Yes, he's handsome." She chuckled before adding, "In a beach bum sort of way."

Gabi pushed her thick, dark hair over her shoulder and grinned. "*Caliente* in every sort of way."

The woman nudged her away from the plate and prepared it for Jessie before carrying it over to the table at the end of the galley kitchen. "You sit. Eat."

Jessie followed her directions and filled her fork with a generous bite. At first taste, she thought it quite delicious. About four seconds later, however, she hopped up from her seat and rushed to the refrigerator. "Just . . . need some water." Fanning her open mouth, Jessie managed, "Now *that* is *muy caliente*."

Gabi chuckled and sat in the chair across from hers, waiting for her return to the table.

"I like your *cuh-lors*."

"My . . ." She repeated it in her mind. "Oh! My colors. You mean the paint colors."

"*Sí*. Very nice."

"Thanks. Danny and Riggs picked them. But I really like them, too."

"Our apartment *es blanco*. White, everywhere."

"You said, 'our apartment.' Are you married, Gabi?"

"No, not married. I live there with my *niños*."

"Children. You have kids. How many?"

"Carlos is ten, and my Miranda, she is six."

"Oh, and you're raising them on your own. That can't be easy."

Gabi blurted out a chuckle. "Easy! No, not so easy. But somehow we manage. It seems like every time I think there is no way to make the"—she used both hands to signify her meaning—"ends to meet, something *wunnerful* comes along."

Jessie silently hoped she had a lot of *wunnerful* headed her way as well.

---

*Jessie mighta been the first female I ever met who shrank away from bein' pretty. As much as she loved all those frilly dresses o' hers and the shoes with the buckles and bows, soon's somebody told her what a pretty girl she was, that child looked like she might die from embarrassment.*

*"I think she likes to play dress-up so people will look at her clothes 'steada lookin' at her," Jessie's mama says to me one day, and I guess I never looked at it like that, but it jangled true when she put it to a voice. "Ah, Daddy, how's she ever gonna meet the right nice boy and get married with all those other flies buzzin' 'round her like they do?"*

*"Her Maker's gonna send her the right one just like He did you," I says. "Just give 'im time to do it."*

*Didn't say so out loud, but in my head I was thinkin', "And I'll keep havin' my talks with the good Lord just to make sure He don't forget."*

# 10

Cynthia Ross slipped into the booth across from Jessie with a smile so broad and white that she almost wanted to shield her eyes. She wore her platinum blonde hair short and, combined with her small, sharp features, she had the look of a little fairy or a pretty elf.

"It's good to see you again, Jessie," she said. "I think the last time was at Piper's birthday party last year at Tuscan Son, wasn't it?"

"I think so."

"I'm really sorry to hear how rough things have been with Jack leaving."

Jessie's heart sank to the pit of her stomach and bobbed around there. Piper had told her?

"As soon as I heard, I called Piper. I thought it must have just been a rumor. You know how that crowd likes to talk."

"And she confirmed it for you," she stated.

"Honestly, I think she tried not to. But I guess I had enough details that she knew she couldn't deny it. I mean, she and I have been friends for years. You know how that is. But then she told me about the wonderful way you've turned things around for yourself. I'm just in awe, Jessie. Honestly, I don't think I could have done it. If Devon left me high and dry like that, I think I'd be crying in my merlot until next summer sometime. What a resilient spirit you have!"

She wanted to laugh right out loud. Leave it to Piper to put the *resilient* spin on the natural disaster that had become her life.

"I don't know," she replied. "I'm just trying to face reality and pick myself up and make a life again."

"Talk about making lemonade, huh?" she exclaimed, shaking her little elf head, those pearly whites beaming. "I think it's amazing. Honestly. Just amazing."

Jessie's grandpa once warned her about people who used phrases like "honestly" or "to tell the truth" to preface their thoughts. "Honesty and truth are probably the last things you're going to get when a sentence starts off by declaring it."

She grinned at Cynthia. After all, did it really matter if she was sincere? In the bigger picture, it really didn't somehow.

"So tell me about your little store idea. How's that going to work?"

Jessie took a deep breath and blew it out playfully. "Well. I didn't really come from money. My family was middle-class Louisiana, you know? I was fascinated by fashion and the designers all my life, don't get me wrong. But it wasn't until I married Jack that I really had access to the finer things. When I found myself left with nothing *except* my labels, I started thinking about those days of yearning for them with no real way of acquiring them."

"It must have been so . . . jarring. You know, to lose it all."

"At first, yes," she fibbed, as if her situation wasn't rocking her to the very core every single day. "But then I met a young lady who reminded me what it's like to make your own way in a world where style costs a pretty penny."

"Who is this young lady?"

Jessie grinned. "Amber Davidson. We met in the ladies' room of Antonio's restaurant." She chuckled and shook her head. "A twenty-five-year-old fashionista who could have been me if Jack hadn't sauntered into my life. I hired her on the spot. I had an employee before I even had a store!"

"So how is it going to work?" Cynthia asked, interest bubbling to the surface of her glossy eyes. "You'll just take the things out of your closet and put them on racks for others to poke through?"

"Well, that's where it starts, I suppose," she replied with a laugh. "But I've been acquiring garments and accessories from other sources as well, so there will be a sort of consignment feature to it. The bottom line, Cynthia, is that women can come into the store and rent pieces for a week or a month at a fraction of what they might pay to own them. And once they've been seen in that Chanel or McCartney, they just trade it in for a little slice of Valentino heaven."

"I did a piece on an online store like that," she recalled. "But I think that was just handbags."

"Right, and eventually we may start an online segment of the business. But for now, I think we're in the right location for a lot of repeat business."

Cynthia laughed, and it had a somewhat bitter edge to it. "Yes, LA is premium real estate for offering the posers what they need to pose."

Jessie hadn't really thought of it in such unflattering terms, but she supposed Cynthia might be right.

"I'd like to do a piece on your store, Jessie."

A slow, giddy excitement floated up inside her. "Really?"

"Are you planning an event for the opening?"

"We're in the beginning stages of that, yes."

"Target date?"

"About three weeks. Why don't you give me your email, and we'll send you an announcement."

"Good," she said, digging a business card out of her Michael Kors bag. "Meanwhile, I'd like to send over my video team to shoot some in-process footage as you get the store ready. I'll schedule them for tomorrow afternoon." She didn't even give Jessie room to answer. "And then we'll do a sit-down in the store at the end of the week. I'll have to check my calendar and talk to George . . ."

Jessie lost the frequency of the chatter as Cynthia continued with directives and observations; her own mind drifted to the store and the shape in which they'd left it.

"Oh! Maybe it would be fun to get some footage of your Malibu house and then do the interview in your apartment in Santa Monica for contrast—"

"No!" That part she heard, and she wasn't having it. "Nothing like that, Cynthia. If you want to do a piece on the opening of the store, I'm thrilled. Grateful, even. But if your planned focus is the riches-to-rags angle where I'm the poor unfortunate soul who was duped, I'm not interested."

Cynthia scrunched up her sharp features and stared at her for a long and frozen moment. Finally, just as Jessie pictured the big interview swirling the drain, Cynthia's expression bounced back to normal. She shrugged and gave Jessie a firm nod. "Okay. I get it. I see what you're saying."

She wondered. "Okay, as long as . . . we're *clear?*"

"Yes. Sure."

Jessie made a mental note to put Piper on it, just to make sure.

"So I'll call you about tomorrow."

And with that, Cynthia Ross slid out of the booth, leaving her cup of untouched coffee behind with Jessie. Short and not-too sweet.

Grabbing her macchiato and her bag, Jessie headed for the door. She dialed Piper before she reached the Taurus.

"How did it go?"

"And hello to you, too," Jessie said with a giggle.

"Sorry. Hi. How did it go?"

"She's doing the story."

Piper's squeal forced the phone away from Jessie's ear on sheer decibels.

"But listen. I need you to follow up on this for me, would you? She's your friend, and I just want to make sure you get her to understand it's not a Poor Pitiful Jessie piece. Please, Piper. I can't take that."

"I'm on it. Where are you headed now?"

"To the store to meet Amber and a friend of hers she met in a writing class at UCLA. The girl is now interning for some big public relations firm on Wilshire, and she's agreed to help us write a press release."

"Ooh, that sounds like fun."

"Why don't you come over."

"Ahh, I'd love to, but I can't. Antonio's mother wants to go put her feet in the celebrity cement at Grauman's."

Jessie cackled. "You're joking."

"How I wish. No. She wants the whole tourist experience."

"Oh! Maybe you can take a walk over to Sunset and Vine after. Show her the hookers and cross-dressers."

"Nice, but no. Afterward we're headed up to Universal Studios."

"For the tour of the lot?"

"No," Piper's voice dropped dramatically. "They film *Extra* there."

"Maybe you'll see Mario Lopez!"

"Uh-huh. That's the plan. She's convinced he's part Italian."

Jessie giggled. "Have a good time."

"You, too."

When Jessie arrived back at the apartment, she found Amber at her front door in animated conversation with two girls; one of them, barely a teenager.

"I'm guessing you're our PR angel," she said to the second one.

"Riley Masters," she replied. Early twenties, tall and thin, cute as could be.

"And you?" Jessie asked the younger girl.

"This is Allie Riggs," Amber interjected. "Your landlord's daughter. I told him she could hang with us while he made a run to the hardware store."

Allie pushed a mane of shiny black hair over her shoulder and took a stab at a smile, but shyness snatched it back quickly.

"Hi, Allie. I'm Jessie Stanton."

The "hi" she returned came out in such a soft whisper that it could barely be heard.

"Let's all go inside, why don't we." Jessie wrestled with the locks and gave the door one swift knee to get it to open. "Come on in."

"You should get my dad to fix that," Allie said softly as she passed.

"You're right. I should."

Except for the bone-straight, glossy mane in contrast with her father's short, kinkier hair, there was no mistaking Allie as Riggs's daughter. She had his deep-set eyes brimming with an odd mix of mystery and playfulness, and his dark even-toned skin. In profile, both of them shared the same flat-bridged noses that flared only slightly, and Allie inherited that little curve of the lips that turned a slight smile into a grin.

"How old are you, Allie?" she asked as she slid her bag off her shoulder and dropped it to the floor next to the sofa.

"Twelve."

"I guess you hear this all the time, but you sure do look like your dad."

Her smile-turned-grin inched upward. "Yeah."

"Doesn't she?" Amber exclaimed. Leaning toward Allie, she added, "And that's a good thing. At least you have a hot dad! My dad is bald with a gut that hangs over his pants."

Allie giggled and covered her face.

"Okay, Riley," Jessie began as she sat down across from her. "Has Amber mentioned how thrilled we are that you're here to help us?"

"Only about a dozen times," she replied. She slid a piece of paper from a case that looked like a pristine leather envelope with a handle. "I got some basics from Amber, and I put together a first draft. There's still a lot to fill in, but I thought we could start with this."

Riley and Jessie moved closer together to review the release while Amber quietly led Allie away with her. Thirty minutes later, they had a final draft that pleased Jessie to no end.

"This is better than I'd even hoped," she said. "How can I thank you for helping me?"

"A free rental or two?"

"You got it!" Jessie answered with a tap to the coffee table.

"Amber told me about a green Christian Siriano dress you have."

"Oh, the chiffon?"

"Yes. I have a special event coming up."

"You're such a tiny thing, and that dress is layers and layers of chiffon circles. You'll get lost in it. I bought it when I was pregnant to cover up the bump and the extra weight." Jessie regretted the admission the moment it landed.

"Oh. You have children?"

"Umm, no. I . . . I miscarried."

*Isabella Rose.*

Riley rested her hand over Jessie's wrist and whispered, "I'm so sorry."

She hadn't thought about Bella in a while now. She swallowed the emerging emotion and tried to smile at Riley.

"Thank you." The lump in her throat choked her a little. "Well, you come in and try the dress. If it doesn't look right, we'll find something that does."

Riley leaned forward slightly and confided, "I'm three months pregnant."

"Oh! That's . . . wonderful. Congratulations."

"My sister-in-law is getting married and I'll be seven months along by then. I'm going to need something fabulous to wear, and Amber told me about the Siriano."

Jessie sighed. "You'll look spectacular in that dress, Riley."

A wave of envy sloshed inside her and swirled around in a standing pool of regret. Her belly had been fat and round when she'd lost Bella at seven months, and she'd bought that dress for just such an occasion—a spring wedding that she'd missed. By the time the couple cut their wedding cake, all that was left of Bella had already been taken from Jessie's body the weekend prior. She found herself hoping it went better for Riley than it had for her and that the pretty blonde got to wear the flowy green Siriano.

A series of stern knocks at the door jolted Jessie forward three years, and she pushed up from the sofa to greet Riggs. To her surprise, Danny stood behind him smiling at her.

"Allie here?" Riggs asked her.

"Yes, come on in."

Jessie padded down the hall toward her bedroom, then muffled conversation drew her to the closet. She pulled the door open to find Amber and Allie sitting on the floor with several handbags around them.

"Hey, those aren't for the store," she cried. "Those are mine."

"I know. I just wanted to show Allie what great style you have."

She couldn't very well follow that, so she sighed. "Allie, your dad's here to get you."

The twelve-year-old clicked her tongue and groaned. "Thanks for letting me come over, Amber." As she scuffled past Jessie, she muttered, "You too."

"See you later, alligator," Amber called after her, and she scooped up the handbags, crawling toward the cubbies to replace them. "How did it go with Riley?"

"She's still here. But I think we have something really good, and she has a whole list of places we can send the release to. And they go by email, so it's free."

"We like free."

"Yes, we do."

Jessie and Amber returned to the living room as Allie squealed, "Dan-ny!" and she sprang forward into Danny's open arms.

"How are you, kiddo?" he asked as he hugged her.

"Good. Did Dad tell you I'm going to marine biology camp this summer? It's down in San Diego and we get to help take care of dolphins and whales and we even get to feed some of the sharks!

There's lots of different kinds of sharks, too. There's blacktips and bull sharks. Oh! And hammerheads. They call them that because if you see them from the front, they look like they have a hammer in their mouth . . ."

It happened just like that, too. A timid young girl who had barely spoken a word since she'd arrived unrolled her tongue and slid down an avalanche of words aimed right at Danny Callahan.

---

Allie had hardly taken a breath in ten minutes, and Danny had to do little more than stand there, nodding occasionally. Riggs had given up on listening minutes prior and headed out the front door, shaking his head.

"Listen," Danny said the instant she allowed him the sliver of opportunity at breaking in. "We have to hit the road."

"Oh!" she exclaimed, turning toward Amber. "Danny lives at the beach, and we're going to have a cookout. Do you want to come?"

Danny didn't imagine this virtual stranger might take her up on the invitation, but she stunned him a little when she replied, "Sure. That sounds like fun."

*Really?*

"Jessie?" Amber asked.

"Oh, no. You guys go ahead. I have some things to finish up."

The thought of spending the afternoon with Amber without their mutual buffer made Danny's jaws itch.

"Burgers and hot dogs at the beach, and you're turning it down?" he cajoled, trying to keep his desperation from showing. "C'mon. We need to talk anyway."

"We do?"

*We do?*

"Sure," he said instead. "I want to do a little catch-up."

It felt like time stood still before she finally shrugged. "Okay. Just give me a few minutes to change clothes. We'll meet you at your place in an hour."

Allie chattered all the way out to her dad's VW bus, continuing until the minute they pulled up in front of the house. He wasn't entirely certain she wasn't still jabbering when she ran off across the sand; the surf may have simply reached up and caught her voice, drowning it.

"I'll fire up the grill," Riggs told him, and Danny headed inside to pull together the food. Frank rushed past him the instant the door opened, galloping out after Allie like a wild horse thundering away from the herd.

By the time he emerged with grill-ready burgers, dogs, and cobs of corn, Riggs called Allie back to the house. While she set out plates, plastic cups, napkins, and condiments on the oversized teak table, he draped the long benches on either side of it with beach towels. Just as he turned the burgers, Amber and Jessie parked behind Riggs' bus.

"Amber!" Allie cried, and she raced toward Jessie's Taurus, tugging Amber—now dressed in cut-off jeans shorts and a bathing suit top—by the hand toward the beach.

Jessie waved and clomped toward him in tall, wedged sandals, her hair pulled back into a bouncy ponytail with large white sunglasses propped on the top of her head. She wore black pleated shorts that fell a couple inches above the knee, highlighting her long, suntanned legs. The bright red tank top layered over a black one with thicker straps revealed far more toned arms and shoulders than he'd imagined.

She held up a plastic container and called out to him. "I brought macaroni salad!"

She flashed a momentary smile as she approached, transforming into an expression of horror when Frank barked and trotted toward her.

"Oh, no!" she squealed. "Danny! Help?"

"Frank!" he commanded, slapping his thigh twice. "Over here."

The Great Dane obeyed, but reluctantly.

"Drinks in the cooler," he pointed out as she reached him. "Help yourself."

"Thanks. Get you one?"

"Not just yet."

She set the container on the table and plucked a bottle of iced tea for herself before she joined him in front of the grill, inching around Frank with an edge of caution.

"That is the biggest dog I've ever seen in my life," she half whispered, as if Frank might hear and take offense.

"Yeah, he's a big boy."

He watched her struggle with the cap on the tea for a few seconds before taking it from her, loosening it, and handing it back.

"Thank you." She removed the cap and took a swig before asking, "So. What did you want to tell me? Jack's an international terrorist, right? He just married me to get into the country and plot how to take over America?"

"Who told you?" he asked, straight-faced as he dug the spatula under a burger and unloaded it to a plate.

"You're kidding," she stated, deadpan.

"Yes. I'm kidding."

"Thank you."

She seemed genuinely relieved. He wished the news wasn't nearly as bad.

"Jack has been under investigation for quite a while now."

She turned toward him and shifted her weight to one hip. "Very funny." After a moment's thought, she added, "For what?"

"Do you know what a Ponzi scheme is?"

She stood there frozen for a few seconds before deflating, shuffling to the table and sitting down. Danny finished loading the plate with burgers and dogs before he followed and sat on the bench beside her.

"I had a horrible feeling it was something like that," she said softly.

"The government has been looking into some missing funds."

"How much?"

"Not yet determined. But it looks like several dozen of his top clients are affected."

"Oh . . . no . . ."

After setting her tea on the table, she wilted, depositing her face in the palms of both hands. Danny leaned back, propped his elbows on the table behind him, and sighed. He didn't know quite what to do, so he did nothing; just sat there quietly. When she finally lifted her head and looked at him, tears had moistened both cheeks.

"How bad is it, Danny?"

He didn't want to say it. "It's pretty bad, Jessie."

Without a hint of what she might do, Jessie collapsed against his arm with a thud and sobbed. After a couple of minutes, it felt unnatural to just sit there like a stuffed swordfish on a wall, so he raised his arm and wrapped it loosely around her shoulder.

*Say something comforting, you idiot.*

He couldn't very well tell her everything was going to be all right because he simply didn't know if that was true. He'd heard people sometimes say things like, "there, there," but he wasn't exactly a "there, there" kind of guy. Nothing else sprang to mind, so he just tapped her gently with his hand a couple of times.

"There, there."

*Nothin' pierces the heart of a man like seein' his grandchild slurpin' up tears. From baby to youngster to girl, sobs comin' outta Jessie near 'bout broke this old man's heart.*

*"It's the winter formal, Grampy! How could he let me think all year he was gonna ask me, then turn around and ask Melissa Klein?"*

*"Melissa Klein!" I just about laughed 'til I cried. "That girl's got buck teeth big as playin' cards."*

*"I know. But Ryan says she understands him better'n I do. Can you believe that? How can she understand him better'n I do? . . . Why do boys always lie, Grampy?"*

*"Well, little girl, because they can. Some boys—and some girls, for that matter, too—just don't know what they got until they don't anymore."*

*"Why does it have to hurt so bad?"*

*"This too shall pass," I reassured her. "Just ride it out 'til it does."*

*"Do you suppose I'll meet a boy one day who won't lie to me?"*

*The hope fire in her blue eyes set a blaze goin' inside me, and I kept a prayer silent in my heart that I'd find the right words to soothe the burn.*

*"Gimme your hands right now, child. We're gonna say a prayer to God about that."*

*She curled up her heart-shaped face and scowled at her old gramps. "I don't wanna pray right now. I just wanna cry some more."*

*"Fat lotta good tears'll do ya without prayers to back 'em up."*

# 11

Let's get a bear trap and try it again," someone shouted from the front door. Aiming toward the corner in the back of the empty store where Jessie and Cynthia Ross sat atop tall canvas and wood director-type chairs, he added, "We'll be ready in ten, Cyn."

"Bear trap?" Jessie asked.

"Metal spring clamps with serrated jaws that hold the lights in place," Cynthia replied without looking up from the interview notes in her hand while a stout woman fussed with her hair.

Amber and Piper stood quietly in the hallway watching as a lanky redhead touched up Jessie's lipstick.

"Are you ready for this, Jess?" Piper asked her.

"As ready as I can be, I guess."

"You'll be fine," Cynthia interjected. "We'll start off with a couple of quick questions about your life before you moved to Malibu." Jessie straightened, but before she could express her concern again, Cynthia raised a hand and wiggled her bright orange fingernails. "I know, I know. You and Piper have both been clear. This is not a riches-to-rags story, I promise. I do want viewers to see that you're creating something for a demographic to which you once belonged before moving into the Malibu crowd, so you have a unique perspective and can identify with them. Better yet, they'll identify with you."

Jessie sighed. "Thank you."

"We've got our establishing shots of the coastline and the boulevard out front. All we'll need is a nice solid A-roll with you today to put it together. We'll leave about ninety seconds clear for editing in what we get at the opening next Friday, and it will air Saturday to wrap up the Champagne Wishes series on *Fashion Trends.* What details have you nailed down for the opening, by the way?"

Jessie cast a quick glance at Amber.

"Oh, it's going to be epic," Amber exclaimed. "We'll have a red carpet on the sidewalk outside with spotlights, and about half a dozen models mingling inside the store wearing Chanel and Valentino and Vera. Oh! And we're planning a raffle where someone in attendance will win a week's rental any time before the end of the year; full ensemble—clothes, accessories, and shoes."

Jessie released the deep breath she hadn't realized she'd been holding. If she were a praying person, she mused, she'd thank God above for that night in the ladies' room when she and Amber had stepped up to the mirror at the same time.

"We've sent personal invitations to every stylist in Hollywood, and a bulk event notice to our local demographic," she continued. "And this afternoon, we have flyers being disseminated all over Melrose Avenue."

"It seems you've thought of everything," Cynthia said. "Let's see if I can't help you cross your Ts."

"Ready when you are, Cyn."

The butterflies sitting at the bottom of Jessie's stomach must have heard the declaration because they began fluttering their wings and taking flight inside her. Cynthia noticed the reaction and touched Jessie on the hand.

"Just follow my lead."

Jessie did just that as Cynthia sauntered across the length of the empty store. The crew had set up two navy-blue wingback chairs, a vintage table with a colorful Tiffany lamp and a small vase of flowers against the backdrop of the wall where one of Antonio's artist friends had come in and painted a quotation mural.

*"Dress shabbily, and they remember the dress; dress impeccably and they remember the woman."* —Coco Chanel

Piper and Amber found a spot by the empty cubbies and racks that Danny and Riggs had completed the night before. Cynthia sat down in one of the chairs and gave Jessie a nod.

"Go ahead. Get comfortable. We'll just get you miked and do a quick sound check before we get started with the interview."

A young man attached something to Cynthia's sweater with a clip before he moved toward Jessie and unceremoniously reached into her blouse to do the same for her.

"Oh!" she cried.

"Afterward," Cynthia continued without notice, "we'll need to get a few cutaways and then we'll get out of your hair."

"Cut-*aways*?"

"Those are just reaction shots George will get of me to edit in later."

"Checking for sound!" someone shouted. "Quiet on the set, please. Rolling for sound."

---

Danny pulled up in front of the store just in time to see the Adornments sign dropped into place in the center of the window by a young Hispanic guy. Jessie and Amber blew out the door to the sidewalk, squealing. He stood back and grinned, leaning on the hood of his Jeep watching as they embraced and hopped up and down like schoolgirls.

Jessie paused her reverie just long enough to flash the sign guy an A-OK before she spotted Danny and rushed over to him and squealed again.

"Isn't it perfect, Danny?" she exclaimed, grabbing his wrist and shaking his whole arm.

"It looks great."

"I have a store!" she cried, and she rushed back to Amber's side to admire the proof. After a moment, she reeled around and tilted her head at Danny. "What are you doing here?"

"I came to finish bracing the racks. Remember?"

"Uh-oh. They weren't ready."

"Not yet."

She and Amber bounced glares off one another before they both broke loose and tore into the store. When he followed, he found them unloading hangers of clothes from the metal rods.

"I'm sorry," she said, breathless. "I forgot."

Danny smiled as he passed them. "I'll drag out the boxes from the storeroom so you can get started unloading those while I finish up the racks."

"Thank you, thank you," she sang to him and continued working.

About six hours later, as the California sun just started its descent, Danny thought the place actually looked like a boutique. Jessie's vision had inched together, and the shelves were stocked, the metal rods bulged with clothes on pale lavender hangers, and a long glass display case with purple velvet trays had been polished and made ready for the adornments for which the store had been named.

"I can't wait to see the bling inside the glass case," Amber commented as she stood up, tossed the paper towel, and stretched. "When will we bring it over?"

"The office safe won't be delivered until Thursday," Jessie told her. "And I don't want it here until after that."

"What's next on the agenda? Shall I get to work setting up the office?"

Jessie sighed and sprawled out on the floor beneath the shelf she'd just finished stocking with handbags. "Nah. Why don't you go ahead home. We'll hit it again in the morning."

"Ten o'clock?"

"See you then."

Danny's cell phone buzzed again as Amber walked out the front door and set the bells to jingling. As she locked the door behind her, Jessie gave a voice to his thoughts. "That thing has been paging you all day long."

He'd been ignoring it most of the day, but now he figured he'd better pull it from his pocket and check the screen.

"It might be something important," she said.

Two missed calls and a text from Riggs, and a missed call from an unknown number.

"Excuse me a minute," he said as he dialed. "Riggs, what's up?"

"Where are you, man? You were supposed to be here an hour ago."

Danny closed his eyes and groaned. "Ah, man. I'm sorry. I'm at the store helping Jessie and I completely forgot. I'll be there in twenty."

He tucked the phone back into his pocket and turned toward Jessie. "I've gotta fly. Riggs has a thing tonight, and I forgot all about it."

"I know, I know," she said with a delightful smile. "My company is so compelling, everything else whipped straight out of your mind."

"Yep, that's it."

"What's he doing?"

"Come again?"

"Aaron. You said he has a thing?"

"Oh. He's organizing a program to supply hot meals and coats to the homeless starting in the fall. He's talking to a group of men about helping."

"Isn't he homeless himself?" she asked seriously.

"Riggs's kind of homelessness is by choice. Not like the street population he wants to help. Do you need anything here before I go?"

"Does he do that kind of thing often? Help people who need it, I mean?"

"Sure. All the time. The way he helped you with a place to crash when your back was against the wall."

"And . . . maybe give cars to abandoned women with no transportation?"

"Sure. You think he gave you that car?"

"You tell me. Would he do something like that?"

One eyebrow rose, and he found himself sort of glaring at her as he considered her question. "You're serious?" He raked his hand through his hair and sighed. "I couldn't really tell you."

"You can't tell me, or you won't?" she asked. "Are you keeping his big secret?"

"Riggs is pretty much an open book, Jessie. I don't think he has a lot of secrets."

"Are you going to answer the question?"

He thought it through for a minute before he answered her. "Riggs has the heart of a missionary, no doubt about it. I know he does good things for people all the time. Unexpected things. But he's never said one word to me about being a car fairy."

"You promise?"

"You have my word."

"Hmm."

"I've really gotta fly. Are you all set?"

"Go." She waved her hand and smiled. "I'm fine." Seemingly as a second thought, she rounded the case again and stepped up in front of him. "I don't know what I'd do without you." She planted a tender little kiss on his cheek and squeezed his shoulder. "Thanks for all your help."

He didn't mean to, but Danny jerked slightly as he pulled back from her. She looked at him, clearly puzzled, and one corner of her ruby lips twitched before she turned on her wedged heels and walked away.

"Have a good evening, Danny."

He stood there after she disappeared into the back office, wondering if he should follow and apologize or explain—although an explanation wasn't exactly ready and waiting—or whether the better side of wisdom came with just walking out the door. Before he had the chance to make the decision, Jessie returned with a leather tote slung over her shoulder and two large overstuffed shopping bags in her hand.

"Oh. You're still here. Did you forget something?"

"No." *Nice, loser. Say something marginally intelligent.* "I mean, you need to lock the door behind me."

"I'm leaving now too. We can go out together."

On the other side of the front door, Danny took her bags and tote and held them while she fumbled with the keys and locked the store. Once she stepped away, he handed them back to her and grabbed the rolling steel security grille and yanked it down. She handed him the keys, and he secured the gate at the ground.

"Thanks."

"Have a good night," he said, and she gave him a nod before heading for her car.

As he climbed into his Jeep, Jessie flew by in her Taurus and waved.

Danny checked the clock on the dash as he turned into traffic. The men's group had already socialized and descended on the snack table, no doubt. Riggs may even have started his talk by then. Still ten minutes out, at least he'd catch the second half if the red lights showed some sympathy.

As he jogged into the fellowship hall, Riggs's voice carried into the vestibule. "In Philippians, chapter two, we're instructed not to look out only for our own interests, but to pay attention to the interests of the people around us. And it's important to note here that Jesus also said that whenever we provide food for the hungry or clothes to those who need them . . . Whatever you do for the least, you also do for Him. It's quite a concept, right?"

Danny slipped into a chair at an empty table in the back and nodded when he caught Riggs's eye. About twenty men had gathered, and Danny looked around the room. Riggs had captured the attention of every one.

"I don't always succeed," he told them with a chuckle. "But isn't that what we're supposed to do? Not because it makes us feel all warm and fuzzy inside, and not because we get anything out of it at all. But because it's part of the commission He gave us as His followers. He left us with a job to do, and acting as His hands and feet is a key part of it. The lesson guide for this week lays it all out for us in Scripture references."

Danny stepped up to help distribute the study guide and Riggs muttered, "Nice of you to show up, bro."

"Sorry. I'm a loser."

"You said it."

About twenty minutes into the study guide discussion, the tone on Danny's cell phone announced a text message.

*From Steph. 911. Lead on Stanton.*

"Let's talk about that," Riggs said to the group. "What's your take on the application of that verse?"

Danny turned around at the door and shot an apologetic glance at Riggs. Instead of the daggers he expected to volley back at him, Riggs just shook his head, smiled, and nodded toward the door.

In the corridor, he replied to the text.

*Where are you?*

*Your place. When will you get back?*

Danny headed out the door and across the parking lot as he typed in his answer.

*On my way.*

Countless scenarios played out in his mind as he raced across town. Had they located Stanton on a beach in Bali sipping a Corona? Had he ever really left the country at all or was he hiding out in a rented penthouse somewhere, spending his millions just as fast as he could count them while Jessie hawked everything she had left?

"I kid you not, Piper." Jessie spoke into her cell phone as she headed out of the bedroom. "He jerked away so hard I'll bet he wakes up with whiplash in the morning."

"Well, what do you think was behind it?" Piper asked, and Jessie let out a little groan as she tied the waistband of her pink Juicy Couture ruffled robe and sauntered into the living room.

"Who knows. I don't care."

"Of course you care," Piper said. "Or you wouldn't be so steamed."

"I am not steamed."

"No? My mistake."

"He's just so . . . irritating."

"This is Danny Callahan we're talking about? The guy who is helping you sort things out with Jack, who helped you find a place to live and a way to finance it? The guy who just spent several days building and painting and—"

"I know, and I appreciate it," she surrendered. "But he's just so . . ."

"Irritating. I see. . . . And what was it about him that was irritating again?"

Their connection broke momentarily and the call waiting tone sounded. Jessie checked the screen.

"Oh, great. That's him."

"What is?" Piper asked.

"He's calling."

"So answer it and call me back."

She poked the button and jumped from Piper to Danny. "Hello? Danny?"

"Is it too late to call?"

His voice kick-started her pulse. "No, I was just on the phone with Piper."

"Jessie, can I come over and talk to you?"

"Why?" she asked, and he groaned subtly. "I mean, if this is about before—"

"It's not. I have news." Her heart fluttered as she waited for him to continue. Finally, "It's about Jack."

"Come on over."

"I'm parked out front," he said.

"Give me five minutes to pull myself together."

Jessie tossed her bathrobe to the edge of the bed and grabbed the first thing she could find: a pair of jeans and a tailored white shirt that hung on the hook on the back of her closet door. She didn't bother to slip into shoes when the soft rap at the front door sounded, and she padded toward it, barefoot.

It took several tries to tug open the door, and Danny stood there facing her with rumpled hair and concern churning his eyes into smoky gray pools.

"What is it?" she asked him.

He lifted one corner of his mouth into a strange smile. "Can I come inside?"

"Oh, yes." She stepped back from the doorway. "Of course. Come in."

The moment she nudged the door shut, she repeated her greeting. "What is it?"

Danny sat on the edge of the sofa and leaned both elbows on his knees, staring at the floor. She watched him heave a deep breath and lift his head, gazing at her almost tenderly. "Come and sit down."

"It's that bad, is it?"

He smiled and patted the sofa cushion. "Sit down, Jessie."

She plodded toward the couch and perched on the arm, looking down at her glossy Cinnamon Kiss toenails and bracing herself for the bucket of icy water about to drop upon her.

"He's in Indonesia?"

"I believe so."

She jerked her head toward him and frowned. "But we sort of knew that, right? You said you had news."

"I do."

She tapped her foot and clawed at the grain of her blue jeans. "Just tell me, Danny. Why are you drawing it out like this?"

"Because . . . I'm not eager to send your life swirling the drain again."

"Oh, thanks. That's a pretty picture. Just be out with it, would you?"

"It looks like Jack was married before you."

"I know. Patty. They divorced the year we met."

"I just need to get some clarification about the first wife so I can look a little deeper," he said, referring to notes he had in his cell phone. "I've got her maiden name as Patricia Lauren Walters. Born in Encino in 1973, which makes her forty-two years old. She stayed in Encino and Glendale until she married Jack, then they lived in Pacific Palisades after the marriage." He glanced up at her. "Sound about right?"

She parted her lips to speak, but no sound emerged, so she nodded.

"Have you met her?"

"Yes. Once, or maybe twice." After a moment's thought, she added, "Twice."

Danny swiped his phone and turned the screen toward her. "Is this her?"

She squinted at the smiling brunette in the photo. "Well, she was blonde when I met her. But, yes, that looks like her." A swell of emotion pressed in on her throat. "What's this about?"

"This is a passport photo for Patricia Lauren Walters taken two years ago. The most recent travel of record was a couple months ago from LAX to the Denpasar/Bali International Airport by way of Taiwan."

Jessie pulled the corner of her lip between her teeth to stop it from quivering as dread surged through her. "They're together? Jack and Patty?"

"I don't know yet. I'm still looking for a paper trail to put Jack there as well. Jessie, did you ever have any indication that the two of them might have stayed in touch?"

She narrowed her eyes and looked up at the air over her head as if she might be able to find something there, quickly scanning for any mentions of Patty that could help.

"She introduced herself to me for the first time at a charity luncheon in Beverly Hills about five years after Jack and I were together. Then she brought flowers to the house after my miscarriage a couple of years ago. Jack wasn't very happy about either instance, but he never mentioned her again that I can remember."

Danny touched the back of her hand. "You lost a child." It seemed like more of a statement of fact than an inquiry. "I'm very sorry."

"Thank you." That familiar eerie chill frosted her heart again. "So what comes next? Please don't tell me you have to go to Indonesia to figure it all out because I'm pretty sure I can't afford that."

Danny chuckled. "Not that I wouldn't like a chance to surf the beaches of Bali in the name of a business expense, but I'll keep after it from here."

She swallowed around the lump in her throat. "Good surfing in Bali, is there?" When he didn't reply, Jessie turned a pleading gaze upon him. A stream of tears sprang out of her eyes, meandering down her aching cheeks as their salty taste plagued her. "Talk to me about the surfing in Bali, Danny. Or about a case you're working on. Or what you had for dinner."

"Seriously?"

She looked away and wiped the tears. "Please. Tell me about surfing."

"Well. Uh, there are some pretty significant storms out in the southern Indian Ocean and, without land masses to block the swells, they hit the shores with waves that spell paradise for any serious surfer." He shifted and released a gentle sigh. "Have you ever been on a board?"

"A surfboard? No," she replied with what she knew appeared as a sloppy attempt at a smile. "Jack either, as far as I know. In fact, in all our years together—some of which were spent living at the beach—I don't think I ever even saw him on the sand more than a couple of times. And one of those was for our wedding."

Jessie turned toward Danny and, for the first time, discerned how incredibly uncomfortable he appeared at the prospect of delivering news like this. She groaned and dropped back into the sofa cushions.

"So was there anything else you had to tell me?" she asked with a bitter chuckle. "Or is my Life Circling the Drain Report complete for today?"

"Sorry. That was a bad choice of words."

"But honest." She sighed. "I bet you don't have very many regrets about your life, do you, Danny?"

"A few."

Jessie closed her eyes and considered his words before turning to him and asking, "Only a few. What's *that* feel like?"

He chuckled and touched her arm. "Seasons."

"Pardon?"

"Everything in life comes in seasons. The good stuff, the bad, the in-between. The one thing you can count on is that—"

"This too shall pass?" she asked him with a grin. "My grandpa used to say that all the time."

"Exactly."

Following a silent pause—so noisy that it screamed—Jessie asked, "What if it doesn't? Pass, I mean."

"But it will."

"What if I get through the bad stuff with Jack, but then I realize I don't like the rest of my life either?"

"Then I guess you just build something else that you do like."

"Well, that sounds exhausting."

---

*I was married to Ellie for near forty years before she slipped away from me. Alzheimer's, they call it. Nothin' shy o' torture is what I say it is. Lookin' into the eyes of the final puzzle piece o' your heart and havin' them stare back atcha like they never even knew ya—that does somethin' to a man's soul. Gets him to thinkin' he might never see the light of day again.*

*Ever' now and again though, just when I thought Ellie might be gone forever, she'd smile. Nothin' earth-shatterin' or nothin'. Just a smile with a squeeze o' somethin' familiar behind it, like she knew me again. Like her light and mine weren't star-crossed no more. Like they found each other in the air between us, a total accident, and yet a slice o' the divine. I'd live off those moments, 'til the next one came 'round.*

*"How'd you know you wanted to marry Granny?" Jessie asked me one hot mornin' in the dead of summer while we nursed some cold lemonade out on the stoop. "How'd you know for sure she was the one, Grampy?"*

*"I caught sight of her light," I told her. "You got your Granny's light, you know. Someday you're gonna cross the sunbeam of some boy, and you'll look at him and just know."*

*"Know what?"*

*"You'll know you wanna be by his side all the time."*

*She curled up her heart face and laughed it up. "What, like 'til the end of time or somethin'?"*

*"Just like that. You wait and see. It'll hit ya square between the eyes while you're lookin' someplace else. Just you wait and see."*

*Jessie pondered that for a time, and all the funnin' dropped clean off her face. "That sounds just awful, Grampy."*

# 12

Jessie hadn't meant to drive over to Danny's house on the beach; she'd just gone out for a cappuccino and a drive to clear her head. After he'd dropped the bomb about Jack the night before, Danny Callahan seemed like the last person on the planet she wanted to see again so soon. But there she was, parked next to his Jeep and wondering what to say about why she'd landed there.

*I just had an urge to see you. I don't really know why*, she thought before laughing bitterly. "Come on, Jessie."

A moving target at the shore caught her attention, and she realized it was Frank, Danny's monstrous cow-dog with the pointy ears and legs nearly as long as her own. The dog paced back and forth in the foam, just where the sand met the water's edge. Beyond the plodding dog, a lone surfer snagged her eye.

Jessie leaned over the steering wheel and strained for a better look. Danny's lean frame seemed almost unmistakable in the muscle-hugging wetsuit as he expertly rode a tall wave toward the shore. She wondered how he balanced so adeptly atop the narrow board, one arm stretched forward like a wing and the other bent casually behind him, his weight leaning on one solid foot and his body hunched slightly over it. She didn't know much of anything about surfing, but he sure did look professional to her.

He rode the board almost straight into the sand, and he hopped off as Frank galloped toward him. He stopped to rub the dog's head for a moment and untangled something from its collar that he used to fasten his own wet mane back into a slick ponytail. She felt uncomfortable, watching him in secret like a voyeur and she decided to back out of the parking spot and disappear. But just as she reached out to turn the key, Danny waved his arm. She turned and looked behind her, then scanned the area, hoping against hope that he'd seen some familiar beach bum somewhere. But when he leaned all of his weight back on one hip and crossed his arms, she could feel him looking straight into her.

*Nothing to do now but face the music.*

Jessie pushed open the door and stepped out. She'd no sooner placed one foot from concrete to sand when the cow-dog spotted her and charged like a bull who'd seen his first glimpse of a red cape. She trotted backward until the fender rammed her, and she rounded the car and watched the dog from the rear bumper.

"Frank! No."

Two simple syllables from Danny, that's all it took. The massive dog stopped in his tracks, glared at Jessie for a moment, and turned around.

Danny picked up his board and tucked it under his arm as easily as if he carried a large envelope or a light briefcase. As he stalked through the sand toward her, Jessie found her heartbeat picking up the pace until it thudded against her chest.

*Boom-boom-boom.*

"What are you doing here?" he asked when he reached the edge of the sand. "Everything all right?"

"Oh, yeah. Fine. I mean"—*Get it together!*—"I . . . I just was out this way, and I thought I'd just stop by . . . and . . ."

"Go for a surf?" he teased.

"Yeah. That's exactly it. I thought I'd hop on a board and hang ten."

He raised an eyebrow and grinned. "Hang ten?"

"Isn't that what you surfer dudes call it?"

"Yeah. That would be a totally righteous term," he said in his best Surfer Dude dialect. "If I was the Big Kahuna and you were Gidget."

Jessie's face broke straight in two and she laughed. Once she pulled herself together, she sputtered, "Wh-what do you know about Gidget?"

"What's more important here," he said as he tossed his board to the sand, "is what *do you know* about Gidget?"

"My mom loved Sandra Dee."

"Mine loved Sally Field. Still does, in fact."

Danny's enormous dog sauntered around his master before approaching Jessie and sniffing her hand.

"Oh," she said, nervous. "Hi there."

"So come on over here," Danny exclaimed. "Step on the board and I'll give you a few pointers."

She looked down at her tailored Dolce Vita sundress with the snug sweetheart bodice and full pleated skirt. Pointing out her apparel with a flourish, she told him, "Uh, hello? Italian plaid linen. I'm not exactly dressed for it."

"I promise you won't get wet," he insisted. Taking her by the wrist, he led her across the sand to his board. "Slip out of your shoes."

She frowned at him but complied, kicking off her jeweled flat sandals.

"Step on," he said, leading her atop the surfboard. "We'll skip the paddling and go straight to the ride, okay?"

"Oh, sure," she said glibly.

His hands came to rest loosely above her hips as he stood behind her. "You've paddled out into the water, and you've navigated into the belly of the wave."

"I hope I'm not what's for lunch."

"You feel the momentum of the board moving faster than your paddling, so you feel confident. You hop up."

Jessie playfully hopped.

"Good. Now keep your body centered, just a slight slant forward."

She allowed him to guide her into position and took on the serious expression she imagined a surfer might wear. Danny leaned around her shoulder to get a look at her face before laughing softly.

"Okay. Plant your feet firmly, with your right one nearer the tail of the board and your left one about midpoint on the board." Standing behind her, he mirrored her stance. "Good. Now don't stand up straight like your mother probably always told you to do. Instead, crouch down slightly with a low center of gravity, like this."

Jessie allowed him to guide her, and his hand touched the bare skin of her arm for just a quick brush, but it jolted her like a live electrical wire.

"Keep your arms out," he continued, "and your eyes up ahead of you. Since your board will generally follow your line of vision, just concentrate on moving forward as you use your arms and feet for balance."

"Like this?" she asked him.

"You're a natural," he said. "Next time, maybe we can try this in water."

Jessie straightened and hopped away from him, off the surfboard. "Water. Are you joking? I don't think so."

He chuckled as she slipped into her sandals and smoothed the skirt of her dress.

"C'mon!" he urged. "Just one lesson, and you'll be hooked."

"What are you, the ambassador for the Surf Santa Monica campaign?"

"If there was one of those, I'm sure I'd be their guy. How about some coffee? You want to come inside?"

"Oh, I don't know."

"Let me just grab Carmen."

Danny picked up his board and sauntered toward the house, his giant dog following close behind.

"Carmen? I thought his name was Frank."

"Frank's my dog," he called over his shoulder as she trotted quickly behind him. "Carmen's my board. She was my first, and I named her after Carmen Electra. My first big crush."

She thought that over. "If I had a board, I guess it would be named Justin," she muttered as she followed him.

Danny stowed his surfboard, still considering her comment. "Justin."

"Timberlake. I mean, I thought I loved Donnie Wahlberg from New Kids on the Block until 'N Sync came around and I spotted Justin. That was it for me. True love that never waned . . . Well, except for that time when he was with Britney Spears, but that's understandable, right?"

"Sure."

"I don't know if I ever got over him, if you want to know the truth."

He nodded thoughtfully.

"Too bad my taste in men didn't carry over to real life. But seriously, look at J. T. now. He grew up so great."

Danny chuckled. "Your earlier crush didn't do so bad, either."

"Donnie Wahlberg?"

"Yeah. Isn't he on that show with Tom Selleck now?"

"I know. Who saw *that* coming?"

---

Jessie angled into the corner of one side of the rattan loveseat and her gaze lingered on Danny's desk, the top made from a flat, colorful surfboard. He walked into the sunroom with two cups of coffee and handed one of them to her.

"Cream and sweetener."

"Thanks. And yours is strong and black."

He grinned. "Nice."

"My grandpa used to take his the same way." She deepened her voice and added a bit of a Southern lilt to it as she mimicked Grampy. "Joe was meant to be drunk strong and black."

"That's not the first time you've mentioned your grandfather," he said as he sat down in his desk chair with a creak. "Is he still alive?"

"In his nineties and still alive and kickin'," she replied with a smile.

"Where is he?"

"Slidell, Louisiana. Outside of New Orleans. It's where I grew up."

"You're from the south, and not even a hint of an accent."

"I worked hard at dropping it when I was in high school," she reluctantly admitted. "I'd sit in front of the television and imitate the *normal* accents for hours."

He tilted his head into a subtle shrug. "Why?"

"I spent my whole life in Slidell, and it felt like a very tiny dot on the map of such a huge, adventurous world. I guess I was afraid people outside of the boundaries of that one little speck would think me simple . . . or backward."

Danny took a drink of his coffee and watched her over the rim of his cup as he did.

His gaze made her uneasy somehow, and she muttered, "Pathetic, right?"

"Not pathetic. It just explains a lot."

"Does it? Well, when you have it all figured out, maybe you could share it with me."

They spent the next few minutes in silence except for the dog's panting as he stretched out at Danny's feet and stared at Jessie.

"So did you want to talk to me about something?" Danny finally piped up.

"What do you mean?"

He chuckled. "Well, I'm trying to figure out why you came over this morning."

"Oh!" She straightened, and her face and neck flushed with heat. "That."

What could she say to that? She'd awoken that morning feeling strange. Lonely. And the only person she wanted to talk to was Danny Callahan.

No. She couldn't say that!

"I guess I just wanted to thank you," she offered instead. "You were so kind to me last night. I mean, I could see how uncomfortable you were having to deliver the news about Jack to me, and you were just . . . Well, I appreciated how you did it, that's all."

Danny emptied his coffee cup and set it on the desk. "You could have sent a text or an email. You didn't have to drive over."

"Oh. I'm sorry. Am I keeping you from something? I should go." She hopped to her feet. Frank, startled, stood up as well.

"No need to rush out or anything," Danny told her, nodding back to the couch. "I was just wondering . . ."

She sat down again and folded her hands in her lap to keep them from trembling. "I guess I'm just feeling a little out of sorts. I was looking for something to think about other than my tumultuous life." She took an aimless scan of the sunroom and sighed. "So what cases are you working on?"

"Nothing very fascinating, I'm afraid. Some background checks. Paperwork and billing to turn out sometime today. And some research."

"What kind of research?"

He smirked at her before replying. "I have a new client who thinks she's being watched. I've gone over her apartment with a fine-tooth comb, and then I remembered this news story I saw a couple months back where a guy was hacking into young women's webcams on their computers and watching them. I thought I'd read a little more about it and then take a drive out to the valley to see her laptop for myself."

"That sounds interesting."

He seemed to weigh her words. "Are you joking?"

"No!" she protested. "I think it sounds interesting."

"It's just a hunch, but I thought I'd look into it." After a long moment of awkward silence, he finally asked, "Do you want to stick around?"

"Do you mind?"

"No," he said and shrugged. "Knock yourself out."

She didn't think he meant that entirely, but something inside Jessie just wanted to stay. She didn't feel like thinking about designer labels or rent-a-look shopping or even attracting wannabes. While Danny made phone inquiries with a couple of techie types he knew, she traded places with him and googled some articles on his laptop. Over the next thirty minutes or so, she learned about webcam hackers, secret nanny-cams placed in everyday items like clocks and stuffed animals, tracking and spying applications for laptops and phones, and even an elaborate video camera setup that landed a Realtor in prison after spying on a female tenant.

"Hey, it's Danny Callahan. Any chance you'll be around for a little while? I've had some more thoughts, and I'd like to have a look at your computer . . . That's great. I'll see you in about thirty minutes."

---

Not quite sure how it happened, Danny exited the 110 to Fair Oaks Avenue with Jessie in the passenger seat. He never let someone tag along while he worked, and now this was the second time Jessie had done it.

"So what's going on with the store opening?" His stab at making polite conversation.

"It's coming right along. Amber's a jack-of-all-trades, and she's handling most of the grunt work. I'm just hobbling along, guessing and hoping that it's going to come together and not end up to be the worst mistake I've made in my life." She snickered and added, "But since there are so many others to choose from, the odds that it will be *the actual worst* are pretty slim, right?"

"We live in hope," he cracked.

"I love these old houses out here," she commented, changing tracks. "Jack and I toyed with the idea of moving away from the beach, and we looked at a couple of restored Victorians east of here. They were beautiful neighborhoods with old gas lamp streetlights and huge flower beds. One of them even had a spiral staircase and a turret!"

"What made you go with Malibu? Jack wasn't a turret kind of guy?"

"Jack was a status kind of guy. He felt our address was important for his professional profile."

"And what about you?" he asked her. "What do you think?"

"At the time, I agreed with him I suppose."

"And now?"

"Now," she said with a sigh. "Now, I'm starting to think I wasted a lot of years caring too much about things like that."

"Says the woman with a new business built from the labels in her clothes."

"I know," she muttered. "Ridiculous, right?"

Danny reached over and touched her arm momentarily before taking the turn to Cassie Clinton's street. He pulled straight into the driveway on her side of the duplex and came to a stop.

"What a cute building," Jessie commented. With a broad grin, she added, "But not nearly as cute as the one I live in."

Danny chuckled. "Sarcasm? I graciously allowed you to join me on another field trip and you're sassing me with sarcasm."

"I would never," she quipped as they climbed out and headed up the brick steps to the front door.

Twenty-three-year-old Cassie answered the door in a sweatshirt, jeans, and tennis shoes. Not a speck of makeup, hair in a messy little bun; she didn't look anything like the girl he'd met when she hired him a week ago.

"Hi, Mr. Callahan. Come on in."

"Thanks. Cassie, this is Jessie Stanton. She's just observing."

She rubbed her reddened eyes and tried to smile at Jessie. "Come to see the pathetic girl with the invisible stalker?"

"Not at all," Jessie said to her, and she rubbed her arm warmly. "If anyone can get to the bottom of this, Danny can. And if you feel the least bit uncomfortable with me here, I can always wait in the Jeep. It's a beautiful day. I don't mind at all."

"You're so sweet," she said with a grimace, as if the realization surprised her. Danny had to admit, he was a little surprised by the sweet gesture himself. Jessie seemed to do that frequently—surprise him. "Come on in, both of you."

Cassie let them in and bolted the door behind them. The sofa was littered with books, crumpled blankets, and a couple of bed pillows. The door to her bedroom stood closed.

"I've been sleeping out here," she announced when she caught Danny surveying the scene. "I just can't go back in there knowing . . . that's where the picture was taken."

"Is that where your computer is?" he asked.

"Yes. Do you think that's how he got the picture? I wondered about that."

"Let's go have a look."

Jessie followed them through the bedroom door and softly asked him, "What picture?"

"Cassie was sent a photograph through the mail, obviously taken in the apartment, probably in the bedroom when she was changing."

"That's horrible."

"He threatened to post it on the Internet and send it to the dean," Cassie added.

"You're in college then."

"Med school at USC."

"What did he want in return?" Jessie asked her.

Danny, thankful for Jessie's ability to distract Cassie, sat down at the small desk and opened the laptop.

"That's the thing," Cassie answered. "I don't really know. He said he'd be in touch to tell me how I could keep that from happening, but I haven't heard from him yet. It's been a week already."

As the two women continued to chat, Danny flipped on the computer and scanned the room for additional technology while it booted up. An iPhone stood docked on the nightstand beside an iPod, its wired ear buds dangling over the edge. The bed had only sheets on it—everything else had obviously been moved to the sofa in the living room—and a tablet sat face down where the pillows should have been. Stacks of textbooks dotted the floor, filled the seat of the chair in the corner, and leaned in clumsy disarray on the desk.

Danny turned back to the laptop and thought about the conversation he'd had with his buddy. "Her computer may have been hacked by a script kiddie," he'd said. "They use malware to take over other people's computer systems. A couple years back in Pennsylvania, a school district did this to spy on students and their families."

Danny produced the notes he'd made from their conversation and reviewed them.

"That's horrible," Jessie exclaimed, and Danny turned back to see that Cassie had chosen to show her the photo the guy had sent.

"It almost had to have been taken from my laptop, right?" Cassie looked to Danny and added, "I've disabled the webcam, just in case that's how he got in."

Jessie studied the picture, then the room as she walked around in silence. After a couple minutes, she muttered, "I don't think it's the computer. Cassie, do you always wear that ring on your right hand?"

Danny and Cassie both glanced at the sapphire band on her index finger.

"Always. I never take it off."

Jessie held up the photo. "So why is it on your left hand in the picture?"

Cassie hurried to her side for a closer look. "Well, that's strange. How could that be?"

Jessie pointed at the large beveled mirror on the wall over the desk. "I think it had to be taken through the mirror's reflection"—Danny watched as Jessie walked it out and stopped in front of the nightstand—"which means it was taken from over here."

Danny stood up and joined them. In an instant, the deed fell directly into place, and he grabbed the iPhone from its docking station as Cassie exclaimed, "My phone!"

He turned it on and flipped it. "I'm gonna need to take this with me, Cass. Can you function without your phone for a day or two?"

"Fine. Whatever you need to do," she agreed with an emphatic nod. "Please, let's find out who it is and end this thing."

"Other than your iPod, is there any other piece of technology that you generally keep on this side of the room?"

"No."

"The tablet?"

"No," she stated. "It's usually in my book bag. I think she's right. From the angle of it, that picture had to have been taken with my phone. Jessie, thank you so much!"

Once they'd said their good-byes and got on their way, Danny turned toward Jessie while they sat parked at the light on Fair Oaks.

"You enjoyed that, didn't you?" he asked her, and she grinned.

"Kinda. But I didn't mean to show you up, Danny."

He chuckled. "Yes, you did."

"Yeah, I did. You're right. Did I hurt your big male ego too badly?"

"I'll recover," he said as the light turned green.

"Seriously," she added, her excitement sending her voice to a higher pitch. "That was so much fun! Hey, I know! I could scrap that whole idea of the store," she teased. "And I'll come onboard with you. Stanton & Callahan—"

"Callahan & Stanton."

"—Private Eyes."

Before he could answer, Jessie began to sing. "Pri-i-vate eyes." Clapping her hands twice. "They're watching you."

"Hall & Oates?" he said dryly. "Really?"

"Private *eeeeeeeyes* . . ."

There wasn't anything he could do about it. No stopping it or stifling it. So a second later, Danny broke into full song right along with her.

"They're watching you, watching you, watching youuuuu . . ."

---

*Procrastination is the grave holdin' the opportunities that passed you right on by. I don't know who said that, but it's sure 'nough a nugget, huh? If I had a dollar for ever' time I said those words to my Jessie, I'd be livin' high on the hog. Take back a dollar for ever' time she ignored me, and I'd be right back under the bridge, lickety-split.*

*The thing about my Jessie is she enjoys a good distraction. Give her somethin' she don't want to think about, and she's sure to find a project that needs her full and immediate attention.*

*"I'm not distractin', Grampy," she'd say to me. "I'm just givin' my mind time to catch up with what to do. Besides, the sooner I fall behind, the more time I have to catch up."*

*That girl's logic is one of life's greatest mysteries.*

# 13

I tried calling you all day yesterday, Jessie. Where were you?"

Jessie looked up to find Piper standing in the doorway to her small office holding two carryout cups of coffee.

"I went somewhere with Danny."

"All day? Why didn't you pick up my calls?"

"Oh, I must have had my phone turned off by mistake." She grabbed her bag from the desk drawer and retrieved her phone. "Yep. It was turned off. Sorry, Piper. What did you need?"

"Amber called me when she couldn't reach you because there were decisions to be made about the opening."

"Oh." Nodding toward the cups in her hand, she added, "Is one of those for me?"

Piper handed her one of the cups before perching on the corner of the desk and staring down at her. "What's going on, Jess?"

She flipped the stopper on the cup and asked, "What do you mean?"

"Are you having second thoughts?"

"About?"

"About the store opening?"

Jessie sighed. Did she dare admit it after she'd come so far, dragging Piper and Amber and even Danny right along with her?

"Sweetie, talk to me."

She took a sip from the cup. Caramel macchiato. Piper knew her so well. About coffee and everything else, it seemed.

"I guess I'm just wondering if I can do this," she admitted. "I mean, I've never started something of my own like this before. What if it flops? I've put almost everything I have into it, and if it doesn't work out I have no other options. You know what Danny told me? It looks like Jack has gone as far as Indonesia!"

Piper touched her arm. "Is he sure?"

"Pretty sure, yes. And guess what else. He has a traveling companion."

"What? Who?"

"Patty."

"The ex-wife? Are you sure?"

"Danny's looking into it some more, but it appears he had some illegal dealings in his business where he was scamming his clients out of huge sums of money, Piper. And when he thought he might get caught, instead of coming to me and trying to work it out—or even run from it together!—he stepped back in time and went to Patty."

Piper set her cup down on the desk and stood up in front of Jessie. Clutching both of Jessie's shoulders firmly, she said, "Look at me. Your confidence has taken a very hard blow. I get that. But it doesn't change who you are, Jess. You can do this. You're going to pick yourself up, dust yourself off, and you're going to start a whole new life. You can do this."

Jessie wilted under her friend's touch. "I don't know, Piper."

"Well, I know enough for both of us. You can do this. Now pull yourself together before Amber gets here. We made some arrangements yesterday that I think you're going to be really happy about."

She didn't particularly want to think about the opening or arrangements or a store filled with designer labels and blood-bought jewelry—given to her by a husband who only wanted to keep up the appearance of loving her.

"Now tell me where you went with Danny yesterday," Piper cut into her thoughts.

"Oh, he had a meeting. He has a client with a stalker." Brightening, she added, "And I think I helped blow the whole thing wide open!"

Piper chuckled. "Blew the whole thing wide open? When did you start talking like that?"

Jessie blurted out a laugh. "I don't know, but it was fun. I could make a pretty fair investigator, I think."

"Why don't you let Danny do the investigating, and you keep going with your new business venture."

"Yeah." She sighed. "I guess you're right. If anyone actually shows up, I'll have some overpriced dresses and pretentious bling for them to see."

"Jessie! You're just scared. It's understandable. But let us not forget . . . that overpriced and pretentious inventory is going to get you back on your feet again. Show a little respect. There's Chanel in the house."

She giggled and tugged Piper's arm toward her until they leaned together in an embrace.

"You're right," she surrendered. "My apologies to the entire fashion community."

---

Danny sat down in the metal chair next to Rafe Padillo's cluttered desk as the chaos and traffic of the police precinct swirled around him amidst the smell of old coffee and an abandoned deli sandwich on the adjacent desk. Cops shouted to one another from opposite sides of the large open room while a female detective covered one ear so she could better hear the person on the other end of her open phone line. A worse-for-wear girl in tight clothes and smeared mascara sat in one of several chairs lined up next to the wall. Danny willed her to quit tapping her platform shoe on the chipped linoleum in such an irritating broken rhythm.

"Callahan," Rafe greeted him as he dropped to the creaking desk chair across from him. "Thanks for coming to the station. I couldn't get away from here today if I was kidnapped and led out at gunpoint."

"I just appreciate you having your guys take a look at my client's phone."

Rafe removed a plastic evidence bag with a note card stapled to it from the pocket of his shirt, and Danny saw Cassie's phone enclosed inside it. "You were right. The phone was hacked through a program called FaceTime with a ghost Apple account."

"I thought Apple products were pretty impenetrable."

Rafe chuckled. "Ain't nothin' impenetrable, buddy. Welcome to the future."

"So is there any way of tracking the guy down?"

"Where is that thing . . ." Rafe shuffled through the papers and notes and file folders on his desk until he produced a business card. "Here it is. This is contact info for my buddy in the Cyber Crime Unit. If you don't hear from him in a week or so, give him a call. Meanwhile, I'd suggest to your client that she get another phone."

Rafe's phone rang, and he lifted a finger. "Hang on a sec," he said before answering.

When it looked like the call might keep him tethered there for a while, Danny tucked the business card into his pocket along with the phone and lightly tapped the desk with his fist a couple of times. "Thanks again."

Rafe waved him off as he argued with the caller on the other end of the line.

On his way across the street to the parking lot, Danny thought about the adept way Jessie had figured out the angle of the photograph. Through the mirror's reflection, of all things. He had no doubt he would have figured it out himself with a little more time, but the speed at which she'd come to it was pretty impressive. There was a lot more to pretty little former rich girl Jessie Stanton than he'd imagined when they first met.

Thoughts of Jessie filled his mind all the way back to the beach, and he found himself grinning like an idiot when a Hall & Oates song serenaded him from the stereo. "Sara Smile" wasn't the same as "Private Eyes," of course; but the beat of the music drummed Jessie into his thoughts deeper still. He'd have a hard time concentrating on the mundane tasks ahead of him that afternoon, but there were three more background checks due to his client by the end of the week.

After arriving home, Danny called Cassie to fill her in before he changed into his running clothes. The *thump-thump-scamper* of paws told him Frank had jumped down from the bed and rushed through the house at the welcome sound of his leash as Danny grabbed it from the peg by the back door.

"Interested in a quick run, buddy?"

The dog's response equated to an enthusiastic, "You bet!"

Ocean View Park had become a regular spot for them. Danny loved the way they fell into stride, Frank's paws in perfect rhythm with the thud of Danny's shoes against the trail. Not too far beneath the split-rail guard fence, the blue Pacific rolled over the sand; and in the distance ahead of them, fingers of the Santa Monica Mountains stretched over the horizon and descended into the surf. On this particular day, a pristine bluish sky smiled down as if it had never been infiltrated by even a trace of undesirable elements like smog or inclement weather.

Once he returned home, he made a few calls and had just set out to do some online research when—

"Danny!" Allie's flip-flops smacked against her heels as Riggs's daughter hurried toward him and hugged his neck from behind the chair. "What are you doing?"

"Solving some mysteries," he said as he reeled around and gave her a proper hug. "What are you doing?"

"Dad's taking us over to see Amber's store. We wanted to know if you wanna come along."

"Technically," he replied, shooting a look at Riggs as he made his way toward them, "it's Jessie's store. Amber just works for her."

"She does? I thought they were doing it together. Anyways, do you wanna come? They're all over there working on setting up for the big deal party."

A third set of footsteps sounded and Danny stood up as Charlotte stepped up next to Riggs and grinned at him. He hadn't seen Riggs's ex—Allie's mom—in more than a year.

"Hi, Danny," she said, and her broad grin lit up the room.

Danny pushed past Riggs and wrapped Charlotte in a bear hug. "You're a sight for sore eyes, Char. It's been way too long."

"Well, Allie's been chattering my ear off about this new friend of hers, and I was hoping for a chance to meet her."

"Check her out?" he teased.

"Okay, yes. Check her out."

"Amber's a sweetheart," he reassured her. "Why don't we all head over together."

The four of them piled into Danny's Jeep, Allie in the front with Danny because she "called it" first. He couldn't help glancing in the rearview mirror intermittently as Riggs and Charlotte chatted amiably. He'd been praying for the two of them for he didn't know how long, and a weight lifted out of his gut to see them together like this.

"If you could call the school sometime this week and sort it out," Charlotte told him softly, "I think it would go a long way."

"Consider it done. What about next month? Have you checked your schedule yet?"

"I just have to put the finishing touches on it and I'll email it to you sometime tomorrow."

Danny couldn't contain the smile that stretched slowly across his face. Charlotte was the love of Aaron Riggs's life, no doubt about it; but Riggs wasn't your typical husband, and Charlotte hadn't found a way to deal with that in their six years of marriage. When she'd given up and turned the last thread of tenacity loose—and Riggs along with it—his longtime friend had never been the same since.

A midnight pounding on the front door had awakened him from a sound sleep, and sent Frank on a stunned tirade against the perceived intruder. "She says she doesn't want to fight for us anymore," Riggs had said the minute Danny opened the door that night so long ago. "I'm wrecked, man. My marriage is over."

*Wrecked* didn't even begin to describe what Riggs had become in the weeks and months that followed. The only thing keeping him walking around had been Allie and his overpowering love for the little girl who idolized her unconventional father. In many ways, Danny had seen every major action over the next year of his friend's life as a battle to prove himself to Allie—and ultimately to Charlotte as well. They'd forged an agreeable relationship; still strained at first, but now sociable several years later. Not that Riggs's feelings had ever changed one iota toward Char. No doubt concealed from the woman herself, but Danny had no doubt about the love looming still.

"Wait 'til you see the store, Mom," Allie exclaimed over the slope of the seat. "And the dresses are like something out of a movie or like you'd see onstage. They're so glamorous!"

"I'm looking forward to that," Charlotte placated her daughter, and she grinned at Danny through the reflection of the mirror.

Danny parked a few doors down from Adornments, and the four of them strolled up the sidewalk to the store. Allie must have spotted Amber through the window because she took off at a full run and stormed inside. When they reached the door, Danny saw Allie hugging Amber. Charlotte must have seen it, too, because she turned back to him and Riggs with a grimace.

"Tell me again that I don't have anything to worry about with this woman."

"I told you, Char, she's a peach," Riggs replied, and he tugged open the door and held it for her. Charlotte shot Danny a skeptical glance before she passed through it.

They'd done wonders with the aesthetics of the small store. Every rack, cubbyhole, and shelf was occupied with inventory, and Jessie appeared at home behind the counter, underneath the

Coco Chanel quote painted on the wall. The floor space between displays was filled with two lines of women flanked by Amber—and Allie, who was now attached to her hip—and Piper.

When Jessie saw him, she smiled and sidestepped the women to reach him and Riggs.

"What's all this? Did you open early?" he asked.

"Oh, no. These are the models we're using Friday night. We're making decisions so we can style them each in a different label. Speaking of—" She raised her arm and waved until Piper looked up. "Let's try your Alexander McQueen on Sophie, huh?"

Danny couldn't miss the new resolve in Jessie, and when she turned back toward him she brought a bright light resembling joy along with her.

"Look at you. I guess you found your mojo about all this?"

She nodded. "Kinda. So what's up? I didn't expect to see you today."

"I just tagged along with them to get a look at the store. You've been working hard, I see."

"Until I can hardly keep my thoughts straight, but I think it's coming together."

"Do you want to take a walk? Clear your head? Maybe let's walk down to the café and grab a coffee?"

She nodded, and the two of them turned to the door.

"Amber? I'll be back in ten minutes."

"Sure thing, boss!"

Nosh, the shop at the end of the strip mall, had the atmosphere of a small French café with white wrought-iron bistro tables, chairs, and benches. Danny covered the cost of a large coffee and a cappuccino, and they carried them to a table next to the chiffon-draped window and sat down.

"There's so much to think about before Friday," she exclaimed, and she had an exhilarated, breathless quality.

"Well, you have lots of support. I'm sure it will be a huge success."

"You're coming, right? You have to be there, Danny."

"Oh, Jessie, I wish you all the best, but it's not exactly my style."

"I know," she whimpered. "But come anyway. You don't have to stay long. I just really want you to be there."

He sighed. "I'll come for a little while."

She beamed and reached out to touch his hand. "Thank you."

"Listen, I've been scouting the trail on the locket you found, and I hit a dead end. If it belonged to the person I think it did, she passed away about five years ago. And there doesn't appear to be any living relative."

Her blue eyes widened and she shook her head. "I was so hoping we could find her."

"Well, I probably did. Just a little too late. Marjorie Sturgeon lived in the apartment with her parents, Robert and Anna Sturgeon, from 1958 until 1959. She became Marjorie Sturgeon Parnell, buried in Tacoma, Washington."

"That's so sad." She traced the rim of her coffee cup with the tip of her index finger and stared down into it for a long moment. "So I guess I can keep it? The locket, I mean. Or should I give it to Aaron, since it's his building?"

"Riggs has no appreciation for it, Jessie. And you're the one who found it in the Priest's Hole. I'll clear it with him just to be sure, but I'd say it belongs to you now."

"Maybe I'll wear it for the opening. Maybe Marjorie will bring me good luck."

Danny shook his head. "I think your luck is your own," he said. "I'm going to take you back. Will you tell Riggs I'll be in the Jeep? I need to make some calls."

"Sure."

*Six days 'fore high school graduation, young Jessie lost her mama. And I lost one of the bright lights of my life. Cancer proved that old sayin' 'bout how a child should never beat their parent to the Pearly Gates.*

*My April missed so much with Jessie, startin' with her gettin' a diploma. Yeah, six days before the ceremonies, she couldn't hold out no longer, and she gave up her ghost to the Almighty. Two weeks after graduation, her fool husband—Jessie's father—packed up his Ford truck and drove straight outta town without a word. No word since neither.*

*Jessie 'bout lost her mind that summer. We sold the house where she grew up and she hadda come to live with her old Gramps. Oh, she still went off to college at LSU in the fall, but her heart just wasn't in it. Before the freshman year was done and buried, Jessie turned eighteen, and she took the proceeds from the family house and used it to move away to California.*

*"Gotta make a new start, Grampy," she says to me. "Gotta go somewhere I never been before."*

*"Does it gotta be in LaLa Land?" I says back.*

*"I know a girl who's goin' to Hollywood. Says I can come along."*

*Arguin' with a child scorned never did benefit nobody. Just an exercise in the futile, I s'pose. So my eighteen-year-old granddaughter, abandoned by both her folks in different ways, went off to LaLa Land to make a new start.*

*The doc doubled my blood pressure medicine that month.*

# 14

Grampy? It's Jessie. How are you doing?"

Jessie's heart fluttered as she awaited his response, and she pressed the phone tighter against her ear.

"Jessie? Is that you?"

"It's me, Grampy. How are you?"

"I'm fine, weather's fine, hotter'n blue blazes," he croaked. "Where you been, child? Started to wonder if I needed to put together a posse."

"I know," she said, sighing as she sank down to the sofa. "I'm sorry. Things have been a little . . . strange. I miss you so much, Grampy."

"Tried callin' you half dozen times, girl. Don't that husband o' yours pay the phone bill?"

"Well, that's part of what's been so strange."

And with that, the dam broke and the tears fell. In buckets. With sound effects. Days, weeks, months' worth of tears tangled up in sobs and hiccups and explanations. Over an hour of explanations, in fact. About Jack, about Danny, Indonesia, and ex-wife Patty. Her grandfather never spoke as many as ten words the whole time. He just let her babble on about the turns her life had taken, the downward spiral of her faith in people—men, in particular—and the familiar emotions associated with diving head first into something new in the hope that it might wash away the pain associated with a man turning his back on her. Again.

"Rentin' your clothes!" he exclaimed, and Jessie laughed. Out of everything she'd just disclosed, this was the item he zeroed in on? "Well, what're you gonna wear then?"

"I'm not renting out *all my clothes*, Grampy. Just the expensive ones."

"Why not just sell 'em then? Use the money to buy a plane ticket back to Luziann."

"I think my days living in Slidell are over," she softly replied. "But thanks for wanting me there."

"Always. Now dry yer eyes 'n' blow yer nose while I tell you 'bout what Maizie Beauchamp up 'n' done yesterday."

Jessie giggled. "That woman's got to be a hundred years old, Grampy!"

"She's still kickin' though."

Jessie wandered through the apartment in search of a box of tissues as her grandfather described the antics of his crazy next door neighbor who—once she got it into her head that he'd been peering in her windows—got a can of black paint and painted over every one of the panes facing his house.

"Like I'd even be interested in peepin' at an old fossil likes o' her."

She found herself laughing, and it felt wonderful. "Grampy, I love you."

"Do ya now?"

"Of course I do."

"Might try callin' more often than just on days that start with H."

"I'm sorry. I'll do better."

"No more cryin'," he declared. "And think about sellin' those clothes o' yours."

Once she disconnected the call, Jessie took a proper look in the mirror and groaned at the sight. It took ten minutes to patch up the damage that had been done, but she had no regrets over it.

Nothing soothed her broken heart like a chat—and a cry—with her grandpa. That's the way it had always been.

On the drive over to the store to meet Amber and Piper, Jessie replayed those millions of heartbreaks that her gramps had soothed with his unique brand of balm. For some reason, she landed chest-deep on the trip she and Jack had taken to Slidell to tell him in person about their upcoming wedding.

"So what do you think of him, Grampy?" she'd asked once they were alone.

"Matters what you think of 'im, child."

"I think he's pretty wonderful. But I want your blessing. Do I have it?"

"When did my blessin' fuel ya or stop ya, either way?" he'd said with a laugh. "You're as headstrong as you always been, and you're gonna marry 'im and I'm gonna give you a kiss and say a prayer."

"Grampy . . ."

"Can't help noticin' though. Seems to me you found yerself a man to replace yer daddy. Maybe give you a chance to change the ending?"

"No," she objected. "No! Jack is nothing like Daddy."

"No? Seems a little like 'im to me, that's all. If I'm wrong, I'm wrong. Least ways, I want you to be happy, whatever that looks like. This man make you happy?"

"Yes," she vowed.

"Then I s'pose there's gonna be a weddin'."

Jessie shook the memory loose and made a conscious decision to deep-breathe the regrets away and focus on the enormity of what awaited her at Adornments. As she steered into the parking lot and approached the store, that enormity snatched her by the back of the neck and pressed in.

Orange cones prevented her from pulling up in front, and beyond them a long, bright red runner led from the store's door, down the sidewalk, and across half the parking lot. Amber and the building manager stood at the end of it directing two workmen. By the time she climbed out of her Ford and made her way to where they stood, the workmen had put several thick metal rods into place.

"This is where our tent will stand?"

"On the spot," Amber told her before thanking the three men and leading Jessie along the border of the red carpet. "Piper's inside with the guy Antonio sent over. He's got five additional waiters coming tonight with non-messy finger foods and a selection of beverages. You've got Cynthia Ross's video guy arriving in three hours, and the models in two. I've put together a checklist for you and left it on your desk. We can go over it, but first—"

"Take a breath," Jessie teased.

Amber released a rumbly sigh. "I'll breathe tomorrow. And so will you. Anyway, I've arranged for the makeup and hair people to hit you after they finish with the models. Piper and I will use the store room to get them dressed while you get fluffed in the office."

"Fluffed," she repeated with a chuckle.

"Do you have your clothes here? If not, I can—"

"I'm good," Jessie interrupted, pausing to wonder how much caffeine Amber had consumed already that day. "Settle down. I'm good."

As they reached the door, Amber froze with a raised eyebrow and the door partway open. "Yeah. You are good. Jessie, just why are you so calm?"

"I'm not. I'm just not at the top of the Richter scale with you."

"You're probably right. Listen, I wanted to run something by you. Can you come back to the storeroom with me before we get into anything else?"

"Sure."

Jessie waved at Piper and followed Amber through the store to the back hallway and into the room where racks of clothes bordered three sides. Amber waved her arm at one of them. "I guess you're wondering where this rack came from," she said, but Jessie hadn't had the time to even notice the unfamiliar items. "These are items I brought over from my own closet to see if you'd be willing—" She inhaled sharply and smiled. "Why don't you take a look?"

Jessie walked to the rack and browsed through them. A black biker jacket caught her eye first and she removed the hanger and held it up in front of her. Paper-thin lambskin with quilted panels on the front and back. "This is beautiful."

"It's Tory Burch. And look at this," she said with a proud smile, pulling another hanger from the rack. Displaying the bright pink shrug with all-over sequins sewn into sheer chiffon, she stated, "This is Betsey Johnson from last year."

"It's darling," Jessie answered, running a finger over the ruffled trim. "It's not like anything else we have in the shop right now."

"That's kind of my point. I was going over the inventory, and since we hit the Melrose area pretty heavily with flyers, I thought . . . Well, I realized we didn't have any pieces that might speak to a younger crowd, maybe the late teens and twentysomethings."

She grinned. "Like you."

"Exactly like me. And the thing is . . . I think I'm one of your key demographics. The hungry fashion wannabes. So shouldn't we have something that will keep them coming back?"

"You're sure you want to sacrifice pieces like this? There must be a dozen items here."

"Sixteen. And six handbags out in front, and some funky jewelry pieces too. I figure if I can get the commission deal out of them like you gave Piper, it's not like I'm really losing money. I mean, if they don't turn over, I can just take them home and hang them right back in my closet, right?"

Jessie replaced the shrug and the jacket and continued down the line of apparel hanging there. Roberto Cavalli embellished jeans; silk crepe de chine Stella McCartney trousers; a graphic print Lela Rose dress with three-quarter sleeves; an illusion-neck peplum dress by David Meister.

"Amber." She hesitated before asking, "Where did you get the money for all of this?"

"I'm one of those girls who maxes her credit cards, who begs and borrows in the name of fashion," she replied frankly. "But I'm going under, Jessie. I thought putting a few hip items on the racks might benefit you, and help me out as well. Why shouldn't this stuff start paying me instead of the other way around?"

Jessie wanted to laugh right out loud, but she suppressed the urge. She'd been wondering more and more lately about that hold her designer labels, killer shoes, and status handbags had on her; especially in the face of losing everything *except* those items. She glanced down at the pale white circle fading around her finger where her rings had once been. She had to admit though . . . she missed her bling.

"I put the jewelry pieces in the case out front if you want to take a look. I just thought all this might help bring a greater variety of customer through the doors. If you'd rather I take them home, I won't take offense."

"No," Jessie said, and she rubbed Amber's arm. "I think it's really good thinking. Let's give the pieces a try and see what the reaction is."

A wide grin spread over Amber's pretty face and she sighed. "I was hoping you'd say that. I assigned myself a consignment number and logged everything into the system, just in case. So if anyone wants to try them tonight, we're ready for it."

"How did you determine the fees?"

"The same way we did the other inventory, based on the sale price."

It didn't even surprise her. Jessie just nodded. "Okay. How about we go over that checklist you mentioned, and then you can get these racks out on the floor."

---

Eager anxiety coursed through Danny as he rounded the corner and spotted the huge white tent in the parking lot in front of Adornments. As he eased into the jammed parking lot, he wondered if he'd made a mistake in promising Jessie he would attend. He hadn't anticipated so many people, instead picturing a few women browsing through racks of clothing and filing out of the store within minutes. But this—

Servers carried trays inside the tent as a couple dozen people milled about. He spotted Piper making the rounds and paused to wave at her, but she didn't notice him.

He opened the Adornments door to another surprise: At least a dozen more people—both women and men—dotted the floor inside, browsing through racks, inspecting handbags and shoes, and crouching over the glass jewelry case Jessie had purchased through eBay.

He heard her before seeing her, and he turned to find her standing at the back corner of the store in conversation with two women.

"I'm impressed with the eclectic mix you have here," he overheard one of the women say as he approached. "I'm regularly styling just three clients right now, and they're as different as sunshine and snow."

"I'd love to get together and talk more about it," Jessie said. "Will you excuse me for just a second? Why don't you let Amber show you the accessories?"

She grinned as she made her way toward him, and she surprised Danny with a kiss to the cheek. "I'm so glad you came."

"I told you I would."

She lifted one shoulder into a shrug. "Still . . . Hey! Wait until you see what I got for my office. It was just delivered yesterday. It's . . . *a safe!*"

"You have a safe?"

"Piper found it. It looks like a bookcase. Wait until you see."

A young woman approached and touched Jessie on the arm. "I'm sorry, could I interrupt you for just a minute. I have a question about a couple of things."

Jessie smiled at him and gave a little tilt of a shrug. "Of course. Show me."

It looked to him like Jessie had found the enthusiasm she had lost, all the concerns she expressed to him about the new venture alleviated—or at least suppressed—by this new surge of energy.

"Oh, hey, Danny," Amber said, breaking him away from watching them as they crossed toward the office. "I didn't expect to see you here. Did you see all the people out there? It's epic, right?"

"Pretty epic."

"Did you see Aaron and his little girl? I think they're out in the tent having snacks."

He nodded. "Thanks. I'll go look for them."

As he headed toward the door, he took note of the various shoppers, many of them gathered around the cubbyholes where the array of purses and such were displayed. Unfamiliar names like Michael Kors, Vivienne Westwood, and Carolina Something were bandied about on clouds of ooohs and ahhhhs that told Danny there might have been something to this idea Jessie had of sharing the wealth of her designer labels with those who couldn't afford them.

"I could SO rock this hobo," one of the young shoppers said with a large tote bag held up before her like a divine scroll.

*Hobo.* Danny would have thought to be called a hobo it would have to look like a kerchief attached to the end of a long stick.

He spotted Riggs chatting up a young woman with wild, kinky hair as they waited in the short line for the bar. As he moved closer to them, the woman turned around—and the sight of her punched Danny right in the center of the gut.

"Allie? Is that you?" he exclaimed, and Riggs's daughter beamed.

"Do you like it?" she asked, flipping her wild hair and tugging on the lapel of the denim jacket with chains draped over the shoulders. "Amber helped me get ready. A real hairstylist did my hair!"

"You look"—he looked to Riggs and gulped—"very grown-up."

"I told her it was a one-time thing, just for today," Riggs said.

"Dad," she groaned. "You said I look cool."

"I don't think I said *cool*. I said *different*."

"But cool," she insisted.

"You look twenty."

Allie grinned. "I do? Thanks, Dad."

"But you're not twenty. You're twelve."

She pushed out a sound that reminded Danny of a cat relieving itself of a fur ball. "I'll be thirteen in nine weeks, Dad."

"Thanks for the reminder."

"I'm going inside to talk to Amber." And with that, she stalked away from them.

Riggs shook his head and sighed. "I just realized she's going to kill me. Watching her grow up is definitely going to kill me."

"Better you than me, buddy," Danny remarked as they reached the front of the line and the bartender looked up expectantly.

"What can I get you?" he asked, and Riggs burst with one loud laugh.

"Two mineral waters," Danny answered for him.

"And make mine a double," Riggs joked.

Once they'd picked up their drinks, a uniformed waitress approached with a tray. "Antipasto from Tuscan Son?"

An array of finger foods arranged on the tray gave off an inviting aroma.

"Try the little calzones," Riggs said. "They're killer."

The waitress placed a small crusty triangle on a cocktail napkin and handed it to Danny. "Anything else?"

"This is fine, thanks."

He popped it into his mouth and immediately raised an eyebrow. "Good grief."

"I know. Between Allie and me, we've sampled everything they have, and we haven't found a clunker yet."

Danny shook his head. "I'd say her opening is a success."

"I'm tempted to buy a dress and some shoes myself," Riggs joked dryly.

"And get yourself a hobo," Danny added.

"A what?"

"A hobo," he repeated and shook his head. "I don't know. It's some kind of big purse."

"Hobo!" Riggs said with a laugh. "What kind of name is that for a purse?"

"I don't know, but young women expect to rock it."

"You know what Allie told me, man? Women can pay like eight hundred bucks or more for one pair of shoes made by someone famous."

"Yeah."

"That's crazy. You know how many pairs of shoes I could buy for eight hundred bucks?"

Like synchronized swimmers, they glanced down at their shoes—Danny's canvas boat shoes and Riggs's rubber flip-flops—then back at one another in perfect unison.

"About eight hundred?" Danny cracked.

"Oh. Ha. Ha." With a second thought, he shrugged and admitted, "Yeah. True dat."

Jessie stood outside the door to the store with Piper, and she noticed a news truck from Cynthia Ross's station with two guys loading video equipment into it. "I guess they got what they needed from the opening?" Jessie asked. "I never even knew they were here."

"They just needed some crowd shots," Piper told her.

Amber suddenly swung the door open and called out to her. "Jessie? Can you come in for a minute?"

She and Piper exchanged smiles before Jessie hurried inside. "What's up?"

"There's someone here you need to meet."

Amber led her toward the counter where a petite young woman leaned over the display case admiring the bling. When she straightened, Jessie was struck by her beauty. Glossy raven hair, milky skin, cinnamon brown eyes—and her apparel impeccable. She thought the woman might be a model or an actress.

"This is Courtney Alexis," Amber said, and the woman extended her hand. "Courtney, this is the owner of the store, Jessie Stanton."

"It's such a pleasure to meet you," she said, and Jessie wondered how such a deep, raspy voice came out of such a tiny person.

"Courtney is a stylist," Amber explained. "She also writes a fashion blog geared toward girls like me with champagne dreams and a ginger ale budget."

"You're in the right place," Jessie quipped.

"I saw the tease on television this morning about the piece they're doing on your opening for this weekend's *Fashion Trends* segment. I remembered a press release I'd received—"

"I sent you that!" Amber exclaimed. "I'm a writer too. I mean, not like you, of course." Flustered, she added, "I've just had a few articles published. Anyway, I read your blog every morning, and I thought who better to get a press release about Jessie's store."

"Thank you, I'm really glad you sent it. This is just the sort of shop my readers and clients would love to know about."

"Courtney styles the up-and-comers," Amber pointed out.

The young woman nodded. "Those girls who have come to town with very specific goals in mind, whether that's in the world of entertainment or the business community, but they tend to arrive looking like posers, if you know what I mean."

Jessie thought she could have used someone like Courtney Alexis when *she* arrived in Los Angeles. Maybe she'd have had more than three modeling jobs before stepping behind a fragrance counter. She didn't find her true style until after she'd married Jack.

"Every few months, I do a three-day workshop at my studio in Hollywood where I teach girls how to look like the job or status they're pursuing," Courtney continued. "I have one coming up in a few weeks, and I had this revelation that perhaps we could take a field trip to your store."

"Are you serious?"

"I'll probably combine it with a stopover at a couple spots down on Melrose, but your place and what you're doing here is pretty unique to this area. I don't know why someone else hasn't done it."

"I would be happy to arrange it." *Happy* didn't exactly cover it. Jessie's heart soared at the idea. "In fact, if you'd like to schedule it before or after hours, we can give them private access."

"What a great idea!"

*Isn't it though?*

"If it works out, I was thinking we could talk about some future opportunities."

"Such as?"

"Well, maybe you could be a guest blogger for me once a month. How would you feel about that?"

"I don't know," she said, but a grin rose quickly. "I mean, I've never really written much of anything—"

"I could help you," Amber exclaimed.

"See? You have a writer right here. And from the looks of her, a very fashionable one."

Amber looked to Jessie like she might pop from joy.

"And I'll help with the nuts and bolts," Courtney assured her.

Amber looked as if she could hardly contain herself. "What a great opportunity to familiarize people with the store."

"And maybe you'd be open," Courtney began slowly, "to offering additional services, such as private styling sessions for your customers."

"How would that work, exactly?"

"You bring me in and I charge a flat fee to any of your customers who want a stylist, and I style them exclusively from your inventory so you get the ensemble rentals."

"That's an interesting thought," she said, not daring to flash a look in Amber's direction for fear of a crack in the cool, professional expression she'd managed to sculpt. "I'd like to talk with you more about that."

"If that works out, I could probably bring in a good deal more label inventory from my designer contacts. They often use me to create a familiarity with their brand among my readers and clients."

Jessie's face ached from grinning by the time Courtney Alexis left the store. Without a single word exchanged, she and Amber simply closed the gap between them and stood side by side, clutching each other's hands, squeezing until the blood flow just about stopped.

*A bonus. As soon as I can afford it, Amber deserves a giant bonus.*

"How much is the rental on this choker?" someone asked from the counter.

"I've got this," Amber said, letting go of Jessie's hand. "Oh, isn't that gorgeous? It's one of my favorites."

As they discussed the deposit procedure and rental options, Jessie stayed glued to the spot, breathing deep and hoping no one spotted her looming loss of composure.

*Jessie looked up at me from where she sat leanin' into the curve o' my arm and blinked those big bright eyes at me. "You know what I think of every time we read this part of* Charlotte's Web, *Grampy?"*

*"What's 'at?"*

*"I think of how you catch those crabs and eat 'em for supper. Why do people do that anyhow?"*

*"It's why God made 'em, I reckon."*

*"I hate how Fern's daddy grabs the ax just because Wilbur was born small. And how he thinks it's dumb that she wants to keep 'im for a pet."*

*"That's a lotta hatin' you're doin'."*

*"Well," she said, thinkin' it over while bitin' on the corner of her lip. "Maybe not hate exactly. But I don't like it. Least ways, her daddy let her keep Wilbur. You won't let me keep even one of those stinkin' crabs."*

*"Nah, and I won't neither."*

*"You're stubborn, Grampy."*

*"Yep. You will be, too, when you get 'round my age."*

*"No, I won't neither."*

*I didn't tell her stubborn weren't nothin' she needed to grow into. Nah, my little Jessie was already there.*

# 15

There are other storefronts like this one across the country," Cynthia Ross narrated over a sweeping shot of Adornments, from the door to the jewelry case to the Coco Chanel quote on the back wall, "where you can rent everything from apparel to accessories. Most of them are based online, but Jessie Stanton's brainchild—Adornments in Santa Monica—opened yesterday to a small crowd of Southern Californians on that never-ending scouting expedition for designer labels at a price they can afford. If *you* need a little Chanel or Valentino for an upcoming event and have already taken out a second mortgage or opened an equity line of credit, you might try paying Jessie Stanton and Adornments a visit. This is Cynthia Ross for the weekend's *Fashion Trends*. Stay stylish, Los Angeles."

Piper, Jessie, and Amber formed a circle and hopped up and down, squealing at pitches that summoned dogs everywhere. In fact, Danny felt pretty sure Frank heard it from out at the beach.

Jessie broke free from them and closed the laptop. "It was so nice of Cynthia to let us preview the piece," she said. Turning to Piper, she added, "Should I send her something?"

"She loves Anna Shea."

"Perfect."

"I'll get on it," Amber declared.

"Keep it under a hundred dollars," Jessie said as Amber rushed past Danny out of the office.

He scratched his jaw. "Anna Shea's a . . . shoe label?"

Piper chuckled and rubbed his arm. "Chocolates. But thanks for playing."

"A C-note for *chocolate*?"

To Jessie, Piper added, "I'll check on the tent and make sure it's cleaned up out there."

"Thank you."

Jessie sported a wide, satisfied grin as she sank into her chair and set her ocean-blue gaze on Danny.

"It was a successful day, yes?" he said, perching on the corner of the small desk. "Feeling pretty good about yourself?"

She shrugged. "Pretty good."

"Here ya go," he said, casually holding up his palm.

"What?" She stared at his hand strangely. "I don't . . . I don't know what that means."

He lifted it into the air and nodded. "Slap it. You look like you're dying to give yourself a high five. I'm here for ya, kid."

Jessie crackled with laughter and flew to her feet, slapping her palm against his with unexpected brute force.

"Feel better?"

She nodded, sniffing. "Kinda. Thanks."

"No problem."

"Oh, and thanks for coming back, by the way."

"For all the good I've been," he said with a laugh. "All I've done is stand around."

Jessie rounded the desk until she parked in front of him and touched his arm. She reminded him of the morning ocean, those blue eyes of hers calling him closer like the Pacific often did.

"I haven't known you long enough for this to make sense," she said, "but I feel like my confidence is attached to you somehow. I feel stronger when you're around, Danny. I'm really glad you were here today."

"Then . . . I am too."

She leaned forward and gently kissed his jaw. Afterward, she only backed away a few inches before rubbing her chin. "Beard burn."

"Yeah, but it's a personal style choice," he teased. "I don't guess anyone would understand that better than you."

"No, I get it. It works for you." She rubbed her chin again. "But would it affect your personal style to use a little conditioner or something?"

He didn't ask her out loud, but he wondered if they actually made such a thing. Conditioner for beards?

"And yes," she said just above a whisper. "They make moisturizer for beards."

"Yeah. Sure," he covered. "There's a product for just about everything, isn't there?"

"Just about," she replied, grinning.

When she still didn't back away from him, something unrecognizable grabbed ahold of Danny and nudged him forward until his lips pressed softly against Jessie's. After a few short seconds, before his hand even made it upward to cradle the back of her head, she jumped. The lagging reality of the situation finally made it to the censors in her brain, no doubt.

"Sorry," he blurted.

"Yeah."

"Really, I—"

"Right."

"I just—"

"Okay. I need to help Amber close up the store," she said, backing away farther. "And I guess you're probably dying to get out of here."

"Well . . ."

"But thank you for coming, Danny."

"Sure."

"I'll see you later."

"Yeah."

He hadn't had a kiss that awkward since high school.

Jessie hustled Amber toward home so she could tell Piper what happened with Danny. She could hardly wait for the front door to close.

"Well, what did you say to him?" Piper asked once Jessie had quickly spilled the details behind the closed door of her office.

"I think I said, 'I guess you'll be leaving now. Thanks for coming.' "

"You're joking."

"Nope."

"Yikes. Well, how was it? . . . The kiss."

Jessie smiled in spite of herself. "He has very soft lips."

"Well, that's something, isn't it?"

"But his whiskers are scratchy. Jack always had such a velvety soft face."

"So you'll get him a Clinique basket for his birthday."

"Yeah, I could do that." Suddenly, her good sense gene kicked in. Always a day late and a few thousand short, it seemed. "No. I'm not going to be still kissing him on his birthday, Piper."

"Why not? When's his birthday?"

"I don't know. That's not the point."

"What is the point then?" she asked with a laser-focused glare.

"I'm not capable of making good decisions when it comes to men. And even if that weren't true, I am married."

"To a deserter."

"Yes. But still married."

"And a cheater."

"Probably. Still. Married!"

"Are you serious?" Piper asked with a sigh.

"If only I weren't."

"Let's say you weren't married. Would Danny Callahan be someone you'd take for a spin?"

"Like a bicycle?"

"No, like take him out for a date to see if you click."

Jessie dropped to the chair and propped her feet on the corner of the desk, crossing them at the ankle. With a grin, she admitted, "Oh, we click."

"Yes?"

"We click all over the place."

"Then—"

"Yeah," she interrupted. "Married."

"I hate Jack," Piper muttered. "I really do."

"You know what my Grampy would say? He'd say, *'That's a lotta hatin' yer doin' there, Pah-per.'*"

"Well, I'm not wild about your Grampy right now either then."

Jessie giggled and shook her head. "Let's head out."

"Okay. How about we swing by the restaurant for dessert and coffee on the way home?"

"From one side of Santa Monica to the other . . . by way of Beverly Hills?" she asked with a chuckle.

"Yes. I'll drive."

Jessie hadn't eaten anything since the low-fat blueberry muffin and coffee Amber had brought her earlier in the day, and her stomach rumbled at the mere idea of Tuscan Son.

"What are you waiting for?" she said as she hopped up and grabbed her bag. "Let's go."

---

"Malibu Fitness. This is Jennifer."

"Hi, Jennifer, this is Jessie Stanton," she told the receptionist on the other end of the phone.

"Oh, Mrs. Stanton, how are you? We haven't seen you in for Pilates in a while."

"I know. I've been crazy busy. I wonder if you could check something for me. When is my membership due for renewal?"

"Sure. Hang on for just a moment and I'll check our records."

While she waited, a knock at the door drew her across the living room to answer it. She found her neighbor Gabi standing on the other side.

"Hi, Gabi." She pointed to the phone in her palm and adjusted the Bluetooth on her ear. "What's up?"

"I just stop by to see about my dish."

"Oh! Come on in." Gabi followed her inside and closed the door behind her. "I've been meaning to return it. The tamales were out of this—"

"Mrs. Stanton?"

Jessie raised a finger and whispered, "—world!" She smiled at Gabi and tended to the phone call. "Yes, Jennifer. I'm here."

"It looks like your membership was up last week."

*Figures.*

"Would you like to renew right now?"

Jessie deflated. She didn't remember the price tag on her gym membership, but she did recall Jack balking at it when she'd joined for the purpose of working out there with Piper.

"No, I don't think so. I've moved further down the beach, and I think I'll have to look into finding a Pilates class closer to home. Thanks, Jennifer."

"Everyone will be so sorry to hear that. I hope you'll stop by and say hello if you ever get back."

"Thanks. I'll do that."

Okay, she would probably never do that. But there was no use in being rude. Or unfurling her recent life story.

As she disconnected the call, she headed into the kitchen and picked up Gabi's Pyrex dish from the counter. "I can't thank you enough for the tamales, Gabi. If I had any skills in the kitchen whatsoever, I'd invite you over and reciprocate. But maybe we can order takeout some night."

"I like that," she said, beaming. "I hear you say you want to find Pilates? There's no Pilates, but there are good yoga *clahsses* at the YMCA on Tuesday and Thursday mornings. Zumba on the weekend."

*The YMCA?* Jessie could hardly picture herself dropping to a mat on the linoleum floor of a YMCA.

"Thanks, I'll think about that. I was headed out, so . . ."

"Oh, okay. I go too."

Jessie picked up her keys and bag. On the other side of the front door, she twisted the keyring around her finger and started to say good-bye to Gabi, but an eruption of noise from the street end of the driveway stopped her flat.

"Would you get a move on? We're going to be late."

Her ears perked as she recognized Danny's voice.

"Keep your shirt on, bro. I just had to lock up the work closet." Definitely Riggs.

The two of them moved into view around the corner of the building, their backs to Jessie and Gabi as they stalked down the driveway toward Danny's Jeep parked at the curb.

"Ay, it must be *Wen-esday*, *sí*?" Gabi commented.

"Yes."

"Every *Wen-esday* right at this time, Danny come over here to get Aaron. I always wonder where they go."

"They meet here?"

"*Chez*. Each *Wen-esday* at six o'clock."

"Hmm. See you later, Gabi."

She didn't exactly *mean to* hurry to her Taurus, speed around the building, and catch up to the Jeep at the light; but when she did, Jessie's curiosity sloshed against her good sense and she called Amber.

As she followed Danny and Riggs out to the boulevard, she asked, "Amber, how are things going?"

"Fairly well. We've had a pretty steady stream of people."

"Any of them result in business?"

"Actually . . ." Amber paused. "Four apparel rentals and three accessories for the day."

"Really? That's not bad. Did you get those chocolates sent to Cynthia Ross?"

"With a gushing thank-you."

"Excellent. Listen, are you all right on your own for a bit longer? I have a quick errand to run on my way over."

"Sure. Do what you need to do. I've got it all in hand."

"Thanks. See you soon."

She questioned herself about half a dozen times on the drive to who-knew-where behind Danny's Jeep. *Jessie, what are you doing?* The answer never came, but its absence didn't slow her down. Following at a safe distance behind them, the adrenaline rushed through her veins at an alarming rate of speed. Investigating an investigator. Not the smartest thing she'd ever done on the fly but, for some inexplicable reason, Jessie simply had to know more about Danny Callahan. Where did he and Riggs go every Wednesday evening like clockwork? She'd just lag behind them long enough to find out the answer, and then she'd turn back. It wasn't like she was going to climb through bushes and spy on them or anything.

Danny steered into the parking lot of a white building with wide brick stairs in the front, but Jessie slowly passed them by. Utilizing the next street to make a U-turn, she backtracked and pulled into the parking lot as Danny and Riggs headed up the steps, pushed through double white doors, and went inside.

United Community Church, the small sign in front declared. Fellowship at 6 p.m. Worship service at 7 p.m.

"Church?" she muttered. This was where Danny and Riggs hurried off to every Wednesday night, rain or shine? "Heh."

She suddenly recalled Danny's explanation of the circle of thorns tattooed around his bicep. "A reminder of my faith," he'd said, and she'd thought it a pretty interesting take on faith. The only religious person she'd ever known had been her grandpa, and he sure didn't feel the need to tattoo anything on his body to remind him.

On the drive back to Santa Monica, she wondered about Danny. Why had he flinched the way he had on that day she'd touched him . . . and then felt compelled to kiss her the next time she did? And what in the world inspired the kind of religious fervor that would make a guy tattoo thorns on his arm?

When she reached the store, just one customer stood at the counter chatting with Amber, so Jessie went ahead to her office. Her intentions of reviewing the receipts for her first couple of days in business took a nosedive under those nagging questions about Danny.

*A ring of thorns.* Like the one Jesus supposedly wore when he was crucified, she supposed, and she opened a browser on the laptop and typed in the first sets of words that sprang to mind: ring of thorns tattoo, reminder of faith, history of tattoos.

She spent the next hour reading about how Jewish law thought tattoos to be an affront to God, and went on to skim various accounts of people's choices behind getting tattooed, and how meaningful they can be in trying to dig down to the heart of someone's personality. She struggled in admitting that there was only one person whose heart she wanted to dig into. So she typed in his name.

DANNY CALLAHAN.

It turned out that the name wasn't all that unique. It also belonged to an American philosopher from the 1930s; a song title by someone named Conor Oberst; various owners of Facebook pages and LinkedIn profiles; and a former Navy petty officer whose wife had been killed in a head-on collision.

Jessie's heart stopped beating for just a moment before it kicked into overdrive, racing and thudding against her chest. She clicked on the first link about the Navy petty officer third class and—sure enough—there was Danny, wearing a crew cut so short that she might not have recognized him except for the familiar steel blue eyes looking back at her from the screen.

He and his wife were driving toward San Diego, presumably back to the naval base after a three-day leave, when they were involved in a head-on collision. The passenger—Rebecca Callahan—was killed on impact. The driver—Daniel Callahan—had a blood alcohol level of .108, well above the legal limit.

Jessie's stomach knotted as she looked back at the night they all dined at Tuscan Son, and he'd quietly exchanged his Negroni for a club soda.

If anything could turn a drinker into a teetotaler, this article about Danny's past—dated September 2006, she noted—surely indicated something that could. The sweet, soft eyes of Rebecca Callahan burned a warm hole straight into Jessie as she considered the horrifying realizations and guilt with which Danny must have had to learn to cope. She couldn't even imagine that kind of torment. It put her straying liar of a husband and his disappearing act into strange and sad perspective.

Two soft raps on the office door preceded Amber's head poking around it. "Knock, knock," she sang.

Jessie closed the laptop and looked up at her.

"Do you have any objections to me bringing in a little card table and setting it up in the corner of the store room so I have somewhere to eat my dinner?"

"That's fine."

"Can you cover the front while I run next door for a salad?"

"Sure."

"Want anything?"

"No, thanks."

Jessie followed her out into the store, and she sat down on the stool behind the jewelry case as the door jingled behind Amber. Less than a minute had passed before the bell clinked again to announce the entrance of two stylish twenty-somethings.

"That's her," one of them muttered, and they both smiled at Jessie. "We saw you on the weekend news," she said more loudly. "We couldn't wait to come in and check out your store."

"Wonderful," she replied. "Feel free to look around, and let me know if you have any questions."

They turned out to be nothing more than lookie-loos, and they left again before Amber returned from a thirty-minute dinner break. Jessie had just started polishing the jewelry display case with the Windex and roll of paper towels Amber had stashed under the counter.

"Have you given any more thought to the website idea?" Amber asked, dragging a second stool closer to her.

"What website idea is that?"

Amber chuckled. "Riley said the store needs an online presence beyond Facebook. Remember?"

"Oh, right. I haven't, really."

"She was here for the opening, but she said she didn't get a chance to talk to you. She's offered to get us set up with a site, and then she'll teach me how to update it."

Taking a moment to reflect on the strange way everything had come together for her, Jessie lost track of her conversation with Amber.

"I've met a lot of great people at my church, but I think she's the nicest. She's always willing to lend a hand when someone needs it."

She blinked back to the moment and tried to think of a more delicate way of asking, but the words tumbled out of her. "Amber? You go to church?"

"Of course!"

The reply tickled Jessie. *Oh, of course.* Like church attendance was as natural as bathing or shopping.

"I go to Emmanuel Christian, out in Van Nuys. Why? . . . Hey, would you like to come with me sometime?"

"I'm not sure we can both be out on a Sunday," she replied. *Never mind that I'm not really interested in—*

"Maybe we could go to an early service and get here in time to open the store at ten."

"Oh, I don't think so. But thank you for inviting me."

"Okay. If you change your mind, let me know."

What was it about the topic of church lately? It seemed to be closing in from every direction.

"Do you ever go to Wednesday services?" she asked casually.

"Sometimes, when I can. I don't suppose I'll be making it now since I close the store during the week. But they have a great Bible study for singles on Wednesdays at Emmanuel."

"Maybe we can work something out if you need that night free."

Jessie nodded, but her thoughts moved to Danny and Riggs, wondering if their Wednesday church attendance was geared toward the single life, too. Perhaps Danny had met a nice Christian girl at one of those Wednesday Bible studies. Someone with warm eyes like Rebecca once had. Someone who kept him coming so faithfully week after week.

"Anyway, do you want me to tell Riley to go ahead and get started?"

Jessie swallowed around the sudden dry lump that had risen in her throat. "Sure. If she's willing, I guess we'd be fools not to take her up on it, right?"

*"Do we hafta go to church again today?" Jessie asked me after she pushed the newspaper away and crawled up into my lap and replaced it.*

*"You don't wanna go, huh?"*

*"Not really. Do you mind an awful lot?"*

*"Nah," I says to her. "I don't mind. Don't mean we're not goin' though."*

*"Why do we hafta keep doin' the same thing, Sunday after Sunday, Grampy?"*

*"'Cause it's somethin' worth doin'," I told her. "No better way to spend a Sunday morning'n thankin' the good Lord for all he give ya."*

*She thought about that for a minute before curlin' up her pretty little face into a knot. "Can't we thank 'im from someplace else?"*

*"We could," I says. "But we ain't gonna."*

*She groaned and whined about it, but she came back all dressed up not an hour later, and she held my hand all the way down Eaton Street and five blocks over to the church steps.*

*"Don't know why God needs me to wear such fancy shoes if we're gonna walk to church, Grampy."*

*" 'Cause He wants to enjoy you all spit-polished and purdy."*

*"But it's so hot out. I wish I could just send him a picture postcard instead."*

# 16

One of those days. As she inched along in traffic, Jessie made a mental "storm list" of the things that had gone wrong.

1. The bathroom sink at Adornments had backed up. She thanked the God who may or may not be out there somewhere that Amber knew what to do before it streamed anywhere near the store floor. Too bad the plumber was already two hours late when she had to leave.
2. Their third rental on the day of the store opening—Manolo Blahnik Swan Embellished satin pumps—came back a day late and an embellishment short. "I don't know where it went," the customer whimpered, tapping the spot where the crystal beaded vine applique had once been. "I just looked down and it was gone. But you're insured for stuff like this, right?"
3. After calling Jessie's insurance broker, Amber returned with the news that her bare minimum coverage for her business did not include damage to a killer pair of Manolos. Why hadn't she thought of wear and tear damage? And why hadn't the broker advised her about it? Ten minutes on the phone with him and Amber volunteered to call around for some guidance on better—and affordable—business policies. Two hours later, she declared that a "BOP package" was

needed. As it turned out, this meant a Business Owner's Policy tailored and bundled to meet specific needs. It also meant several hundred dollars more each and every month to expand from simple worker's compensation and liability to Manolos and Chanels.

4. A review of the week's receipts had further painted a bleak and pit-in-the-stomach thud of a picture of her financial future.

A violent shake cut her storm list of the day's events suddenly short, and Jessie gasped as the Taurus tremored beneath her and, after one sharp jolt, stopped right in the middle of the westbound lane of Wilshire Boulevard. Screaming horns at various octaves serenaded her distress, and a guy in a red Porsche shouted something at her as he squealed around her.

She threw the gear into park, turned off the ignition, and then twisted it back on. Not a sound. Two more tries resulted in the same irritating silence.

"Stupid Ford!" she muttered, feeling around her bag for her cell phone.

The horns and shouts of afternoon traffic were sliced by the occasional obscene gesture, all while Piper's phone went straight to voice mail. She debated calling Amber, knowing she'd have to close the store to come and get her, so she dialed Danny instead.

"My car broke down," she whimpered when he answered. "I'm in the middle of Wilshire with everyone yelling at me, and I don't know what to do."

"Wilshire and what?" he asked immediately.

"Uh . . ." She looked around. "Past Third, almost to Second."

"Sit tight. I'm not far."

*Easy for you to say*, she thought above the cacophony of horns and a siren. But she did appreciate his authoritative, I'll-take-care-of-it-ness.

A uniformed police officer appeared at her window and motioned to her to open it.

"Shift it into neutral," he told her. "We're going to push you up there."

Two officers and a guy who looked like a road worker in jeans and an orange hard hat pushed the car while Jessie steered it through halted traffic and into an adjacent parking lot.

"Can you call your auto club?" the cop asked her.

"I've called a friend to come and help. He'll know what to do."

She detected a quiver of amusement at the corner of his thin lips, and she grimaced. The ridiculous thought of making an excuse by explaining her entire life situation to him flitted across her mind, but she brushed it away with a sigh as he waved and headed back toward Wilshire. By the time Danny arrived twenty minutes later, she'd worked herself into full-blown embarrassment. She yanked the door handle, climbed out of the car and flew toward him, leaving the door gaping open behind her. When she slid her arms around his neck and hugged him, his laughter rumbled against her.

"Thank you for coming! I know I should know what to do. I'm an adult person, right? It's not like I haven't had a flat tire or a dead battery before. I have. Once, I even overheated on the 101 and I called AAA. I don't know why I—"

"Hey, Jessie," he interrupted, and he placed hands on both her shoulders and held her there in his gaze. "Let's have a look, okay?"

She wilted a little and nodded. "Sorry. The cop was just so . . . condescending. Yes. Okay."

He leaned into the open door and tugged until the hood popped. She stood back and watched him, her arms dangling at her sides like some sort of alien, completely out of her element. She couldn't help noticing how handsome—and manly!—he looked, hunched over the inner workings of her Ford like that. After poking a couple of things and inspecting a couple more, he peered up at her.

"Slide behind the wheel and turn the key when I tell you to."

She did as she was told, trying—and failing in the effort—not to scrunch down for a better look at him through the opening in the hood.

"Okay, give it a try."

When the engine didn't turn over, he pushed his straight blondish hair back with one hand while wrapping it into a short ponytail with the other and securing it with a thin band. The stubble on his face—a shade darker than his hair—glistened with perspiration as the afternoon sun found it.

"Try once more."

She did, to no avail. Danny let the hood slam shut and wiped his brow with the back of his hand as he walked up to her door.

"Now what?" she asked.

"We'll get it towed over to my buddy's garage and I'll drive you home. I think it's the fuel filter, but he'll know better. I'll give him a call."

Jessie sighed and picked up her own phone as Danny used his.

"Amber, it's Jessie. I'm having car trouble. Can you stay a little longer and close up the store on your own?"

"Sure, boss. No problem."

"You have your checklist?"

"I transferred it to my phone. I'm good. Do you need me to pick you up?"

"No, Danny's here. He'll give me a lift home."

When Jessie disconnected the call, she leaned her head back and sighed, watching Danny as he spoke to his friend.

"He can't get here for a couple of hours," he said, tucking his phone into the torn back pocket of his faded jeans. "I'm going to tuck the key on top of the front tire, and he'll send the truck out when it's available."

"What if someone sees you? They'll steal my car."

Danny leaned his weight back slightly on one leg and grinned. "Pretty attached to her, are you?"

"Yeah. Okay. But she's the only ride I've got."

After the key had been secured and they were in Danny's Jeep and on their way, he turned to her while waiting at the light. "I was headed out to Newport Beach for a quick meet with a friend. You want to come along and I'll drop you home afterward?" When she hesitated, he added, "It'll take a few hours round-trip, if you're free."

She shrugged. "Okay. Why not? You can't believe what a disaster this day has been. I could use the diversion. Thanks."

Jessie tried to imagine the friend Danny might meet in the upscale community of Newport Beach. She envisioned another surfing buddy like Riggs . . . or a former client—now a friend—living in the lap of luxury . . . or perhaps a friend who operated the ferry around Balboa Island. What she never imagined was Stephanie Regnier and a table at the Burgee Bar inside the Balboa Yacht Club.

"Steph, I'd like you to meet a client of mine. This is Jessie Stanton."

Steph's gray-blue eyes lit up slightly as she raised one dark blonde eyebrow into a perfect arch. Danny hoped she wouldn't mention Jessie's illusive husband, and she didn't let him down. "Jessie. It's good to meet you."

"You too."

Once they'd settled at a table and ordered cold drinks, Steph shifted toward Danny. "So what do you think? The Commodores Gallery is their smallest room, and my mom has already put down a deposit. It holds up to sixty people, and the views are amazing." Turning to Jessie, she added, "The wedding is on the beach at my folks' place, but I guess we're thinking of this place for the reception. I don't really think we need anything quite so fancy, but my mom's been planning things, and she likes it."

Jessie looked from Steph to Danny and back again. "I'm sorry. Wedding?"

Was it his imagination, or did the pulse in her reddened throat start palpitating? The poor thing had that reaction to the mere mention of a wedding? Jack Stanton really did a number on her.

"Danny's my . . ." Steph chuckled. "My what?"

"Groom?" Jessie exclaimed, and her neck jerked so violently toward him that he thought he heard it snap. "You're getting married?"

"Oh, honey," Steph said, cackling. "Are you joking? Me and Danny?"

Danny leaned toward her and smiled. "Steph is getting married. I'm her—"

"Guy of Honor," Steph completed. "That's what we're calling you."

Jessie exhaled noisily and leaned back into the chair. "Ohh."

"My groom," Steph repeated with a laugh. "Can you imagine?"

He couldn't. But it did give him a little shot of delight at the idea that Jessie had reacted that way.

Steph pulled up a picture on her phone and extended it toward Jessie. "This is my fiancé. Vince."

"Cute," she commented. "When's the ceremony?"

"Next month."

"So you two have known each other a long time?" she asked them.

"Since we were kids," Danny told her. "We were neighbors, went to the same school."

"Neighbors," she repeated. "You grew up in Newport?"

He snorted accidentally. "Pegged me for Long Beach, did ya?"

"Well . . . no . . . I . . ." She gulped. "I'm just surprised, that's all."

They took a walk around the club and stopped in for a look at the small room Steph had in mind. She was right about one thing; the views were pretty spectacular. On their way out to the parking lot, the two women chatted about the idea of a reception at Steph's folks' house versus making everyone drive over to the club while Danny set his sights on the view.

"We're taking out my dad's new boat this weekend," Steph said, tugging at his arm to get his attention. "You interested? I'd love for you to meet Vince."

"Yeah," he said, nodding. "Which day?"

"We're thinking Sunday."

"I'll give you a call."

"Jessie, can you make it? We'll make a day of it."

"Oh, thank you," she replied, and Danny's ears perked up. "But I've just opened a store in Santa Monica. I don't think I can get away on a weekend this soon into it."

"That's a shame. But what about the wedding? I'd love for you to come. I'd bet anything you haven't seen this guy in anything more formal than jeans or a wetsuit."

Jessie giggled. "I'm trying to picture it . . ."

"I'll send you an invitation and hope you can make it."

"Thank you so much."

"It was great to meet you," Steph said before pulling Danny into a hug and placing a firm peck on his cheek. "Thanks for coming, Danny. Any thoughts to share about the reception?"

"A few," he replied seriously. "There needs to be a lot of food. And a big cake."

"Thanks, genius."

"Oh. And get a good band. Live music, no spinners."

"About the venue, moron. Here or at my folks'?"

"This place is great. But I vote for Rob and Jean's house. Just a trot in from the beach instead of everyone driving over here."

"Good," she said, and she shot a smile Jessie's way. "I'll blame him when I break the news to the folks. My mother thinks the sun rises and sets in this one."

Jessie grinned, and Danny couldn't help wondering about it. She looked a little like she had a secret pressing on the confines of those sparkling eyes of hers, just dying to get out.

"I'll call you later," he told Steph as they separated, and he opened the passenger door of his Jeep for Jessie. "Hey, mind if I snap off the top?"

She gazed at him strangely. "Pardon me?"

"The Jeep. It's getting to be such a great day, I thought I could zip off the roof."

"Oh. Okay."

Jessie unexpectedly jumped out of the car again and took one side while he took the other. After the soft top was folded up and stowed, they climbed back in. Danny pulled a cloth band out of the box behind the driver's seat and handed it to her.

"It can get a little windy."

"Thanks. We'll be adorable with matching ponies."

She took the band and slipped it over three fingers. Raking her shiny hair back from her face, she smiled at him as she fastened the ponytail. On the second pass through the band, she let the ends of her hair remain tucked under it, producing a funny little mess of hair at the crown of her head.

*Ah, sheesh. Adorable.*

The desire to pull her close and kiss her nearly overwhelmed him, and Danny sucked the thought right back in and deposited it under other ones about traffic on the 405. Looking away from her as quickly as he could, he turned the key and backed out.

When the magnetic pull of having Jessie in the seat next to him tugged at him like a force of nature, he resisted by pushing a few buttons on the dash and cranking up a little James Taylor.

A few bars into "Shower the People," Jessie smiled at him. He caught the sunbeam out of the corner of his eye. "I love James Taylor!"

"Yeah?" He glanced over at her, but it equated to staring into the sun and he looked away.

"Is this his *Best of* CD?"

"Yeah."

"You know what song I like best of his?"

He meant to ask which one; instead, it just came out as a bit of a grunt.

"Carolina on My Mind," she said.

He liked that one too. He always changed the lyrics in his head to "*California* on my mind."

She chuckled. "I make up my own words though. *California* on my mind."

He grimaced and turned to look directly at her. "Seriously?"

*She's . . . beautiful.*

"Weird, right?" she said, misinterpreting his expression. "I always knew I wanted to get out of Slidell, and Southern California was just this pie-in-the-sky sort of Nirvana of glitz and movie stars, so I started dreaming about coming here long before it was even a real possibility. So I had *California on my mind*."

Danny sighed. "So how do you feel about it now? Cali still on your mind?"

"Well. My personal glitz is now otherwise engaged," she joked. "But I've had a good bit of it in my life since coming to LA. Not so pie-in-the-sky Nirvana any more, and if I could go back in time I might not marry the first handsome guy in a Mercedes who asked. But I do love it here."

He nodded. "It's a beautiful place, this California."

"Yes, it is," she said softly, and he glanced over to catch her staring off into the distance with a warm, dreamy haze in her eyes.

About thirty minutes into the drive back to Santa Monica, the Eagles harmonizing with the wind-blown hum and dusky remnants of sunset ahead of them, Jessie touched his arm softly. "You know what we should do, Danny?"

He raised one eyebrow at the question, keeping his focus on the freeway. "What's that?"

"Right where we exit, there's this amazing little hot dog stand."

Danny let out a chuckle. "Herbie's?"

"Yes!" she exclaimed. "Do you want to stop? My treat!"

"How do you know about Herbie's?"

She pouted at him for half a second and asked, "What? You think I didn't exist before I met Jack?"

"Exist, yes," he said on a laugh. "Stop at hot dog stands?" He glanced over and looked her up and down for effect. "No."

"Well, that's not the first time you've been wrong about me, I'm sure."

He shrugged. "Fair enough."

They placed an order for two chili dogs with jalapenos for him and a foot-long monster with chili and onions for Jessie, a couple of lemonades and a giant bag of fries to share between them. They quickly set out on their way with bulging bags of deliciously unhealthy junk food.

Jessie squealed when, instead of parking next to his house, Danny drove his Jeep past it, right out onto the sand. The California sun just barely peeked up over the ocean horizon, leaving muted streaks of pinks and blues in its wake, and Jessie yanked the cloth band out of her hair and let it fall around her shoulders.

"I haven't had one of these in years!" she declared, digging into one of the paper bags with the colorful HerbieDogs logo emblazoned on it. "Wow, you're really going to eat these peppers? They reek."

"Not like your onions," he teased, and she sniffed and turned up her nose as she handed him one of his dogs.

"Here," she said, passing his lemonade. When she picked up her own drink, she lifted it and touched his cup with hers. "To ocean breezes and HerbieDogs!"

"I'll drink lemonade to that."

A few beats later, he felt her gaze on him again. Strange how it burned into him like that. Turning to cast a glance at her, he asked, "What's up?"

"Danny . . . I . . . hope you won't think I'm . . . Well, I don't even know why I did this, really. But . . ."

He knew what was coming. Was she actually going to admit it?

"I Googled you."

His swagger dropped with a thud. He didn't know anything after all. "You what?"

"I Googled you. I saw the articles about your accident. And . . . your wife."

He balanced the lemonade cup in the spokes of the steering wheel and set the last bite of his dog on a napkin on his leg.

"I don't want to make you uncomfortable—"

"And yet."

"I just wanted to tell you how sorry I am about what happened. Really, so sorry."

He stopped grinding his teeth long enough to mutter, "Thanks."

"She was really lovely." When he pivoted toward her with a confused expression on his face, she clarified. "One of the articles had a photo."

He nodded and turned away from her again, gazing out at the water as if he cared about the view.

"It must have been horrible."

Did a guy really need to comment on being solely responsible for the death of someone he loved? "Yeah."

"Is that when you stopped drinking?"

Danny's gut burned as he looked down at the remnants of his food. He shook his head and groaned. "I don't drink anymore," he managed. "You know what else I don't do anymore? I don't talk about it."

"Okay. Sorry." After a minute of silence, she touched his arm and added, "I really just thought . . . Well, I won't bring it up again."

He shifted and looked at her for a long and frozen moment, weighing his words before he spoke. "I'd appreciate that."

"But you know, if you ever wanted to talk—"

"Thanks," he cut her off.

Throwing back the last of the dog, he wadded up the paper and tossed it into the open bag sitting against the gear shift between them. He pulled out his phone and checked it for a message from his buddy about Jessie's car, but there wasn't one.

Turning over the ignition, he said, "I'll drive you home."

"No," she objected, and she reached across him and flipped the key, shutting off the engine again. "I don't want to leave like this. I've had such a wonderful time with you, Danny. I haven't felt this lighthearted in I don't even know how long. Just because I was dumb enough to ruin it and bring up something like that . . . Don't let it change things, okay? I'm sorry. Really."

He sighed, yanked the band from his hair, and leaned back into the padded seat. He let the ocean breeze caress his face while his brain worked on zapping the bitter regret flooding his thoughts again. Rebecca's suntanned face had been the apparition tormenting him again lately.

Danny restarted the Jeep, reversed back toward the house, and parked. "You sit here a minute," he said. "I'll be right back."

"Okay," she replied as he climbed out and trekked toward the house.

Ten minutes later, Frank galloped across the sand toward the shore—casting one thoughtless bark over his shoulder at Jessie—as Danny dragged a wheeled cart behind him.

"What's that?" Jessie cried when she saw him, and she slipped out of the Jeep.

"C'mon," he said with a nod, and he headed toward the patio. "You feel like s'mores?"

"How fun!" She did a funny little hop toward him atop those heels that had to be four inches tall. When she finally gave up and stepped out of them, she hurried over to him and stood by eagerly. "What can I do?"

He tossed a towel at her. "Brush the sand off the chairs."

As she followed his instructions, she told him, "My friends and I used to have bonfires at the river in Slidell all through the year, but in all the time I've lived in California, I've never once had a bonfire at the beach."

"This isn't exactly a bonfire," he said with a chuckle. "Bonfires are illegal on most of the beaches in Southern California. Not all of them, but . . . Well, you lived right on the water, so you know."

"Are they illegal here?" she wondered aloud. "Jack wasn't exactly a beachy type of guy, so we never would have done anything fun like this anyway."

He thought how sad that seemed, particularly since she appeared to take to it like a duck to a stream. He stoked the small flame in the pit and opened a bag of marshmallows. "Come on over here," he said, poking one with a skewer and handing it to her.

A few short minutes later, he couldn't take his eyes off her as she giggled and squashed a gooey mess between two graham crackers and tried to stuff it into her mouth.

"Oooh! Hot!" she managed to exclaim over a full mouth.

"Yeah, fire," he joked dryly. "Hot."

She plopped down in the chair next to him and laughed. Lord help him, it sounded like music to his ears.

"You know what?" she piped up. "I forgot all about my car. Do you think it's ready?"

"I haven't heard from my friend, other than a text early today that he got it back to the shop. I'll call him tomorrow and, if it's ready, I can pick you up in the morning and we'll go get it before you head to the store if you want."

"That's sweet, but I'm having breakfast with Piper in the morning. If you tell me where your friend's garage is, I can have her drop me."

He nodded. "I'll update you in the morning when I know something."

"I hope it's something easy," she added. "And cheap."

"Yeah," he said as he took a bite of his s'more. "You can't be without a car in LA, can you?"

"Uh-uh," she answered.

"How else are you going to follow somebody to see what they're up to if you don't have a car?"

She froze, wide-eyed. "Huh?"

"Well, that's why you followed me and Riggs on Wednesday, right? To see what we were up to?"

The melted chocolate and marshmallow flopped right out from between the graham crackers in her hands and landed on one of her bare feet with a splat!

*My Jessie never did like surprises.*

*No, fact is from the time she was old enough to point her finger at somebody, she was directin' traffic. Liked the world orderly and purdy like them dresses and shiny shoes o' hers. Her mama used to say, "Wish my cupboards looked as purdy as my lil girl's closet."*

*"They could, Mama," she'd say. "You just gotta spend time on it ever' now 'n' then or the mess can git away with ya."*

*The thing about growin' up though is how things don't stay lined up and purdy like that. Sometimes it don't matter 'tall how much time you spent organizin' and sortin'. Sometimes a twister comes in 'n' makes a mess, lickety-split. If you ain't used to surprises, they can toss your world around somethin' fierce.*

*From then to now, I been prayin' that the good Lord helps my Jessie develop a tree that kin bend so she don't snap like a twig when a twister swoops in.*

# 17

Jessie's tongue seemed to swell up inside her mouth. Big enough to block things like words. And breathing.

Danny propped his elbows on his knees and leaned into them. "I am an investigator, Jessie. You think I won't notice an amateur following me like that?"

When Frank sauntered over to join them, he became suddenly distracted by the alluring fragrance of the mess she'd made on her foot and made a beeline straight for it.

"Frank," Danny reprimanded, and he shooed the dog away. "Go on."

The Great Dane obeyed by inching to the corner of the patio and flopping down, but certainly not willingly.

Jessie set the empty graham crackers in her hands on the wheeled cart between them and picked up a partial roll of paper towels. She tore off several and started cleaning up the mishmash of chocolate and marshmallow on her foot, her mind racing with discombobulated ramblings she hoped would come together into some sort of plausible explanation. Because the humiliating truth of it just about choked her.

"I shouldn't have," she managed. "I'm sorry."

"Why did you?"

Jessie cringed. She only wished she knew why.

"Gabi told me you and Aaron go somewhere every Wednesday night at the same time," she said, holding the messy wad of paper towels and s'mores debris in front of her with both hands.

Danny stood up and took the towels from her, depositing them in a plastic bag dangling from the side of the cart. He unfurled several more, saturated them with a sprinkle from a bottle of water, and crouched down in front of her.

"So instead of asking me about it when your curiosity got the best of you," he said as he dabbed at stickiness splayed over her cheek, "you decided to play Sam Spade."

"Not my finest hour," she admitted as he rubbed the damp towels over her chin.

"And when you saw where we were headed? What then?"

"What do you mean?" she asked him. "Mystery solved. On to the next one, I guess."

Danny narrowed his steely eyes and looked straight into her soul, fueling icy fingers to walk straight up her back and into the hair at the nape of her neck.

"So we've addressed my wife's death, my faith, and subsequent church attendance. Is there anything else you'd like to know?"

Even though she knew the question was rhetorical, her brain seemed to miss that fact as it scurried with the cacophony of questions she'd been harboring.

"If I thought you meant that and weren't just trying to trick me . . ."

"No trick," he said. He stood up and wiped his hands with the towels before depositing them in the bag with the others. "What would you like to know about me, Jessie? What are those burning questions I see simmering?"

She clucked out a bitter chuckle, staring at her knees as he sat down in his chair again. While the ocean sang a lullaby in the distance, the crackling fire provided the percussions to an otherwise uncomfortable silence.

Danny finally broke it. "Come on. Lay 'em on me, girl."

Jessie lifted her eyes and gazed at him for a moment. "Well," she began, chastising herself for it. "I know you said you didn't want to talk about the drinking anymore, but I'm just wondering . . ."

When she hesitated, Danny sighed. "Well, don't stop now. What are you wondering?"

"Did you quit . . . because of the accident?"

"Yes."

His candor astonished her. "Right after?"

"Yes. I haven't had a sip of alcohol since that night, and by the grace of God I'll never have one again."

Pressing her luck, she shifted toward him and looked him directly in the eye when she asked, "Do you go to AA meetings or something?"

"When necessary, I do."

"Is that when you found religion too?"

He returned her gaze for an instant that felt to Jessie as if the whole world had frozen over. Then he said, "I didn't find religion. I found God. Within a year of the accident."

"Isn't that the same thing? Religion and God?"

He surprised her by smiling. "You'd think so, wouldn't you?"

She chuckled and nodded. "Yes."

"I guess I used to think that, too. But religion is man-made. My relationship with Jesus Christ is intensely personal. It's changed me in ways another person might not be able to understand until they sell out to Him, too."

She let that sink in for a minute. "And that's why you got the thorn tattoo?"

He nodded and gazed out at the dark ocean at the end of the carpet of sand. "Yeah. Kind of a reminder of the faith that's changed me. To sort of say, 'This is permanent. It's not going away.' I can never take back what I did before I found my faith, but going forward . . . I'm accountable."

"You know, the Jewish faith looks at a tattoo like it's against their law. I don't think you could even be buried in a Jewish cemetery."

He snickered. "You don't say."

"Jesus was Jewish. How come you'd get a tattoo as a reminder of knowing him when it's against his religion?"

When he didn't answer right away, a swell of nervous acid sloshed in her stomach. Maybe she'd gone too far. Maybe—

"That's a big question," he told her. "But the short version answer is that Jesus came to finish the Jewish faith, and everything was changed after he came."

"So the thorns on your arm," she said, pointing at his bicep. "They represent the crown of thorns Jesus wore?"

Instead of answering, Danny turned toward her and smiled.

"What, you're surprised?" she joked. "I know who Jesus is."

He looked away, nodding slowly. Finally, he leaned forward again and—without looking back at her—he said, "Tell me."

"Tell you what?"

"Who Jesus is. To you, I mean. A great historical figure? Some deluded guy who meant well?"

"I . . . don't . . . know. I mean, I know what they say He did."

When Danny turned his gaze back on her, Jessie felt like he'd flipped a light on behind his eyes at the same time. "That's it," he said. "The difference between religion and faith. You and me, we're the difference."

"I don't understand."

"You know what they say He did. I know what He *absolutely* did all those years ago and what it means still, today."

A strange lump of emotion rose in her throat, and she found it oddly disconcerting that she couldn't be quite sure why.

"Are you ready to head home, Jessie?"

*Am I ever!*

"Yes."

Danny stood up. "Give me a minute to stow the cart and my dog, and I'll meet you at the Jeep. Don't forget to grab your shoes." He slapped his thigh, and Jessie jumped. "Frank! Come on, buddy."

---

Parked at a stoplight just five minutes from home, Danny's cell rang and the screen announced Jessie.

"Didn't I just drop you off?" he joked when he answered the call.

"Can you turn around and come back, please?"

"What's up?"

"There's someone here I think you need to speak to, Danny. Please. Can you please come back?"

He checked traffic in both directions before squealing into a U-turn. "On my way."

His pulse thumped with the fast beat of a Third Day song on the radio, and a hodgepodge of imaginings painted dark streaks of varied possibilities across his mind. He'd come to know Jessie well enough to recognize the subtle drop in the octave of her voice when she became scared or worried, and there had been a pretty significant lower register on that last call. He couldn't help imagining a scenario where he arrived to find Jack Stanton himself standing in Jessie's living room.

Instead, when Jessie let him in—greeting him with wide eyes filled with a haze of standing tears—he found a familiar woman sitting on the couch, sipping tea like an old friend.

*Raven hair, pudgy nose, probably in her forties . . .*

"Danny," Jessie said, "I think you've met Claudia Stern?" The blank look on his face spurred her to continue. "Claudia was Jack's assistant."

"Of course," he said, nodding. "I'm sorry. How are you, Ms. Stern?"

"I'm well, thank you."

He looked to Jessie and asked, "Catch me up?"

She sat down in the chair where a half-empty cup sat on the table in front of her. When she motioned to him to sit down on the other side of the couch from Claudia, he leaned on the arm instead.

"Claudia saw the piece about the store on the news."

"I'd been thinking about you so much already, Jessie," the woman said. "And when I saw the news footage, it gave me a lead on how to contact you. I meant to come around to the store tomorrow, but I did a little research and found this address listed on your fictitious business name filing. And, well, I just couldn't wait until tomorrow."

"Will you tell Danny why you were so inclined to get in touch with me?" She looked at Danny and blinked, leaving behind a gloss of emotion in her eyes.

"After you and I met when Mr. Stanton took off, and you told me Jessie was as much in the dark as I was, I got to thinking about how horrible it must have been for her. He left her high and dry as well, and it certainly had to be much worse for her than for me."

Jessie's eyes brimmed with meaningful and discernible concern as they locked with Danny's.

When Claudia didn't expound, Jessie sighed and took over. "Claudia felt especially bad because of the terrible news I surely received."

"Terrible news?"

"Claudia learned that Jack has another wife."

Danny nodded. "Patty."

"Right. Except Claudia believes that Jack and Patty are *still married.*"

Danny dropped from the arm of the sofa to the seat with a thump. "Can you tell me why you believe that?"

"Because Mr. Stanton told me so."

*Like pulling a bad tooth out of the mouth of a skittish cat.*

"When did he tell you this?"

"When he called me last week." She maneuvered her dark hair away from her face and sighed. "Well, wait. It's not what he said exactly. Let me clarify."

"Please. Jack Stanton called you."

"Yes."

"And?"

"And he asked me to go to the safety deposit box."

Danny sighed in frustration. "The safety deposit box?"

"Yes. For business purposes, he'd listed it in both our names some years ago. In case something happened to him, he told me. I had a key, but I never used it until last week. Anyway, he said there was an envelope there for me, which he wanted me to take, and then destroy the rest of the contents."

"So you did as he asked you."

"Yes. Well, no. I mean, I went there, and I emptied out the contents, and I found an envelope with my name on it."

"What was inside?"

She leaned forward as if telling him a secret. "A considerable amount of money." She cleared her throat before continuing. "And a letter asking for my forgiveness."

"And the rest of the contents?" Danny inquired, trying to rein in the impatience tapping at his throat.

"I wouldn't normally betray a direct request from Mr. Stanton, I hope you understand. But something just felt off about it. So I went through the documents to see what was there before destroying them. That's when I saw it."

Jessie stood up and walked into the kitchen without a word. Danny looked after her as she stood there facing the counter, motionless, her arms folded in an X across her chest.

"What else was in the box, Ms. Stern?"

She reached down and pulled out a file folder tucked between the couch and the cushion. Handing it to him, she whispered, "I'm afraid I've thrown Jessie for a loop. Is she all right?"

He didn't answer. Instead, he opened the folder marked Personal and reviewed the documents inside.

The letter of apology to Claudia was on top.

*. . . Things have gotten out of hand, and I find myself with no other alternatives . . . While I feel confident that you realize I am not the man they may try to make me into soon . . . After all our years together, I hope you can forgive me for leaving without a word . . .*

He turned it over to examine the remaining documents.

A marriage license between John Fitzgerald Stanton and Patricia Lauren Walters.

A petition for divorce for the same, citing irreconcilable differences.

Jack and Jessie's marriage license.

A letter drafted on the letterhead of Spence & Spence, Attorneys at Law.

*. . . As we discussed on the phone yesterday, I've conducted a full records search and I cannot find any indication that your dissolution of marriage to Patricia Lauren Walters has indeed been finalized. In consideration of the timeline of your second marriage next week, I am not sure a full investigation and resolution can be accomplished beforehand. I suggest postponing the nuptials until we can contact Ms. Walters-Stanton and legally resolve this issue.*

*Please advise the following . . .*

Danny flipped over to the next page in the file; a sheet of pale pink linen stationery with an ornate *P* engraved at the top. The letter, written in a wide, round—clearly female—hand, appeared to be a love letter from Patty to Jack dated a full five years after his marriage to Jessie.

*. . . I've loved you always and I love you still . . . I'll never give you a divorce, Jack, so please don't ask again . . . I feel sure we can work things out between us . . .*

"He knew before our wedding that he was still married to Patty," Jessie said, and his eyes darted up to find her standing across from him, her arms still folded and the tears once standing in her eyes streaming down her cheeks. Her shiny dark hair—glistening with thin strands of gold and caramel—fell toward her heart-shaped face, making her look weary and frail. "Why? Why did he marry me anyway?"

"He probably thought he could get the divorce in time, and—"

Her sobs sliced his words—and heart—in two, and she dropped to the chair and buried her face in her hands. Claudia went to her before Danny had the chance, and she embraced Jessie, rocking her as she spoke to her softly. "I know, honey. I know. It's going to be all right. You don't need him, you never did. You're going to be fine."

Danny pulled out his cell phone and dialed. "I'm calling Piper to come over and stay with you tonight."

"No, Danny. She's—"

"It wasn't a question," he said as Piper answered on her end. "Piper. Danny Callahan. Can you break away and come over to Jessie's? We've had some news and I think she could use a friend."

"Of course. I can be there within the hour."

"Better plan on staying the night if you can."

"Oh, dear. Okay, I'll see you soon."

Danny walked Claudia Stern to her car and thanked her for bringing the information to light. He didn't mean it entirely, of course, but he also knew that the infliction of pain was necessary for Jessie.

"Truth is power," Rebecca used to say. "But before the power sometimes comes the pain."

Spot on. But then she usually was.

"Do you suppose I'm doing anything wrong in keeping the money?" Claudia asked him through the open window of her sedan.

Danny shrugged. "He's being investigated for fraudulent activities involving a great deal of money," he said. "I think your best bet is to contact a lawyer."

"I'll do that. Thank you."

He stood there watching her drive away, another of the women left confused and brimming with questions in the wake of Jack Stanton. When her car had disappeared from sight, he remained planted to the concrete drive, his arms folded as he looked up into the dark, cloudy night sky.

*Justice comes from you, Lord. I know that. But if you could see your way clear to give me an opening for just one good punch at the guy . . .*

Danny snickered. What kind of prayer was that?

*Help her, Lord. Only you know what that means or what it will look like, but help her. I don't know how much more she can take.*

He hadn't seen Piper's car until she parked on the street next to the driveway and slammed the door behind her. The heels of her shoes clomped on the pavement as she jogged toward him.

"Danny. What's happened?"

The worry for her friend paled her peaches-and-cream complexion and creased her forehead beneath spikey strawberry-blonde bangs that she'd brushed aside. Her greenish eyes glistened with anxious questions.

"Jack's assistant paid her a visit," he said.

"Claudia?"

"Yeah." Danny shook his head and sighed. "Long story shortened, it seems Jack quite possibly wasn't divorced from his first wife when he married Jessie."

"What! That's not possible."

"But it appears to be the case."

"So in addition to being the biggest creep on the face of the earth—a liar and a thief and a con artist—Jack is also a bigamist?"

"Looks that way."

"Where is she? Inside?"

"Yes."

"Alone?"

"For the moment."

"Well, come on," she exclaimed. "Let's get in there."

"You go ahead. I'm heading out."

"Why?" Piper sang. "She needs you."

"She needs *you*," he softly corrected her. "Go on. I'll call her in the morning."

---

"You had cookies in the freezer!" Piper said, looking so proud of herself for finding them. "Turns out they're oatmeal raisin. I think. Anyway, I zapped them in the microwave, and they're not half bad. Here, have a cookie and drink your tea."

Jessie couldn't help herself and she laughed. In troubling times, Piper always thought a sweet snack and a cup of hot tea held the answer to every conundrum, provided a balm for every wound. She was a lot like Jessie's mother in that way. While Grampy fought every battle with a prayer and a good word, his daughter wielded cupcake swords and shields made of comfort food.

Piper sat down next to her on the couch and brushed Jessie's hand with hers. "Do you want to talk about it?"

Jessie shook her head and nibbled on a warm cookie instead.

After a minute or two, Piper sighed noisily. "We could look at the upside."

Turning toward her friend with a frown, Jessie asked, "There's an upside?"

"Yeah. You won't have to go through a messy divorce." The hopeful lilt in her voice fell flat on Jessie. "Oh, and he'll probably go to jail for a really long time once they catch him. So you won't have to see him ever again."

She didn't admit it out loud, but there may have been some credence to that. It was something at least.

"But he's in Bali," she recalled aloud. "Sipping a mai-tai on the beach with Patty, laughing about how they got away with all of it and escaped to a country with no extradition. They're in the clear, Piper."

"Oh, sweetie. These things have a way of working themselves out. It might only *look like* he's gotten away with something. Maybe he can run to Bali, but I don't think he can hide there forever."

Jessie took a sip from the cup of tea and sighed. Reality was like an overfilled bouncing ball—plunking down on her hard, then propelling upward away from her, only to spring back and pack a harder punch. As the force of it pressed down on her again, knocking the wind clear out of any degree of peace she might have thought she could get her hands on, Jessie's heart palpitated. Then came the swell of anger, raging over her like a tsunami wave.

"He doesn't even like the beach. I mean, we lived fifty yards from the sand and I could never get him out there. Now he's in

Bali? . . . With *Patty?* Patty drove him crazy, Piper! And you know what this means, don't you?" Jessie didn't give her a chance to reply. "If we were never married, it means I'm not entitled to anything in a divorce. Because unmarried people *don't get a divorce.* I'm not going to recoup anything he took. Look around you! The only assets I have are the ones you see here. I'm not going to get my life back, Piper. It's gone. He took it! And it's gone forever."

"You also have the store," Piper pointed out, but the menacing scowl Jessie shot at her caused her to retreat into the corner of the sofa momentarily.

No one wanted to help more than Piper did, Jessie knew that. *Shame on me.* Regret spread over her until her skin tingled. "Sorry," she said, shaking her head. "I'm sorry."

Piper sighed and reached out for Jessie's hand. "Sweetie, you're building something there. Something out of literally nothing. You can be proud of that."

Jessie fell back into the sofa cushions with a groan. She hadn't really realized how she'd pinned her hopes on the idea that, even if Jack wanted to divorce her, she might get some sort of monetary leg up out of it.

"Using a pin on your hopes to attach 'em to somethin' else," Grampy used to say, "can be a pretty dangerous thing 'cause you stand a chance of pokin' a hole right in 'em."

Jessie clamped her eyes shut, staring into the black behind them as her hope-filled balloon popped and slowly deflated, zigzagging away from her, leaving nothing behind but a noisy raspberry that represented her life.

---

*I could always pretty much read my Jessie like a book. When she was workin' her way up to tryin' to win me over to her way o' thinkin', she dropped her eyes and glared at 'er feet fer awhile. But when she found herself holdin' on to the last couple inches o' rope, she looked to me with a certain sparkle in them eyes, askin' me to make a knot in it for her.*

*I knew when she came home from her first semester o' university—right in the middla the week, and with her poster of that boy Justin Timberland along with her—somethin' was sure up.*

*"Grampy, I don't like college at all," she finally says to me over top o' the eggs on her plate. "I've tried to like it, I really have, but I just can't do it. I don't fit."*

*"And you got an inklin' where you might fit better? You plannin' to join one of those boy bands like InStyle?"*

*Jessie smacked my arm, playful-like. "In-Sync," she pronounced real slow. "I've just been thinking that the money we got from Mama and Daddy's house . . . instead of using it for tuition when I don't even know if I want to be there any more . . . it might be better used in helping me to make a new start. I know a girl from my modelin' class who's goin' to Hollywood. Says I can come along."*

*I never had nothin' against new starts, mind you. I think they're a good thing when a soul can get one. But they're never easy. They don't roll along in front of you like a bolt o' carpet bein' unfurled. There's a lotta bumps in the road to a new start. Jessie never did understand that.*

# 18

It's a pretty solid car, your Taurus. Your trouble was just as Danny suspected. We replaced the fuel filter, and checked the injector. It's fine. It's not keeping the engine from firing, but the connector on top of the injector was a little worn so we replaced it."

Jessie tried to lift the corners of her mouth into a polite smile, but she couldn't quite manage it as she asked the one question that had been plaguing her. "How much do I owe you?"

"Just see Joey at the front counter for your keys."

Jessie flashed a glance at Piper before turning back to the good-looking guy in greasy coveralls. "Really, I'm willing to pay you for the repair. And for the tow you provided."

"Forget about it. It's taken care of."

"I don't understand."

He sighed and smiled strangely. Finally, he said, "Look, Danny took care of it. You can take it up with him."

She bit down on the corner of her bottom lip. "I'll do that. Thank you."

After she picked up her car keys, she and Piper walked out to the parking lot together.

"Thanks for breakfast," she said. "And for the ride over. And for staying last night."

Piper smiled at her and pulled her into an embrace. "No problem. Call me later?"

She nodded. "I will."

Instead of taking the left toward the store when she reached it, Jessie turned right and headed straight out to Danny's place at the beach. She pulled into the drive and saw his Jeep parked there, and her stomach did a little flip. When she got out of the car, she removed her sunglasses and used them to pull back her hair by propping them on top of her head. She spotted Danny and his cow-dog immediately out on the sand.

Just as she started to head toward him, she stopped long enough to peer down at her Coach caged sandals with four-inch stilettos wrapped in python-printed leather. After pushing down the exposed zipper at the back of each shoe, she stepped out of them, carrying them along rather than trying to traipse through the sand.

Danny's wet hair fell straight and long. He wore a dark blue wetsuit, unzipped and removed to the waist to reveal his muscular, suntanned torso. He faced the water, cross-legged on top of a surf board, the dog at his side mirroring his perfect, erect posture. Something about the way they sat there—silent and motionless—caused Jessie to reconsider the interruption. As she moved around Danny, she saw that he wore black tinted sunglasses that gave no indication of whether his eyes were open or shut.

Just as she parted her lips to speak his name, he smiled. "Hi, Jessie."

At the sound of his voice, Frank popped up to all four of his massive paws and panted at her, his large pink tongue dangling over the side of his mouth. When the dog moved next to her, Jessie rubbed one of his smooth, pointy ears.

"He's so soft."

"Don't tell him that. It makes him feel less manly."

She giggled. "I don't want to bother you, but I just picked up my car from your friend's garage."

"Oh, good. It's running well?"

"Fine. I just . . . He told me you paid the bill."

"Yeah, I covered it. No worries."

"Danny, I can't have you doing things like that. I want you to—"

"This again?"

"I want you to add the cost to my bill for the work you've done."

"Are you firing me?" The corner of his mouth twitched.

"Well, I don't suppose there's really any more need to sort things out, do you?" she asked him. "He's not my husband. I don't need a divorce and I won't be entitled to any alimony or anything. Why do I need to find him?"

"Or why would you want to?" he said with a chuckle. "But let's find out if you're actually married to him or not, shall we? Just a little more digging."

She chuckled, absently running her hand through Frank's fur where her fingers fell right to the height of his back.

"Okay. Well. I guess that's a good idea."

Jessie took a couple of steps to leave, then stopped and just stood there, feeling a little like a dope.

"Was there something else?"

"Well." She swallowed around the lump in her throat and inhaled sharply. "The thing is . . ."

"Yes?" he prodded, standing up and grabbing his board and walking away from her.

She tried to keep up alongside him toward the house, screwing up her courage as they went. But . . . Did she even want to know? Maybe it was best to let sleeping secrets lie.

He stopped and turned toward her with a grin. "What is it, Jessie?"

"Well. Okay." One more deep breath. "You're the one who gave me the car, aren't you?"

Danny's smile didn't fade in the least as he adjusted his sunglasses and continued toward the house. "What makes you ask that?"

"I've been thinking a lot about it," she said. "You're always doing things for me. You wouldn't let me pay you for the work you did at the store. You covered my car repairs—"

"And that makes me a serial gift-giver, so I must be the one who bought you the car. I must be very rich. Do go on. This is entertaining."

"Well . . . You were raised in Newport Beach, which probably means your family has money."

"Does it?"

"Well, you were able to get into Balboa Yacht Club when we went to meet Stephanie. And—"

"What's your point, Jessie?" he asked as he stowed his surfboard on the mounted rack.

"I think you're the one who bought me the car. And I want you to confirm it."

"If I'm so rich . . . ," he said as he stalked over to the outdoor shower. He paused to turn on the water and grab the handheld attachment. Jessie found herself mesmerized by the muscles bulging on his arms, chest, and broad shoulders.

Had he finished his statement? His muscular shoulders had distracted her.

"If I'm so rich," he began again, and Jessie jerked her eyes away from him, "why did I get you a Ford? You'd think I'd be nice enough to just pick up the lease on your Jaguar."

"BMW," she corrected him.

"Right. Since it's only money."

Frank sauntered into the line of fire as if he'd been told to do so, and Danny rinsed his coat with the water, spraying away a stream of sand.

"Maybe you're not BMW rich, but you could easily be used-Ford well-to-do," she suggested, and he grunted out a chuckle and shook his head.

"Because if my family has money, that automatically means I do."

Danny shut off the water valve and replaced the showerhead before grabbing a large dry towel hanging on a hook a few feet away. The morning sun lit up the sprays of water that he shook from his hair and that Frank simultaneously shuddered from his black and white coat. As Danny pulled the towel over his head like a hood and massaged the residual moisture away, Jessie found herself gawking at him again, zeroing in on the way his bicep bulged around the crown of thorns.

"Well, if you're not going to answer me," she said, shaking her attention away from him, "I have to get to the store." She took a couple of steps, then stomped her foot as she turned back toward him. "Oh, and I'll be driving there in the car you gave me, by the way."

"You don't say."

"Have a nice day, Frank," she quipped as she stalked away.

Jessie tossed her shoes and bag to the passenger seat, and she drove over to the store in bare feet. She was still in the parking lot, leaning on the hood of her car as she tried to zip up the back of her shoes, when a raspy woman's voice called out to her.

"Jessie Stanton!"

She stepped down on her shoe and raised her hand to shield the sun from her eyes. The dark-haired, fair-skinned woman waving at her seemed very familiar.

"It's Courtney Alexis," she exclaimed as she closed the distance between them. "We met at the store opening?"

*The stylist/fashion blogger. Amber introduced us.*

"Courtney," she said as the petite girl reached out to give her a hug—instead of the air kiss she expected. "Good to see you again."

"You too. Listen, I'm styling one of my clients for the Teen Choice Awards, and I was thinking about a couple of pieces I saw here."

"Really. Well, come on in and let's see what we can find."

As they headed through the door, Courtney said, "Are those Cavalli embellished jeans I saw at the opening available?"

"Let's have Amber check."

"Oh my gosh, I love those shoes!" she squealed, and Jessie realized she'd honed in on her sandals. "Are those Coach?"

"They are."

"The Josey heels, right? They're so chill. How are they on the feet?"

The moment Amber spotted her, she blurted, "Courtney! You came back!"

Jessie chuckled. "And so did I."

"Oh, sorry, Boss. I'm happy to see you, too." Completely unconvincing. "Courtney, I loved your blog this morning." She turned to Jessie and explained, "She wrote about the biker chic trend and how it weaves in and out of style every so many years."

"Speaking of which," Courtney said, then she stopped herself. "I'm sorry. Thank you, Amber. I appreciate that." Shaking her head, she regrouped. "I remember seeing a lambskin Tory Burch jacket when I was here before. Maybe that would work with the Cavalli jeans for my client."

Both pieces had come directly from Amber's closet. No wonder she darted out from behind the counter. "I'll get them both for you!"

"What size are they?" she asked Jessie, but Amber trotted back with both pieces in time to answer.

After Courtney inspected them as if panning for gold nuggets, she asked, "Would you consider pulling them for my client? In return, I'd like to bring my workshop girls for a private styling session next weekend. There are fourteen of them enrolled, and I thought we could come by around seven on Friday. I know you close at eight, but if you could keep the store open for them a little longer, we can do a private session and try to get you some business out of it at the same time."

"That's a great opportunity for us," Amber cut in with an enthusiastic nod.

"I agree," Jessie said. "Amber, why don't you bag the jeans and the jacket. What about shoes? Do you know her size?"

"Eight and a half."

"Why don't you go ahead and browse. I think we might have a couple of options."

"I'll show you," Amber volunteered, and she led Courtney over toward the shoes.

"Amber, tell me a little more about your writing. Are you a fashion writer?"

"Primarily, as it turns out. Last month, I had an article in *Today's Style Magazine*."

"I write for them now and again, too."

"Oh, I know!" Amber gushed. "I have the issue here with me if you'd like to see it. Have a look at the shoes, and I'll go grab it."

Amber floated back toward the office while Jessie's mind reeled. Fourteen women scrounging up three figures for a weekend workshop on affordable style would surely appreciate what Adornments had to offer. She swallowed the excitement threatening to come out of her throat in an unceremonious screech of relief. Maybe teaming up with Courtney Alexis would help her break even for the month. Or at least closer to it than she was without Courtney's style recruits. And the idea of reaching out to her blog subscribers with word about her store; well, that could only add to the benefit of their connection.

Courtney chose two possibilities from the selection of shoes and, while Amber put together the necessary paperwork, Courtney returned to the front.

"Are you free for a little lunch?" she asked Jessie.

Her morning had disappeared, and she'd only just arrived, but . . . "Sure."

Jessie's budget passed before her eyes when Courtney suggested lunch at The Ivy at the Shore. She and Piper used to lunch at their sister restaurant—The Ivy on Robertson Boulevard—on a regular basis. Oh, how she loved their grilled vegetable salad with mesquite lime chicken; just thinking back on it caused her mouth to water. But a thirty-dollar lunch-sized salad wasn't in the budget these days. She hoped all the way over to Ocean Avenue that a side green salad and a glass of water wouldn't break the bank.

"They have the most amazing crab salad here," Courtney said as they waited for their table, and Jessie winced. She never had learned to eat crab without a guilty conscience. "They make their own Thousand Island dressing. Have you ever tried it?"

"I'm not big on crab."

"Well, hopefully you'll find something appetizing. I want to talk some business, and this is my treat."

*Her treat. Goodie!*

A broad smile wove its way upward, and Jessie muttered, "I'm sure I'll find something." She could taste that lime chicken before they even sat down.

Once the menu reached her hands, Jessie's eyes went instinctively to the SALADS heading.

*Grilled zucchini, asparagus, corn, avocado, tomatoes, and scallions on a bed of baby lettuce leaves . . . topped with mesquite grilled lime chicken.*

"I'm in heaven," she said.

"Oh, good. You've found something?"

"Mmm." She nodded. "The grilled vegetable salad looks really good."

Once they'd ordered, Jessie leaned back in the cushioned rattan chair and sighed. Other than the occasional meal at Antonio's amazing restaurant, she didn't imagine she'd be dining on cuisine like this too often in the future. And even though the casual décor of this location was no match for the more elegant, non-beachy atmosphere in the Beverly Hills restaurant, the other one didn't have that exquisite ocean view that happened to include—on this day anyway—Gerard Butler at a table by the window and Reese Witherspoon lunching with girlfriends near the bar.

"Have you given any more thought to the idea of becoming a guest blogger?"

She almost hadn't heard her. "Oh. Well, a little."

"And?"

"And I'm intrigued. Why don't you give me a little more of an idea about the expectations."

"I prepared some guidelines for you," she said, sliding a linen paper out of her case. "Each blog post is a maximum of 1,000 words, written on the fashion-related topic of your choice. I'll need a short bio—no more than 150 words—and the URL to your Adornments website."

Jessie realized the palms of her hands had begun to perspire.

"I can email this information to you, of course, along with examples of some past guest blogs that I've published. I have a readership of about 750,000 and—"

"Seven hundred—?"

"I know. We hovered at a couple hundred thousand subscribers for years. It's probably tripled over the last eighteen months, for some reason."

Jessie absently traced the rim of her water glass with the tip of her finger. "That's quite an audience. I'm encouraged by the fact that you had a growth spurt like that. I can only hope Adornments will have a similar one."

"I hope to be part of making that happen for you." Courtney seemed so sincere about that, and Jessie felt like her heart had been squeezed slightly.

"Any idea how much of your readership is located in Southern California?"

"Around 100,000, as far as I can tell."

She lifted one eyebrow and smiled at her. "Courtney, you're giving me a great opportunity here."

"I can't really explain it, Jessie," she said, and she reached across the table and touched Jessie's hand softly. "I just have a feeling about you."

"Does it feel anything like indigestion? Other people have remarked about that."

She chuckled and raked her black hair with the fingers of one hand. The way it feathered back into place made Jessie think of a shampoo commercial.

"Can I confide in you about something, Jessie?"

"Absolutely."

"I have the opportunity to adopt a little girl who came over from Moldova. I've wanted children my whole life, and this feels like one of those divine appointments, if you know what I mean."

She didn't entirely . . . but—as usual when someone mentioned children—Bella drummed across her mind like an old wagon on a bumpy road, leaving tiny, fragmented dregs of envy behind. "Courtney, how wonderful for you."

"There's a lot to consider about becoming a single parent at this juncture. I mean, I certainly never intended to do anything like this without a husband, that's for sure. But this precious little eight-month-old needs a home, and I have one to offer. Anyway, I was praying about what to do"—*Again with the religion?*—"and that was the very afternoon I stopped in to check out your store and met you and Amber. I just can't shake the idea that, if things work out between us, maybe between you and Amber and one other person I have in mind, I could keep the blog going without having to spend every waking moment consumed with it. I'd like to spend at least a year with my daughter. Then after the baby and I get used to each other—assuming it works out for all of us—maybe having other people involved will afford me the time to take on more styling clients."

Courtney stopped talking and shook her head. "Am I overwhelming you? I'm so sorry. Shall we talk compensation?"

Jessie gulped. *Wait. She's going to pay me, too?*

Jessie and Amber spent the rest of the afternoon hashing and rehashing Jessie's lunch with Courtney Alexis, expounding upon what might come of such a great—and completely unexpected—connection. For Amber, the chance of growing in her writing aspirations seemed like a blessing dropped right out of the sky and into her lap. For Jessie, it brought a bit of a different ingredient.

*Nice to see ya, hope. It's been a while.*

"It's been such a great day!" Amber sang. "Can you believe everything that's happening?"

"I can't wait to tell"—she'd almost said, "Danny." Recovering, she said—"Piper!"

"And she's going to *pay us for this?*" Amber cried the instant she returned with two muffins and a stack of paper napkins. "Pay us."

"That's what she said."

Jessie laid out the information sheet Courtney had given her on the glass case. "I made notes about the money on the back of the info sheet. Have a look and watch for customers? I want to go call Piper."

But the first number she dialed was Danny's.

"So it's like pennies from heaven," Riggs told him. "The first chick who's been able to reach you in years, and now she's not married. She's attracted. You're attracted. You gotta brush away the sand and see what's there."

"It's not that uncomplicated, Riggs."

He paused to consider a better way of telling his friend what a simpleton he was when his cell phone buzzed a perfectly timed interruption. From Danny's expression, his *simple-minded friend* quickly deduced, "It's her, right?"

"It's her," he confirmed, staring at the screen.

"Answer it, you moron."

Danny inhaled sharply and pressed the button. "Hey, Jessie. What's up?"

Completely oblivious to the conflict he'd been battling for the last two hours, Jessie hit the ground of their conversation running. She bounced from a blogger she met to a lunch she had to a job offer she'd received that included Amber.

"And the pay isn't bad, Danny. I mean, I'm not much of a writer, but if there's anything I know about, it's fashion, right? And she has about a hundred thousand subscribers to her blog right here in the LA area who will read my posts and maybe want to know more about the store, and—"

When a fraction of a pause allowed it, he interrupted. "Can I ask a question?"

"Of course."

"When was the last time you took a breath?"

Complete silence . . . followed by a stream of giggles that reminded him of musical tin cans attached to the back of a moving car.

"I know, right? I'm just overwhelmed with this feeling of . . . I don't know what."

"Hope?"

She sighed softly before replying, "Exactly."

"It's a good thing, hope."

"A very good thing."

"I'm happy for you, Jessie."

"Thank you, Danny. That means . . . Thank you." She breathed in so deeply that he almost felt the vacuum of it through the phone. "Have you been able to find anything else out about whether I'm a married woman?"

"I spent most of the morning digging into that very thing, in fact. I can find no record of a divorce dissolution between Jack and Patty in any California county south of Sacramento."

"I guess that means I'm . . . *single*."

"I believe that's what it means. I've got one more statewide search I can do this afternoon, but I have a meeting across town first."

Jessie sighed. He had the feeling her previous euphoria didn't mix well with harsh reality.

"We'll sort this out," he vowed, and she snickered.

"Oh. I know."

"Don't let it color your enthusiasm about everything else. Do you know how many women in your predicament have nothing at all to fall back on? But you were able to take a ridiculous situation and spin it into something, Jessie. That's no small feat."

"Thank you, Danny. Well, I won't keep you. I just . . . The minute I got good news, the first person I wanted to tell . . . was you."

Danny closed his eyes and bit his tongue. No way could he tell her what that meant to him, how much he wanted to have that role in her life. Not until he untangled all the knots. Not until he knew for certain that she was unattached. And not until he sorted out the faith issue. Getting involved with someone who didn't share his faith seemed like a black cloud of trouble looming up ahead. Too many things to think about so late in the day.

"Oh! I forgot. Your friend Stephanie called the store while I was gone and left a message inviting me to go sailing with you guys on Sunday."

A whoosh of acid pushed through his gut. "Did she?"

"I wanted to find out what you thought about that. I mean, all things considered."

"I remember you telling her you can't get away on a weekend so soon after the store opened."

"I did. But she called and invited me again, and I thought maybe it would be fun. But I wanted to talk to you about it first. See what you think."

Did he dare admit how much—despite everything—he wanted her to come?

"I thought some fresh air and sunshine would kind of refuel me," she said. "Clear my head and think about things. And besides, I really liked Stephanie."

"Yeah, she goes by Steph."

"Oh. Steph."

Danny watched Riggs as he pulled half a dozen items from his refrigerator. "Hey!" he called out to him, covering the mike on the phone. "Albertsons is up the street if you need to shop for groceries."

"I'll make some for you, too."

"Danny?" Jessie said with a grin in her voice. "Would you rather I don't go Sunday?"

He sighed. "No, no. It's fine. If you're up for it, I can pick you up. Say, around noon?"

"That's great, Danny. Come to the store."

"Will do."

"Thank you. I'll call Steph back and tell her, and I'll see you then."

The second he disconnected the call, Riggs cast him an amused glance. "I'm makin' us a couple of vegetable omelets. You want cheddar or mozzarella on yours?"

"I'd probably want cheddar," he said as he got up from the chair and grabbed his keys. "If I was going to be around to eat it, that is."

"What, you're out?"

"I have a meeting."

"Oh. Well, you're going to miss the greatest omelet known to mankind then."

Danny shook his head and turned toward the door. "You better do those dishes before I get back," he called back.

"Yeah, yeah, yeah. I'll do the dishes, dear. Have a nice day."

Frank followed him to the door, and Danny patted the dog firmly on the back. "You're staying. Go lay down." Calling out to Riggs, he added, "Give Frank some of those eggs."

Frank seemingly understood, because he hustled back to the kitchen.

"That's right," Riggs growled. "Who's your daddy, huh? I'll hook you up with some eggs, won't I, Frankenstein?"

"No onions."

"Are you still here?"

During the drive over to Beverly Hills, Danny's head swirled with questions about how best to open the conversation ahead of him. He hadn't yet landed on the answer when he parked across the street from Tuscan Son and jogged over to the entrance.

A dark-haired girl greeted him at the door. "I'm sorry, sir. We're closed from three until five to prep for the dinner crowd."

"I'm not here to eat," he replied. "I have an appointment with Antonio Brunetti."

"Oh, of course. Follow me."

Antonio's spacious office screamed Tuscany, from the rustic furnishings and stone floor to the carved crown molding and textured walls—painted a deep shade of gold and landscaped with framed photographs of his winery, his family, and happy shots of his stunning wife.

"Mr. Brunetti will be right with you. Make yourself comfortable."

A suit jacket folded over the arm of the dark green leather couch with antique brass nail heads told Danny that Antonio wouldn't be gone long. He wandered over to the credenza behind the desk and checked out several pieces of colorful Italian pottery displayed around the centerpiece: a large ornate frame holding an exquisite photograph of Piper wearing a colorful scarf loosely over her head, and standing in what looked to be an olive garden. The sky behind her was streaked with vibrant colors that seemed to match the scenery.

"She is quite beautiful, my wife, yes?"

Danny nodded before he turned around. "That's a compelling photograph."

"I took it the day she visited my family's vineyard for the first time," Antonio told him through his thick Italian accent, and he walked over to the credenza and picked up the frame. "I knew that day everything had changed. I just didn't realize how much." After replacing the picture, he sat down behind the desk. "Tell me what can I do for you today, Daniel."

He walked around one of the weathered, leather-upholstered chairs and sat down.

"Well, Antonio, I'm hoping you can help me make a decision on the best way to handle something."

"Please. Let me help."

"Jessie asked me to do a little research for her, and now that I have the information I'm not sure what to do with it."

Antonio shifted in his chair. "Oh? And I can assist in making your decision?"

"Sure can," he replied. "So do you want to tell her, or shall I?"

*Never did take to Jack Stanton when Jessie brought 'im home. Tried. Just couldn't. Somethin' about him just weren't right. He didn't look at my girl like a woman worth treasurin'. Instead, I got the feelin' he got a blue ribbon fer her at the county fair.*

*"She's so beautiful I couldn't take my eyes off her," he says to me about the first time he spotted Jessie in the store.*

*"Jessie's a beauty all right. But her beauty ain't nothin' in the whole picture of how she is," I told 'im. "Hope you can appreciate that." And he looked at me like I just fell off the turnip truck and dented his fender for the trouble.*

*When Jessie called and told me the whole story of what he done, cryin' like she did, well, I just listened, didn't say much. After that phone call though, this old man hit his creaky bad knees and talked it over with the good Lord himself. Asked fer some angels sent her way to keep her from divin' into the wrong direction like she sometimes does. Asked fer helping hands from all directions to help her get back on her feet. Asked fer some good sense for that girl and a godly man the next time around if she wantsta storm the gates of marriage agin. A man who'll give her some babies, with a lick o' sense, who'll look at her like she deserves insteada like a prize pig from the fair.*

*Then I called the doc. Blood pressure zoomin' agin.*

# 19

Don't let me forget," Steph said as she handed Jessie a tray for the glasses. "I brought you an invitation to the wedding. I hope you can work out your schedule and come."

"Thank you. I hope so, too." She placed the tray on the granite counter and looked around at the beautifully appointed galley kitchen. "When you said you were borrowing your dad's boat," Jessie teased, "this is not what I pictured!"

"Disappointed?" Steph asked her.

"No!" she clucked out with a giggle. "Not at all."

"Pretty fantastic, right? It's my dad's. A fifty-three-foot Regal, new on the market. My dad's got a boat addiction."

"They don't have a twelve-step program he can get into?"

"If only. My mom would pack him up and drive him there herself."

Jessie stood over the high-gloss galley cabinetry, filled the four hard plastic glasses with cubes of ice, and placed them on a tray.

"This kitchen makes me want to cry," she said. "Puts mine to shame."

"Wait until you see the bathroom. It's ridiculous." Steph finished filling the glasses and headed up the stairs. "I've got the drinks. Can you grab the snacks?"

"Sure." Jessie picked up the large tray of fruits, cheeses, and crackers.

"There's another one on the counter," Steph told her. "Can you carry that too?"

She peered into the plastic container brimming with cookies and cupcakes, and she moaned. "Oh dear!"

"They're from SusieCakes. Have you been?" Steph asked as she led the way up the stairs to the deck. "They're over on Westcliff."

"No, I haven't," Jessie replied, following.

"You're in for a treat."

Danny's melodic laughter harmonized with Vince's, and Jessie followed Steph up the stairs to the deck. She noticed Danny's muscular, suntanned legs beneath the long Bermuda swim trunks, his ankle loosely propped on the opposite knee. He had rolled up the sleeves of his white T-shirt and sat there casually chatting with Steph's fiancé in the side-by-side leather helm chairs, Vince at the wheel.

"We have snacks," Steph sang, and Jessie couldn't help noticing how she beamed when Vince's gaze met hers. "What can I bring you, baby?"

"Whatcha got?" Vince asked as Steph and Jessie unloaded the trays to the rimmed table.

"Cheese, fruit, crackers. The usual."

"When are we going to fire up the grill?"

"That's for dinner. You just had lunch two hours ago."

Danny and Jessie exchanged grins as Steph and Vince continued.

"Right. That was two hours ago. I'm a growing boy."

"Well, you'll grow just fine on this. Shall I make you a plate?"

"Nah, we're just a few minutes from the cove we found last time. I thought we could light there for a while, maybe go snorkeling, or take the Jet Skis out."

Jessie had put on a bathing suit under her sundress, but the idea of removing the dress somehow filled her with dread. People wore suits all the time—especially in Southern California!—but the idea of wearing one in front of Danny and his friends brought an unexpected deluge of insecurity and fear.

Danny got up and walked over to the table, grabbed a chunk of cheese, and plopped it into his mouth before sliding across the leather bench seat next to Jessie.

"SusieCakes?" he asked Steph.

"Yep. You know my mom."

"Yeah. Jean's always got my back."

Danny smiled at Jessie before snatching up one of the glasses and downing half of the beverage. He pushed his dark sunglasses upward, raking his hair back with them as they slipped into place at the top of his head.

"So, Jessie, I'm so glad you worked it all out with your store so you could come today," Steph said, and she plunked down across from them. "It's such a perfect day to be out on the water."

"It certainly is."

They'd left the marina behind, and the magnificent waterfront homes dotting the landscape of the harbor as well. A small colony of sea lions frolicked at Newport Bell Buoy, and ahead of them a school of dolphins raced smoothly through the blue-green water to form a swimming path ahead of the boat's bow. The spectacular coastline along Newport and Laguna Beach blended into a horizon of blue sky and cotton ball clouds. Jessie inhaled slowly and held it there for a moment, a salty taste at the back of her tongue. She finally released the breath, exquisitely slow.

"It's captivating, isn't it?" Danny asked her, breaking the spell of the boat's hum and the sea breeze.

"Yes," she breathed. "Medicine I didn't even know I needed."

"The Pacific has a way of filling that role for me, too."

Vince steered them around the curve of the coast into a secluded cove framed by rocky cliffs and overhanging greenery. He anchored them a fair distance from the shore before joining the others at the table and sliding across the bench seat next to his fiancée.

"Thank you so much for inviting me along," Jessie said with a grin. "It's a gorgeous day."

"Not as gorgeous as this one," Vince replied, staring into Steph's eyes.

Jessie watched the two of them play off one another; Steph popping a grape into his mouth, and Vince pecking her cheek with a kiss before he swallowed it. She wondered what love like that felt like, where one person found it while another married their sham of a Prince Charming.

"So, how did you two meet?" she asked them.

"We work together," Steph answered. "I'm an intelligence analyst and Vince is the head of Tactical Collection and Reporting for the Bureau."

"The Bureau?"

"Federal Bureau of Investigations," she clarified. "We work for the FBI. Danny didn't tell you?"

Jessie's stomach dropped an inch or two. "No, I don't think he mentioned it."

She raked back her hair and smoothly turned toward Danny. "This is your friend at the FBI?"

"The very same."

"I thought you were just neighbors, that you grew up together."

"That, too."

Steph snagged Danny's attention and she shrugged with a sweet wince. "Sorry."

"No problem."

"Then you know all about my fake husband, I guess."

Steph smiled at her. "I know some. I'm really sorry for what you've been through, Jessie. Nobody deserves that kind of wipe-out in their lives. But if it helps—"

"Yeah, I haven't talked to her about that yet," Danny cut in.

Jessie's heartbeat quickened. Her eyes burned. A deliberate tingle stalked up her spine and into the hair at the back of her neck.

"There's news about Jack?"

Danny seemed to consider her words for several beats before he finally nodded. "He's been taken into custody."

"What? When?"

"He reached the States last night," Steph interjected.

"He's . . . here?" She jerked toward Danny and tried to catch her breath. "Is he in California?"

"He's being detained by the FBI at the moment. We won't know more until things get sorted out."

"But he's here," she repeated.

"Yes."

She turned to Steph and immediately blurted, "Can I see him?"

---

Danny felt Jessie's arms around him tighten as their Jet Ski pounded through the surf, and he hoped the heavy spray of water might rinse away those thoughts of Jack probably still pelting her with hot remorse. About fifty feet to their left, Vince and Steph zoomed along, parallel to the small waves, and Vince waved at Danny, pointing to the shore. Danny understood and nodded fervently.

He slowed the Jet Ski as they neared the shore, and cut the engine before shifting and calling back to Jessie. "Let's climb off."

She hopped down into the hip-deep water first, and Danny followed suit before guiding the Jet Ski toward the sand. He opened the storage compartment beneath the seat and produced two large beach towels and her sandals that he'd stowed there. She lagged behind him out of the water and stepped into the towel he held outstretched before her. He'd been able to sense her shyness about wearing a bathing suit in front of him, so he figured she might appreciate it. She knotted the towel in the front as she slid into the shoes.

He reached out his hand. "Let's take a walk."

They ambled along the beach in silence, except for the roaring music of the ocean—her small hand clasped inside his larger one—until they reached the stretch of sand that narrowed toward the rocks.

"Is that a tide pool?" she asked, pointing it out a few yards out. "I've heard about them, but I've never seen one up close."

Danny offered his hand for support, and they made their way across the slick rock until they reached the edge. They both crouched down, and Jessie peered into the water.

"What am I looking for?" she asked him, examining the water standing in the kidney-shaped pool, left behind when the tide rolled out. "There are little creatures and stuff in there, right?"

Danny chuckled. "Look over here," he said, pointing out the green and red flowery mass gently rocking beneath the water. "These are sea anemones. They look like plants, right?"

"They're not?"

"Mm-mm. They're considered the flower of the sea because of their appearance, but they're actually meat-eating animals. They spend their whole lives in one place, and only eat by waiting for their food to swim by them."

She leaned down for a closer look. The rushing hum of the surrounding water lulled them as they gazed into the water.

"What are those things all over the rocks over there?" Jessie inquired.

"Barnacles. They're a sort of crustacean."

"What, like a lobster? Or like the stuff on the bottom of boats?"

He smiled. "Both, but a very distant cousin to shellfish. They don't swim around. They just attach themselves to hard surfaces."

"Like rocks."

"Rocks, yes. But also the shells of turtles, the backs of whales."

She looked up at him with widening eyes. "And they're a living thing?"

"They are."

"That's really sort of amazing, isn't it?"

"I'm mesmerized by sea life myself," he told her. "I often wonder how anyone can see all of this and not believe in the God who created it."

Jessie's smile hit him like a heat-seeking missile. "You really believe, don't you?" she asked softly. "With everything inside of you, you believe in God."

"With everything," he said, nodding.

She returned her attention to the glistening water, completely immersed in the world thriving just beneath the surface.

"How are they made?" she asked him. "The tide pools, I mean."

"When they're this close to the rocks," he said, "they're usually formed because the rocks were baked by the sun during the lowest tide."

"Look!" she exclaimed, pointing out the small creature inching along on the bordering rock. "It's a baby crab."

"The tide pools in this area provide a home for them. I've seen sea stars and mussels in similar ones."

"It's so cute." When Danny chuckled, she glanced up at him. "What's so funny?"

"I guess I didn't see you as someone who might think a crab is *cute*."

"Yeah," she said with a smile. "I've always had a fondness for them . . . much to my Grampy's chagrin. He liked to eat them, and I tended to pet their shells and give them names."

Somehow, he could see that.

"Hey. Let's cop a squat," he suggested, pointing out a ledge of flat rock above the pool.

Danny offered her his arm, and she clutched it as they climbed up on the ledge and sat down next to each other. Jessie removed her sandals and held them in her lap, dipping her feet in the shallow water beneath them.

"When were you going to tell me about Jack?" she asked after a few minutes of silence.

"After I found out what the full story is."

"You didn't think I might want to know that he's back in the country?"

"I just wanted to give you all the information, Jessie. Right now, I don't have that yet."

Jessie sighed, and the emotion she conveyed caused an anxious rumble at the base of his ribs. Danny ran his hand through his damp hair and propped his sunglasses on the top of his head. With a smile, he reached out and removed her glasses and handed them to her.

"I want to look into your eyes for a minute," he told her.

She giggled. "Okay." She nibbled the corner of her lip before muttering, "You're kinda scaring me a little, Danny."

"Well, hang on to your hat, sister. This might get scarier."

"What is it?"

He inhaled sharply, bracing himself. "I've finished my search and I can tell you with a reasonable amount of confidence that you were never legally married to Jack Stanton."

At least half a minute of silence ticked by, but it felt more like half an hour. Finally, without looking directly at him, she said, "I guess my name isn't even Jessie Stanton then, is it?"

He chuckled. "This is the first takeaway from what I just told you?" She shrugged, and he said, "Well, I guess not. So what *is* your name?"

"Jessie Hart."

"Ahhh." He nodded and smiled at her. "Now that's a name that suits you. Jessie Hart. I like it."

"I never minded it too much."

Another eternity ticked by while he searched for the words he'd thought he knew by heart, the ones he'd been planning to say to her ever since she called to say she wanted to accept Steph's invitation. But they were lost to him now, swirling around somewhere in her eyes, hiding in the depths of those blue pools of light. Instead, something else came out. Something entirely lame.

"So I guess if I want to kiss you, I don't need to fret too much. I'd be kissing a single woman."

"I guess so. Is that what you want to do?" she asked, and she tilted her head and shot him a charming little sideways smirk. "Why? Why do you want to kiss me again, Danny?"

"I can tell you this," he admitted. "When I finally confirmed that Jack had never divorced Patty and he'd married you illegally, despite the fact that I should have felt really awful for you . . . all I could think was how relieved I felt instead."

When she turned her gaze directly on him, he felt the weight of it somewhere down in the base of his gut. Danny knew there was no force on earth that rivaled that cobalt sword. Jessie's simple gaze pierced him to the core.

"So?" she whispered.

"Excuse me?"

"So?" she repeated. "Are you going to kiss me or not. I mean, you've done enough talking about it, I think. Shouldn't you just make up your mind and do something already?"

Danny chuckled, lifted his hand to the back of her neck, and massaged it as he gently guided her closer. When their lips touched in a soft kiss, he could almost hear the snap of the sparks between them as they intensified into a fire, and the fervor burned a path all the way to his soul. The emotional frenzy, in fact, transported him back to a rainstorm that had cropped up on him one summer day, catching him half a mile from the shore, the winds and waves tossing him about, burning his skin and setting his pulse to racing, land beckoning but still so far out of reach . . .

He hadn't felt that way in such a very long time. In fact, a secret belief had whispered to him for several years now that he never would again.

When they parted, Danny felt disoriented, like his equilibrium had been knocked right on its ear; he couldn't catch his breath. And yet, Jessie—the antithesis of the derangement within him—appeared peaceful. When her eyes fluttered open—exquisite sky-blue content—he saw serenity in them, peace in its purest form. Her reddened lips twitched slightly into the curve of an angelic little smile.

"I haven't been kissed in such a long time before you," she admitted in a low, raspy tone. "In fact, I'm not sure I've *ever* been kissed the way you kiss me."

Danny worked his fingers through her damp, tangled hair and smiled at her, their faces just inches apart.

"Again, Danny," she muttered. "Kiss me again."

# Epilogue

*Ain't nothin' on God's green earth more satisfyin' than answered prayer. That's what I got when my Jessie called home to catch me up on the things happenin' in her life out there in LaLa Land. That counterfeit husband o' hers might just meet Brother Justice and—if that ain't enough—Jessie done met the man I been prayin' fer all these years.*

*"He's like no one I've ever known, Grampy," she told me.*

*But if she hadn'ta said it, I'da known anyways. The good Lord changed my Jessie in her troubles, no doubt about it. I knew them blinders would drop off her eyes eventually if I just took enough blood pressure medicine to keep me prayin' fer my girl.*

*"He's a God-loving man like you, Grampy."*

*'Course he is.*

*"He makes me want to be better. And stronger."*

*'Course he does.*

*Comes a time in everybody's life when the prayers of the people that came before 'em start to get answered. And the Lord 'n' me been chattin' for years upon years. All that other stuff was just bumps in the road that took my Jessie to use the good sense the good Lord gave 'er. Set her priorities right. Drop the blinders off her eyes and see things how they really are.*

*No, ain't nothin' in the world like answered prayers, and the Lord's got a way of whisperin' in a sack of ears when somebody needs the fervent prayers of righteous men. And women.*

*Yeah. Tonight I'll be thankin' God for the ones He answers as well as for the ones He don't. Jessie's old grandpa is gonna sleep sound tonight.*

## Group Discussion Guide

1. What are the various qualities about Jessie that reveal she might be more than the trophy wife she appears to be at the beginning of the book?
2. Danny isn't the typical romantic hero. What did you think of him when he first came into the landscape of Jessie's story?
3. What purpose does Jessie's grandfather serve to advance the story and, most important, to advance Jessie's growth?
4. Did you have misgivings about Aaron Riggs? What did he do to change your feelings about him, if you did?
5. Out of the circle of female friends surrounding Jessie (Piper, Amber, Courtney), what does each of them bring to Jessie's life that she can't grow without?
6. How did you react to Jessie as the dramatic events involving Jack unfolded? How did you feel about Jack's actions?
7. Did you feel that the evolution of Jessie and Danny's relationship seemed like a natural one? What would you say were the three key turning points for them?
8. When Danny's past was revealed, how did that change the way you saw him?
9. What did Jessie gain after she lost all of her material possessions?
10. If you could choose one scripture that represents Jessie's life lessons in the book, what would it be?

Want to learn more about Sandra D. Bricker
and check out other great fiction from
Abingdon Press?

Check out our website at
www.AbingdonFiction.com
to read interviews with your favorite authors,
find tips for starting a reading group,
and stay posted on what new titles are on the horizon.

Be sure to visit Sandra online!

*http://www.sandradbricker.com/*

*https://www.facebook.com/SandraDBricker*

*https://twitter.com/SandieBricker*

# A Note to Readers from Author Sandra D. Bricker

I was thinking. Who doesn't love a good cliff-hanger? If you watch daytime dramas, you know it well. Every Friday afternoon, a shoe hangs over the head of a beloved character, and viewers have to wait until Monday to see whether it drops. And how our hearts fill with dread as the season draws to a close on our favorite television shows. You mean we have to wait until September to find out if the proposal will be accepted, the lie found out, the misunderstanding untangled?

For Jessie, her life—at long last!—has taken a positive slant. But there are two more books to her story. How about a little glimpse of what Jessie and Danny have to deal with in the next installment of their story?

We hope you enjoyed reading *On a Ring and a Prayer* and that you will continue to read Abingdon Press fiction books. Here's an excerpt from book 2, *Be My Valentino*.

# Be My Valentino
# A Jessie Stanton Novel
# Book 2

Jessie gazed at the people gathered around the warm and beautiful table near the hearth on the back wall of Tuscan Son. Beneath the yellowish glow of the chandelier overhead, she tallied the ways that each and every one of them had played a part in getting her to this place. To the top of the insurmountable mountain, where she could finally look down at the path she'd taken and see it for what it was. The road toward her destiny.

Piper—her beautiful friend. Jessie wondered what she'd ever done to earn a friendship like that one. Piper had carried her to the bottom of the mountain that Jessie felt sure would be the end of her, and Piper looked up and saw only possibilities.

"Your confidence has taken a very hard blow. I get that," she had said with confidence after Jack disappeared. "But it doesn't change who you are, Jess. You can do this. You're going to pick yourself up, dust yourself off, and you're going to start a whole new life."

Like in most things, Piper had been right. Against all those horrifying odds.

Beside her sat Amber. If Piper was the driving force to begin the climb up the mountain, Amber was the pickax that helped clear away the clutter.

"I'm your girl," Amber had said to her when they met for the first time to talk about the future. "I'm available today. Do you want to take me home with you and show me your closet?"

What if she hadn't gone into the ladies' room that night, at the precise moment that she did? She might never have crossed paths with Amber Davidson, Force of Nature.

Next to Amber sat Courtney Alexis, the raven-haired angel who had taken a turn at carrying Jessie's backpack up the side of the treacherous mountain when it became too heavy to bear. Jessie's first guest blog for Courtney had garnered more than 200,000 views . . . and 87 new Adornments customers. After Amber's first blog and Jessie's second, six designers had sent inventory to the store in the hope that Adornments' new stylist might introduce them to a demographic they might never have known otherwise. With just a few more weeks from the delivery of her bouncing baby girl, Courtney's gut feeling about her had changed the course of Jessie's life . . . and taught her what it meant to renew a dream.

After a full day of painting the nursery and laughing over trying to assemble a Bellini crib on their own—and finally summoning the big guns with a call to Danny—Courtney had reached across the floor and jiggled Jessie's hand. "You're going to be doing this for your own nursery, Jessie. I just know God's heard your secret dreams and will bring you the babies you yearn for."

Far too soon in her relationship with Danny to start talking about babies, but still . . . the hope of becoming a mother had been rekindled in her, and she felt a joyous assurance in Courtney's words.

Next to Courtney, Antonio smiled and gave Jessie a little wink.

"Okay, the truth is," he'd told her that afternoon, "I have been blessed beyond measure in my life. This kind of blessing is not meant to be hoarded. I may have encouraged Piper to help out with the furnishings and a couple new appliances. Just to give you solid footing to make your leap to the next phase of your life. Did I tie a big red ribbon on a used car for you? Yes. I admit it, *carissima*. I've been found out, and Danny insists that I tell you. But you needed transportation. You are *famiglia* to Piper and me, Jessie. This is what we do for *famiglia*, for the ones we love."

Next to Antonio sat Aaron Riggs, the rope-and-pulley for this climbing expedition her life had become. As she watched him, Riggs leaned into his chair, tossed back his head, and unabashedly laughed. That was something she'd come to love about Riggs. There wasn't a false bone in the guy's body. He lived in a van, for crying out loud; and made no excuses about it either. He did whatever he had to do in order to provide everything his daughter needed in life; lending a helping hand to others came second on the list; he was a distant third.

And Danny.

Jessie's heart melted a little as she looked at him. If life had moved a mountain before her, Danny was the summit she had finally reached. When he glanced up and met her gaze, he narrowed his steel eyes and smiled at her . . . and the world stopped rotating in that moment, and everything in it fell away. There was only Jessie and Danny, and her chest squeezed with heartfelt emotion.

*How did this happen?* she asked herself in wonder. *How did this man happen to me?*

She'd found so many things to love about Danny, so many qualities that made him the most unique person she'd ever met. Laid-back and cool, sweet and funny, a warm and golden heart encased by a Christian faith that she both admired and feared, wondering if she might find something like it for herself one day. Her grandpa had faith like that—completely confident and utterly submissive at the same time—but for some reason, she'd largely dismissed it in younger days. But now . . . after everything . . . it tugged at her from somewhere deep inside.

Nearly everyone at that table with her had a deeper faith and followed some invisible guide; a guide that had somehow led them straight to her, equipped them with the net she would so desperately need, and the tools to make them ready to catch her when the moment arose. Even while chastising herself for the cheesy sentiment, Jessie suddenly imagined that back room of Tuscan Son restaurant—filled with the tools and helpmates without whom she might never have reached it—as some consecrated place and moment where everything she needed had intersected sublimely together.

She almost laughed out loud at her own dramatic emotion. Instead, however, she picked up the Toscana glass tumbler of tea sitting in front of her and stood up. "I need to say something to you all."

The various pops of chatter faded away, and all eyes nestled sweetly on Jessie.

"When the tsunami came and washed me out of the life I had known," she began, pausing for a moment to form the words. "Well, I didn't think there was anything left for me. But what I've learned because of each and every one of you at this table is that . . . new beginnings aren't possible until old obstructions are destroyed. Bit by bit, every one of you has helped me stand up again and move forward, and because of you I've found something I never thought was possible for me. I'm not sure there are words adequate enough to thank you."

Danny stood up and rounded the table, finding a place beside her. He kissed the side of her head and placed his arm loosely around her shoulder. When she looked up into his eyes, Jessie evaporated a bit under his warmth.

"Raise your glasses," he told them all. "Let's drink to the new future of Jessie Hart."

Glasses of wine, tea, and club soda were lifted all around the table. Jessie felt as if a shower of joy had begun to rain down on them as she raised her own glass.

"A new future," she repeated. "I love that."

And just as the last clink of glasses was heard, another voice chimed in.

"Hello, Jessie."

As she turned and looked into the familiar gray eyes of Jack Stanton, a horrified Jessie dropped her glass and it crashed on the floor.

She'd seen it in the movies, but never felt it for herself. That moment where the live wire of horrified shock meets the damp floor of reality, and the sizzling begins. The background moves toward a person until he or she becomes more sharp and clear than the foreground, and something far behind begins to swirl around and around until they can't stand to focus on it any more. The eyes of the movie character usually rolled back in their heads about then, and a slow-motion shot dollied along with them as they fell to the ground, unconscious.

"What are you thinking?" Piper exclaimed as she jumped to her feet and blocked the way between Jack and the table. "You have no right to come here. Not after all you've done."

Jack had long ago dubbed Piper as Jessie's "mama bear," and she could see from the somewhat amused expression in his eyes that he remembered why.

Raising both his hands in a mock-surrender, he told her, "I just came to talk to Jessie for a minute."

Jessie's dinner rose halfway to her throat on a wave of burning acid.

"I don't think so," Piper said. "Do the police know you're here? Maybe we should call them and let them know where to find you."

Jack lifted his pantleg to reveal what looked like a large, square-faced watch strapped around his ankle. "As you can see, the authorities know where I am every minute."

"And yet you're roaming around anyway."

He shifted his eyes from Piper to Jessie as he said, "You have nothing to worry about here."

Jessie jerked toward Danny, looking up at him with panic and churning emotion cresting. "Did you know about this?"

"I didn't," he muttered, just to her. "Steph called earlier and left a message, short and sweet. But I didn't have time to call her back."

Danny's friend Steph worked for the FBI as an intelligence analyst, and she'd utilized her handy connections to help them in their quest to find Jack. Jessie groaned under her breath and turned her focus back on Jack, who didn't look any worse for wear now that she took a moment to notice. He wore a casual black blazer over a black sport shirt and jeans. If you could even call what looked to be never-washed, still-creased dark gray denim trousers "jeans." Apparently, he'd had time to go wardrobe shopping before popping in to ruin her evening with friends.

"Jessie?" he inquired. "Can we talk, please? For just a minute?"

*A minute? That's all you think it will take to explain yourself? Sixty seconds?*

She swallowed around the acid that had pooled at the base of her throat. "I can't imagine that you could have anything worthwhile to say to me, Jack. I think surrendering my car, selling the house, and leaving me nothing but some cheese puff snacks in the cupboard kind of said it all for you."

He hesitated, taking a few seconds to glance down at his shoes. "Jessie, please," he finally piped up. Holding up one hand, fingers splayed, he added, "Five minutes."

"You haven't even earned five *seconds* of her attention," Piper snapped. And with that, Antonio squeezed his wife's arm and made his way toward Jack.

With a nod from Danny, Riggs got up too, and the two of them rounded opposite sides of the large table and followed Antonio as he escorted Jack to the door. Jessie exhaled the breath she hadn't known she'd been holding and deflated into her chair. An instant later, Piper was on one side and Amber on the other.

"Are you okay? What can I get you?" Piper asked.

"Do you want me to drive you home?" Amber chimed in. "Danny can follow after he takes care of this."

"I'm okay. I just need to"—she rolled her hand as if to push oxygen into her nose as she breathed in deeply—"recover."

"It's a shock. Anyone would be shocked," Piper said, and she grabbed Jessie's hand and held it for a moment. As Antonio and

Riggs walked back to the table, she gave a sigh of relief. "Look. He's gone now. It's okay."

"Where's Danny?" Jessie asked them, rising to her feet.

"He said he had to make a call."

"And Jack?" Piper inquired.

"In his car and on his way," Antonio replied.

"What did he say?" Jessie said, reeling. "What did he want?"

"He's under the delusion that he can make things right with you in a few words," Riggs cracked, sinking back into the chair he'd occupied throughout dinner. "I think we set him straight."

Jessie craned her neck to get a glimpse of Danny when he stepped into view, then stopped again, his cell phone pressed to his ear. The instant their eyes met, she hurried across the restaurant toward him, touching his arm when she reached his side.

"Is that Steph?" she asked quietly, and he nodded.

"Thanks, Steph. I'll check in with you tomorrow."

She waited until Danny tucked the phone into his pocket. "What's going on? He's been arrested?"

"They got a tip that the alias he might have been using was flagged on a flight into the States."

"Why didn't someone let me know?" she whimpered. "Instead of letting me be blindsided like that. And how did he know where to find me?"

"It all happened pretty quickly, and Steph didn't hear about it until after he'd already been detained. He was only just arraigned last night, and he had to surrender both passports and wear the jewelry provided by the feds."

"Is Patty with him?"

"I don't know. Steph is going to gather whatever information she's free to share and we're going to meet up tomorrow."

"I want to be there."

"Okay," he said with a nod. "I get it."

"But if he could find me here, does he know where I live now? Will he just walk up to my front door later?"

"It won't matter," Piper said as she joined them. "You're coming home with us tonight."

"Oh, Piper," she replied, "I can't. I have a blog due to Courtney tomorrow, and I've got to finish it up tonight."

"Danny, will you talk some sense into her?"

"No need to worry," he reassured her. "Riggs and I are swapping rides. He'll go back to my place for the night, and I'll park his van on the street and keep watch."

Piper sighed, her relief showing in her smile. "That's great."

"Danny, you don't have to—"

"I am aware. But stakeouts are old hat to me. It's a piece of cake. Now I'm going outside for a minute to make another call."

"Who?" Jessie asked, wide-eyed.

"Rafe. He can help grease the wheels to get us started on a restraining order."

"Good thinking," Piper said. "Let's go back inside and relax for a few minutes while Danny does his thing, yes?"

Jessie nodded and followed, stopping halfway across the restaurant to cast a look back to Danny for one comforting moment.

"I really do think I'm falling in love with him," Piper muttered softly, and they exchanged a grin.

"Yeah," she replied with a sigh. "Me, too."

---

Danny swiped the page on his tablet, then swiped it back again when he realized he hadn't retained a single word he'd just read. Despite his anticipation for the release of this third book in a popular series of suspense fiction, he just couldn't seem to concentrate on anything except the unexpected and jarring resurgence of Jack Stanton.

The guy turned out to be more imposing than Danny had imagined. Tall, muscular, a little chiseled in the jawline. And far more suntanned than any of the pictures he'd seen. Apparently, Stanton had been enjoying his exile to the fullest. Maybe those visions Danny had of him on a Bali beach sipping exotic drinks weren't so far off after all.

He wasn't hard to picture standing on top of a high-end wedding cake with Jessie at his side, or sauntering about that 3,000-square foot Malibu rug he'd pulled out from under his wife.

*Wife.*

The reference left a bitter taste at the back of his throat. More than just the simple aversion to thinking of Jessie as anyone else's *wife*, Danny found it particularly repugnant to envision this particular person tied to her until death they did part. Or until abandonment and possible divorce.

He reminded himself as he gave up and switched off the tablet that there was always the possibility that they'd never been legally married in the first place. He couldn't gauge how detestable it made him that he found a strange degree of comfort in that pain for Jessie, but he harbored the secret notion that it should be a relief to her as well.

His startled reaction to the sudden rap on the window sent the tablet flying out of his hand to the floor on the passenger side. He looked up to see Jessie's face beaming at him from the other side of the glass.

*Man oh man, she's beautiful.*

He reached across the seat and pushed the stubborn door of Riggs's old van until it creaked open. "You scared the living breath out of me."

"I'm sorry. I thought maybe you'd like some coffee," she said, lifting a travel mug with a ribbon of steam emerging from the opening on top of it.

"Thank you."

He reached across the seat to take it from her, but she slipped into the van instead and yanked the door shut behind her before handing him the cup.

"I couldn't sleep," she told him, her eyes trained on the deserted, dimly lit street. "My mind is just racing with . . . all sorts of thoughts."

Danny inched over to the edge of the driver's seat and angled toward her. The instant he stretched out his arms, she did the same on the passenger seat and fell into his embrace.

"I'm so glad you're here," she whispered.

"Not going anywhere," he returned, and he planted a kiss on the top of her head as he held her.

"Danny, can I ask you something?"

"Always."

"Do you think Jack is . . ."

He waited, but she didn't complete the thought. "Do I think he's what?"

Her voice was raspy and emotional as she finally said, "Dangerous?"

Where had that come from? He'd scammed clients, jilted Jessie, absconded with every cent they'd had, but dangerous?

"Why do you ask that?" he inquired, nudging her away slightly so he could get a good look into those crystal blue eyes of hers. "Has he ever hurt you?"

"No," she answered then shrugged. "Not physically."

"What makes you worry about your safety?" He twisted a lock of hair near her face around his finger and moved it back.

"I guess I just realized everything I thought I knew about us—Jack and me—was a lie. It wasn't real. So how do I really know what kind of man he's become?"

"I can tell you this," Danny reassured her. "You know what kind of man I am. Would I ever let him hurt you again?"

Her smile appeared edged with timid confidence. "No."

"We'll get to the bottom of all of this," he promised. "And you're going to be free of Jack Stanton sooner rather than later."

She wriggled toward him and planted her head underneath his chin with a sigh. "When you say it, I almost believe you. You're good at that."

"Yes, I am," he teased.

After a few minutes of comforting silence, Jessie tilted her head upward and stared into his eyes.

"What?" he asked, and she smiled.

"You know what else you're good at?"

"So many things," he replied.

"Yes. But would you kiss me? I feel safe when you kiss me."

Without another random word, Danny leaned down and placed his lips on Jessie's. A muffled sigh came from deep within her throat, and he raked his fingers through the silky hair at the side of her head. When their lips parted, she snuggled beneath his chin again and softly moaned.

"Thank you, Danny."

"For?"

"All of it. Every bit of being you. Thank you."

He chuckled. "Glad I could be me for you."

"Me too," she said, sincerity apparent in the expression. "I've never had a Danny Callahan in my corner before. It's startling . . . and a relief, really."

"Yeah. I get that all the time."

The two of them sat there in Riggs's questionable-smelling van for an hour or so as Danny sipped his coffee and Jessie talked through the details of the blog post she'd just completed. He didn't have a clue what it all meant in the great scheme of the world of fashion, of course, but she seemed adequately distracted by it, and that was all he really cared about.

"Do you want me to walk you to the door?" he asked her.

"No. I thought I'd dazzle you by making the journey all by myself. Want to watch me?"

"Sure. Make it entertaining for me?"

"Sure thing," she chirped, and she quickly pecked his lips before pushing out of the van.

At the edge of the sidewalk, Jessie raised her arms to an imaginary partner and gave him a comical glance before she waltzed up the middle of the driveway toward her apartment door. Danny's laughter followed her, and he watched closely until he felt certain she was tucked safely inside.

Two very round headlights appeared at the corner a short time later, and a sedan-shaped car moved slowly up the street toward him. When it passed the apartment building without altering speed, Danny leaned down and watched the car's retreat in his side mirror before dialing Rafe on his cell.

"Hey, Detective," he said when Padillo answered, the familiar hum of the precinct behind him.

"Hey, Callahan, where you at?"

"You wouldn't believe me if I told you."

"What's up?"

"Jessie Stanton's husband—I mean, *Jessie Hart's* husband—is back in town," Danny advised. "Anything you can do to help us hurry along a restraining order?"

"I thought he was living high in Costa Rica."

"Bali. It's a long story, but he's back in the States, modeling some ankle armor courtesy of Uncle Sam."

"But you're still worried he'll try to make contact?" Rafe asked.

"He already has. Walked right into a public restaurant and tried to have a chat with her. Fortunately, we were able to dissuade him, but only for the time being. Can you help lead the way toward an order of restraint?"

"Text me his details and I'll make a call. Hang in there, and I'll try to get back to you tonight."

"Good deal. Thanks, Rafe."

Danny keyed in the vitals the second they ended the call.

*John Fitzgerald Stanton. Driving late model green hybrid Accord. Picked up by feds for fraud, embezzlement, possibly bigamy. Ankle bracelet while pending prosecution.*

An odd-shaped car turned the corner and cruised up the street. It bore no resemblance to the Accord he'd seen Stanton drive away earlier in the evening, so Danny barely gave it a glance. He bent down and retrieved the tablet Jessie had picked up and stowed under the dash. Just as he started to take a second stab at reading, another set of headlights rounded the corner of Pinafore Street. The form could possibly be an Accord, but he couldn't be sure. He tossed the tablet to the passenger seat and slouched down anyway.

The car swerved into the driveway to Jessie's apartment building and cut the lights before the engine. Danny's pulse went from a soft drum to urgent pounding as the dark shape of a man emerged from what could definitely be an Accord. Tall . . . broad-shouldered.

*Yep. That's Stanton.*

Danny pushed open the door and it cracked, metal against metal, drawing the attention of the unwelcome visitor. As he turned toward the sound, Jack stepped into the yellowish bath of light from the street lamp. Danny closed the distance between them and stood face-to-face with Jack Stanton for the second time that day.

"What are you doing here?"

"I came to speak to Jessie."

"I thought we covered this at the restaurant," he said evenly. "What could you possibly have to say to her at this late date?"

Stanton sighed and, shaking his head, peered down at the uneven concrete driveway. "That's between me and my wife."

There was that word again.

"You sure do toss that wife label around lightly, don't you?"

"Look," he said, slamming the car door shut, "this is really none of your business. What are you, the new boyfriend? That's . . . well, it's adorable."

Stanton's sarcastic lilt set acid to churning in Danny's gut, lifting a foamy fire into his throat. "Almost as adorable as you leaving one wife to flop on a beach with another. Grow tired of the little umbrella drinks, did you? Oh, wait, no. You probably didn't have much choice in the matter. You received your return flight ticket courtesy of the FBI, I believe."

As Stanton turned away from him, Danny quickly padded every pocket with open palms in search of his cell phone. When he finally found it tucked into his shirt pocket, he grabbed it and redialed Rafe. Just as he answered, Danny spotted Stanton already at Jessie's door.

"Rafe!" he exclaimed, sprinting up the driveway. "We need some help over at Jessie's apartment on Pinafore. Stanton is—" His words came to a grinding halt as Jessie opened her door. "No! Jessie, go back inside."

"Callahan?" Rafe bellowed over the line. "What's going on?"

"Go back inside and bolt the door."

He watched helplessly as Jessie's terror-ridden face curled up and she pushed the door shut; but his insides flopped with a thud as Stanton pushed it open again, charged inside, and closed it behind him.

CPSIA information can be obtained at www.ICGtesting.com
Printed in the USA
LVOW06*0658290315

432301LV00001B/3/P